PRAISE FOR

Think post-apocalyptic. Think zombies. Think action horror. Then turn all of that on its head and dig deeper to expose what this book is really about: the tragedy of losing one's identity when the joy of language is lost.

In Hyenas, Sellars has written a tragi-comedy, poignant and riddled with metaphor, and in doing so has provided the most unique What if? scenario I have ever read.

Catherine McCarthy, author of *Immortelle*

Relentless, disturbing, and moving, HYENAS is a superb spin on post-apocalyptic nightmares: Terrifying monsters, sympathetic characters, and a zombie-fighting militia led by a Beatles obsessive. What's not to love?

Peter Atkins, screenwriter of
Hellbound: Hellraiser II* and *Wishmaster

A post-apocalyptic tale that is unlike any other I've read! HYENAS was a hell of a good time! Action packed, with a unique premise that turned the typical post-apocalyptic story on its ear. I'll state it bluntly: I want a sequel!

Strongly recommended for fans of dark fiction, post apocalyptic fiction and horror!

Char's Horror Corner

Sellar Evokes both classic literature and classic horror in this post-apocalyptic debut novel.

What at first seems to be a zombie scenario, somewhere between Dawn of the Dead and 28 Days Later, masks a dynamic portrait of literature and disability. Of course, fans of the adrenaline and gore of more traditional post-apocalyptic zombie fare will find themselves right at home here.

A stirring addition to the zombie canon.

Kirkus Reviews

MICHAEL SELLARS was born in Oldham and moved around the North West, settling in Liverpool at the age of three, where he's lived ever since.

Via the gateway drug of 70s era Doctor Who, he developed an appetite for the creepier elements of his local library's catalogue, and devoured everything assembled by Mary Danby, Christine Bernard and Richard Davis. Aged eleven, an encounter with a mis-shelved copy of Stephen King's 'Salem's Lot introduced him to the hard stuff.

Although he'd always enjoyed writing stories, it wasn't until his early 30s that it occurred to him other people might want to read them. He subsequently published short stories in the magazines Fusing Horizons, Nocturne, Forgotten Worlds, Murky Depths, and Morpheus Tales, as well as the anthologies From the Trenches and Best Tales of the Apocalypse.

He has self-published the cosmic horror novella Things Not Made and collected his published fiction (as well as a few new tales) in Heartfelt Horrors.

Follow Michael on Twitter @HorrorPaperback

HYENAS

MICHAEL SELLARS

Northodox Press Ltd
Maiden Greve, Malton,
North Yorkshire, YO17 7BE

This edition 2022

1

First published in Great Britain
by Northodox Press Ltd 2022

Copyright © Michael Sellars 2022

ISBN: 9781915179098

This book is set in Sabon LT Std

This Novel is entirely a work of fiction. The names, characters and incidents portrayed in it are the work of the author's imagination. Any resemblance to actual persons, living or dead, events or localities is entirely coincidental.

All rights reserved. No part of this publication may be reproduced, stored in a retrieval system, or transmitted, in any form or by any means, electronic, mechanical, photocopying, recording, or otherwise, without the prior permission of the publishers.

This book is sold subject to the condition that it shall not, by way of trade or otherwise, be lent, re-sold, hired out or otherwise circulated without the publisher's prior consent in any form of binding or cover other than that in which it is published and without a similar condition including this condition being imposed on the subsequent purchaser.

For Ray, Reuben, Marcy
and Kristina with love.

Chapter One

The hyena dragged a filthy finger across the spines of Angelou, Arnold, Ashbury, Auden and Betjeman. It hesitated at the breach where Blake would have been had Jason Garvey not liberated him five weeks before, and then it moved onto Browning and Byron.

Jason Garvey — Jay to his friends, few and all dead or worse — was crammed under a display table just four feet from the browsing hyena, close enough to suffer its rank odour despite the thick woollen scarf covering his mouth and nose. He was almost close enough to reach out and touch the tattered hem of its grime-shiny, bloodstained jeans and the dead worm of lace trailing from Reeboks on the verge of splitting, disintegrating.

The corner of a leather wallet peeked out of a torn back pocket and, despite his clattering heartbeat, Jay couldn't help but think of all the things that might be in there. Evidence of the hyena's former humanity: driver's licence, credit cards, money he would never spend, passport photos of a wife or girlfriend or children. Jay tried not to think about what the thing might have been before the Jolt, tried not to think of it as human at all. If he started thinking about the possibility that there might be some pale but retrievable remnant of an actual person beneath that stinking crust, behind those murderous eyes, he wouldn't be able to use the kitchen knife gripped in his trembling right hand, a hand greased with sweat despite the freezing cold. In his left hand, gripped equally tightly though of considerably less use, was a copy of Northrop Frye's *Fearful Symmetry*. This was the reason he'd left the warmth and relative safety of his blanket and foil-lined hidey-hole on the third floor, a room that Jay assumed had functioned as some kind of break area for the Waterstones staff. Moments after he'd slipped the book from its place in Literary Criticism, he'd heard the hyena come bounding up the spiral staircase. He'd had only a couple of seconds to get himself out of sight, assuming he'd somehow given himself away and the thing had come for him. Instead, it had shuffled up to the Poetry section and had started *browsing*.

The hyena snarled, snatched a volume of Byron and, still facing the bookshelf, away from Jay, dropped into a cross-legged seated position. There was still a little snow on its hunched shoulders, but it was melting fast. It turned the book over and over, this way and that, as if looking for a point of entry, then prised the pages apart. Jay saw there was a chunk of flesh missing from the back of its arm, just below a tattoo of the Liverpool Football Club crest; the wound was livid with infection. The hyena looked down at Byron's words and let out a snort which sounded like satisfaction, then sighed, its breath clouding around its matted head.

Jay could feel the onset of cramp in his right calf. His lower back was beginning to protest, a sharp, persistent pain that insulted his twenty-seven years. He knew he wouldn't be able to last much longer but he had no desire to confront the thing. He'd only found himself face-to-face with a hyena once before and it had come very close to ending badly for him. A well-aimed boot to the hyena's balls had saved his life but he'd earned himself a dislocated arm. The memory of *re*locating it still made him wince.

What's it doing? he thought. I mean, what the *fuck*? The world ended five weeks ago. There shouldn't *be* any more surprises.

The hyena ran its fingertips over the page, as if it were reading Braille. Another snort of satisfaction, another sigh, another reeking breath-cloud. Then, with surprising delicacy, it tore the page from the book, pushed it into its mouth and began to chew, emitting little grunts of pleasure.

It swallowed with some difficulty then tore out another page. This one it rammed into its mouth, chewing furiously.

The Byron looked to be at least four hundred pages. Jay put all thoughts of *what the fuck?* out of his mind and began to shuffle backwards, an inch at a time He could no longer see the hyena but could still hear its lips smacking together, its grunts. He was almost out, when the hood of his parka hissed against the underside of the table.

The hyena stopped chewing. Jay froze, held his breath. One, two, three, four seconds of silence. Five, six. The hyena started chewing again. Jay dared to breathe only when he absolutely had to. He was surprised the hyena couldn't feel the vibrations from his juddering heartbeat through the carpet-tiled floor.

He was about to begin inching backwards again when the hyena spat the pulp from its mouth and let out a vicious snarl. Jay thought it had heard him, *sensed* him, but then, as it began tearing at pages and scattering them about, it became clear that it was the volume of poetry that was the source of its fury.

Jay eased his way out from under the table, stayed on his knees for a few seconds, then peered over the display of Mind, Body and Spirit books.

The hyena was looking right at him. *Glaring* at him. Pages from Byron seemed to hang in the air. White flecks of chewed paper peppered its sparse, knotted beard. It pulled back cold-sore infected lips to bare yellow teeth. It was human in every respect — filthy, ragged, diseased, but human — except for its eyes. Its eyes were just rage. Jay noticed the remaining arm of a pair of spectacles tangled-up in its hair just above its left ear. Then it leapt up onto the table, scattering books.

Jay lashed out with the knife, a backhanded arc, warning the hyena off. The thing only grinned.

Jay turned and ran toward the spiral staircase.

If he could get back to his hidey-hole, lock the door, maybe he could wait it out. He had water and food (okay, mostly crisps, muffins and Kit Kats), blankets, a Calor gas heater. The hyena would starve, freeze or just get bored and fuck off.

But it wasn't fucking off now. He heard it launch itself from the table, books thudding to the floor. Certain the thing was going to land on his back — he could almost *feel* it, suspended in the air above him — Jay made a sudden left, away from the stairs.

It was a wise decision: the hyena crashed to the floor where Jay would have been had he continued moving forward. But now the thing, rolling onto all fours, was between him and the stairs. Between him and his hidey-hole.

Jay swiped back and forth with the knife.

The hyena laughed: high, harsh, barking. It was a sound with which he was all-too familiar; usually it was faint, distant. The last time he'd heard it at such close proximity, his arm was being wrenched out of its socket and it had taken all his will just to remain conscious.

Still laughing, the hyena leapt.

Jay knew that if he simply stood his ground, held the knife out, the thing would impale itself. But his belly was hot and oily with fear, his heartbeat a series of painful detonations. He lurched to the right, lashing out with the knife as he did so.

The hyena's body struck his outstretched arm. Jay spun like a turnstile, so fast he couldn't keep his balance. He fell onto his back, hard enough to knock the wind out of him. The knife flew from his hand.

He lifted his head in time to see the hyena scuttling toward him on all fours. A string of saliva hung from its lips, lashing about.

Jay rolled onto his side, his front, got to his feet. He started away from the hyena, toward the stairs.

A moment later, the hyena slammed into his back, its hands gripping his shoulders, its feet pushing into the backs of his knees.

Jay went down again. His forehead struck the floor. There was concrete beneath the thin carpet tiles, and the impact was so hard sheet lightning filled his vision for a second, leaving behind a sickly green-yellow afterimage. He kept his head tucked in, and for the moment the hyena contented itself with raking at his back and shoulders, shredding the outer material of his parka, but Jay knew it would soon tire of that. Hyenas liked to tear at flesh, to break bone, to kill for the sake of killing.

Fighting nausea from the blow to his head, Jay pulled his legs under him, pushed his feet flat against the ground and with a weightlifter's grunt of exertion, stood and threw himself backwards. He managed to turn himself slightly on the descent, so his shoulder slammed into the hyena's chest at the same moment its back hit the floor. He saw and smelled the breath forced from its lungs, a noxious fog. The hyena released its grip.

Jay jerked up and stumbled forward. Regaining his balance, he sprinted toward the stairs.

He thought the hyena might take a few seconds to recover. He thought wrong. He could hear it already, coming at him, laughing, closing the distance. He'd only climbed three steps when his hood was yanked back. The collar of his parka cut into his throat.

Jay spun round, lashed out. He hadn't even realised he was still gripping Northrop Frye's *Fearful Symmetry* until the corner of its thick spine struck the hyena's temple. The rage left its eyes for a moment, replaced by a crazed bewilderment, and then it was tumbling backwards, head over heels, down the stairs. The book followed after, Blake's 'Ancient of Days' becoming a blur of orange and yellow as it cart-wheeled. And then both of them — book and hyena — were gone, out of sight, round the curve of the spiral staircase, and there was silence.

Jay waited, his eyes trained on the spot where the hyena had flopped and twisted from view. His heart punched at his chest; his lungs felt shredded. He gave it a full minute then sat down on the steps and sighed.

'Christ.'

He probed the rapidly forming egg in the middle of his forehead and grimaced. A small price to pay. He flexed the arm which had been dislocated, as if to remind himself how lucky he'd been this time. Looking over each shoulder, he could see wads of grey stuffing erupting here and there from his shredded parka. He was going to need a new coat. Which meant going out. Out there. With the hyenas.

'Shit.' He flexed his arm again, allowed himself a faint smile. 'Still. Could be worse.'

A wave of exhilaration washed over him. He was

grinning now.

There was a bullish snort from the floor below. The smile dissolved. The hyena lurched into view, its face glossed with blood. It was the hyena's turn to grin. Most of its front teeth were missing; one was embedded in its lower lip. It barked laughter, dropped onto all fours and galloped up the stairs.

A part of Jay, a small part, knew it would be better to stand his ground, to opt for fight rather than flight; to deliver a well-aimed boot-tip to the hyena's face once it was within range. The hyena was too fast, too relentless, to be outpaced. If he turned his back on the thing, it would run him down long before he reached his hidey-hole. Probably before he reached the third floor, and he would die here on these stairs with no knife or Northrop Frye with which to defend himself.

For a second, he almost dug in and stole himself for battle, but then the hyena spat out what could only have been its own severed tongue. Jay turned and fled, his bladder suddenly shrieking to be emptied.

The stairs shook with the hyena's violent footfalls. Its ragged panting became louder, closer. Jay threw himself up the stairs, following the hyena's example and using his arms as much as his legs.

He was almost at the top step; he could see the door to his hidey-hole beyond the shelves of Military History, Politics, Religion, Geography and Transport. For a second, he allowed himself to entertain the possibility that he might make it, but then he felt the hyena's febrile heat, saw the roiling clouds of its insufferable breath unfolding all around him. He gasped, inhaling its stink. The hyena laughed.

Jay somehow managed to keep moving *and* brace himself for the inevitable impact.

From somewhere further down the stairs, there was a mechanical *clack*, then a hiss like a sudden puncture.

The hyena's laugh halted abruptly, replaced by a gargling cough. The inevitable impact didn't come.

Jay turned in time to see the hyena swoon to one side, attempt to steady itself on the banister, fail and crumple forward. A metal rod about half a metre long and no thicker than a pencil protruded from its lower back, a bloodstain blooming from the entry point.

Another mechanical *clack*.

Further down the stairs a white-bearded old man in a black Crombie and a black woollen hat, both of which glittered with a sprinkling of snowflakes, was pointing a harpoon gun in the general direction of Jay's torso.

'So,' said the old man, and that single syllable was enough to establish his credentials as a born and bred Dubliner. 'You're not going to be making any trouble for me, are you now, boy?'

Chapter Two

―――

Jay wasn't sure if the blood was rushing to or from his head, only that his legs were weakening. Darkness was crowding in from the edges of his vision like the burning map from the opening credits of some swashbuckling show he used to watch in the summer holidays as a kid. He sat down, his buttocks thumping painfully against the top step, and put his head between his knees. It was all he could do to keep down his breakfast of an Eccles cake and half a pint of UHT chocolate milk.

The old man laughed, but there was no cruelty in it.

'Well, boy,' he said. 'I think that about answers my question. No trouble at all.'

Jay raised his head and watched the old man advancing through the receding darkness. He'd lowered the harpoon gun. He shook Jay's hand and smiled. It was the first human smile Jay had seen since the Jolt.

'Dempsey,' said the man. He was tall and broad, at least half a foot over Jay's five ten, and built like a rugby player, second row. His face was etched with cuts and stained with bruises. He looked like a boxer who'd won his fight, but only on points. 'And you'd be?'

'Jason. Jay. Jay Garvey.'

'So, Mr Garvey, you wouldn't happen to know a thing or two about sailing, would you?' He placed the harpoon gun on the floor next to him and began rummaging through a green canvas shoulder bag.

'Sailing?' said Jay. 'Not a thing. Why?'

Dempsey produced a large bottle of Lucozade and uncapped it.

'I've found a boat. A sailing boat. It's got a motor but that's for shit. Pretty sure it's the only practical, serviceable boat left on the Mersey.' He passed the bottle to Jay. 'Sip it. The sugar will help.'

Dempsey reached down and yanked the harpoon from the hyena's back, wiping the shaft clean on his thigh. Blood bubbled up from the hyena's wound, steaming, and the darkness began to crowd in on Jay once more. He took a sip of Lucozade and was thankful that it was largely flat; his stomach would have reacted badly to anything fizzy. The darkness began to retreat.

'The only boat left?' he said.

'Looks that way.' Dempsey sat down next to Jay. 'Sergeant Pepper did for the rest.'

Sergeant Pepper did for the rest? It sounded to Jay like a random selection of words strung together in imitation of a sentence. He began to wonder if this Ahab-figure might be mad. He'd certainly had *his* fair share of out-there moments since the Jolt.

'Sergeant *Pepper*?' he said. 'As in The Beatles song?'

'Sergeant Pepper, as in the deranged, self-appointed leader of the militia.'

'Militia?'

Dempsey raised an eyebrow then scrutinised Jay's face, as if waiting for him to laugh and give the game away. Then he smiled and shook his head.

'How long have you been cooped-up in this bookshop?'

'Since the beginning,' said Jay. 'I ventured out once, for supplies. It didn't work out so well.'

'Since the beginning?'

Dempsey flashed Jay an incredulous grin.

'Yeah. Since the beginning. Since the Jolt.' He took another sip of Lucozade. It was probably just some soft-drink variation of the placebo effect, but he was starting to feel better. Or maybe he was drawing comfort, sustenance even, from the simple fact that he was talking to another human being for the first time in weeks.

'The Jolt? Is that what you call it? Good a name as any, I suppose. Fella I took up with not long after this all kicked off, Campbell, he called it the Stroke. Said it was like the whole world had a stroke. Everybody at once. The Stroke. I prefer not to call it anything. He's dead now, Campbell.'

'What's this militia? And Sergeant Pepper? Really?'

'I don't know his real name. Some bloke who got himself organised from day one. Which wouldn't be such a bad thing if he hadn't made it his mission to save every Beatles related landmark in the city. I mean, don't get me wrong, I *like* The Beatles but there are more pressing matters than creating a secure perimeter around Penny Lane, you know? Plus, he's not much of

Hyenas

a fan of democracy, our Sergeant Pepper. If you're not with him, you're against him, and he's the one with all the guns, if you get my drift.'

'You said Sergeant Pepper did for the rest. For the rest of the boats?'

'He burnt them. Scuttled them. He doesn't want anyone getting out of Liverpool who can be press-ganged into his Magical fucking Mystery Tour. Anyone trying to leave the city is a traitor, far as he's concerned. Boats were the only safe way out. The roads are completely impassable, and who wants to be trekking cross country when night falls, with all those *things* out there?'

'Hyenas.'

'Hyenas? Oh, because of that laugh of theirs?' He laughed himself. 'What is it with people and naming things?' He stood, settled his bag on his shoulder and picked up his harpoon. 'Point me to the sailing books.'

Jay got up and was pleased to find his legs fully functioning. He handed the Lucozade back to Dempsey.

'Sailing books?'

'Turns out sailing a boat isn't as easy as you might think. Complicated. All those little ropes and whatnot. I'll be needing a bit of instruction and seeing as you've eschewed your proud maritime heritage, that means I'll be turning to a book for help. First time for everything, I suppose.'

'Sports books are on the first floor, at the back,' said Jay and started down the spiral staircase. 'You'll find sailing stuff there, I think.'

'Lead the way.'

It was dark toward the back of the shop, with only a little light from the front windows making it that far in. Jay scanned the sports books. The faces of Gerrard, Torres, Saha and Dalglish, gazed at him from a middle shelf and an unimaginably distant past. Someone had tried hard to create a balance of red and blue but had been unable to hide their preference for the warmer end of the spectrum.

'There you go,' said Jay, pointing. 'Sailing.'

There were only five books.

Dempsey slid the first book from the shelf and turned to the back cover.

'Autobiography,' he said and let the book fall to the floor with a dull slap.

The next one. 'Humour,' said Dempsey with something like disgust. 'Yachting humour? Christ, the world was fucked up long before the Stroke or Jolt or whatever you want to call it.' The book landed on top of the first.

The next. 'This is more like it.' Dempsey flipped back and forth through the book for a few seconds. 'But not enough like it.' Another one for the discard pile.

The fourth book. 'Another fucking autobiography. These sailor-types think they're just *fascinating*, don't they?' Book number four joined one to three.

Dempsey hesitated before reaching for the final book, as if fearful of disappointment and what that would mean for his escape plan, but the moment he had the book in his hands, his face lit up.

'You beauty!' He kissed the book's cover, then flicked

through it.

Peering over Dempsey's shoulder, Jay saw that the book consisted largely of photographs and labelled illustrations.

'This is what I was after,' said Dempsey, grinning. 'Your basic 'How to Sail a Boat if you're a Gobshite Who Knows Sweet Fuck All about Boats' manual.' He shoved the book into his bag. 'So, Jay, do you suffer from seasickness, at all?'

'Sorry?'

'Seasickness? Are you prone?'

'You want me to come with you?'

'I'd be lying if I said my offer was entirely altruistic, Jay. It's a one-man boat but we'll make better headway if we take it in shifts. Besides, what were you planning on doing? Staying in your foxhole and waiting for the cold to kill all those bastard things off? Because that isn't going to happen. The cold will only kill off the weak ones, leaving you with the really strong, vicious fuckers once spring comes. And think of the disease that's going to arrive along with the warm weather, all those dead bodies starting to rot and the rats having a fucking field day. It's going to be positively medieval, boy.'

It was Jay's turn to grin now. He'd thought the old man would just take his book, harpoon and Lucozade and piss off. It hadn't even occurred to Jay to invite himself.

'I'll take that smile as an affirmative, then, shall I?' He slapped Jay on the arm. 'Good lad. Let's get your stuff and be off. The sooner we're out of here, the sooner we're on the water.'

'I'm up on the third floor,' said Jay and headed off. 'I've not got much.'

Dempsey followed.

Jay was stepping over the threshold of his hidey-hole, scanning the neatly stacked volumes of Blake he couldn't possibly leave behind, when, from the top of the stairs, Dempsey pointed out what Jay, in his eagerness to be gone, had failed to notice.

'Jay?' he said. 'Where's the hyena?'

Chapter Three

'No blood going down the stairs,' said Dempsey, turning slowly on the spot, harpoon gun sweeping back and forth. 'Which means it's up here somewhere, with us.'

Jay was still standing at the threshold of his hidey-hole, looking out now into the shop.

'Christ,' he said. 'It never fucking ends, does it?'

'Don't worry. It can't have much left in it. You just concentrate on getting your gear together. I'll sort this little bastard out.'

Jay backed into the middle of the old staff break area. Dimly illuminated by a battery-operated lantern, it looked like a cross between a teenager's bedroom and a derelict's retreat. Clothing, food wrappers, and empty soft-drinks cans were scattered about. A rumpled sleeping bag lay on top of a makeshift mattress made from the seat cushions taken from the green leather sofa which was abandoned against the far wall. Next to the sleeping bag was a small Calor gas stove. In one corner, a red plastic wastepaper bin — which would have been emptied had it not been for Northrop Frye and subsequent events — steamed slightly. Tin foil and blankets had been thumb-tacked to the walls, and the room was noticeably warmer than the shop floor.

Hyenas

Still keeping one eye on Dempsey, Jay grabbed the khaki 40-litre backpack that had doubled as a pillow and began stuffing it with his William Blake collection, his Sony Discman, crisps, muffins and a couple of pouches of Capri Sun.

The insistent reek radiating from the wastepaper bin reminded Jay of how much he needed to pee. He clipped the pack shut, wriggled into the straps and bounced up and down a couple of times, distributing the weight evenly across his shoulders.

The simple act of thinking about his bladder seemed to have the effect of admitting more fluid into it. The urge to relieve himself had become a priority.

He looked back out through the doorway; he couldn't see Dempsey, but he could hear him muttering to himself. There was no sign of the hyena. Maybe it had simply crawled into a dark corner somewhere to die.

Jay grabbed the wastepaper bin, took it out of sight of the doorway, giving himself some privacy, and set it down on the floor, against the wall.

Jay was letting out a series of diminishing sighs, when there was a crash from the shop floor. Dempsey cried out. Then, the distinctive, guttural laughter of the hyena.

'Shit!' Gritting his teeth, Jay tried to force his bladder to empty itself but there seemed to be no end to it. He tried to staunch the flow but the most he could achieve was occasional stuttering interruptions.

'Little bastard!' Dempsey bellowed.

There was the sound of a scuffle, then a clattering.

Jay pictured the harpoon gun tumbling down the stairs,

Dempsey unarmed.

'Fuck!' He glared down at his penis. 'Come on! Come on!'

'Bastard!' Dempsey roared. Then, punctuated with progressively wetter thuds, 'Will. You. Just. Die. You. Little. *Fucker!*'

The hyena snarled. Dempsey grunted. A heavy thud. Shuffling footsteps approached the doorway.

Dempsey, please, let it be Dempsey.

From further off, nearer the stairs, Dempsey half shouted, half panted, 'It's headed your way, boy.'

The hyena stumbled over the threshold and into the centre of the room. It turned to face Jay, its jaw hanging impossibly loose; its nose looked like something scraped from an abattoir floor. It coughed out laughter, the sound squeezing the last couple of drops from Jay's bladder.

Scuffling backwards, Jay zipped up his pants, almost circumcising himself in his eagerness to retain at least some dignity.

The hyena's eyes rolled back into its skull and it fell forward, arms hanging limply at its sides. Its face hit the floor with a coconut-shy crack. The wallet slid from its back pocket and flopped open. Jay saw a driver's licence, a very human face, clean-shaven and smiling, recognisable despite the absence of thick dirt and dried blood.

Jay skirted round the body, refusing to take his eyes from the thing, certain it would spring to its feet. He grabbed the lantern and all but ran from the room.

Dempsey was sat near the stairs, grinning at his bloodied fists. 'I might have a bus pass,' he said, 'but I'm still fucking handy.' He gave Jay a mock scowl. 'And what, might I ask, happened to the cavalry?'

'I needed a wee,' said Jay and immediately regretted his use of the infantile 'wee', wondering where the hell *that* had come from. Maybe it was because he'd felt like nothing but a frightened child since the Jolt.

'Oh, well, that's all right, then,' said Dempsey, getting to his feet, still grinning. 'When a man needs a wee, he needs a wee.' He started down the stairs. 'Come on, then. Let's be off. Unless you think you might be needing a poo-poo.'

Jay pinkened.

'All right, you sarcastic old bugger,' he said. 'It's been a long day.'

'And it isn't even nine a.m. yet, boy.'

Jay smiled. It was nice, being ribbed for an embarrassing slip of the tongue. Like pub banter, merciless but affectionate. Normal. He followed Dempsey down to the ground floor.

The harpoon gun lay on the bottom step. Dempsey picked it up and checked it for damage.

'Seems okay,' he said and expelled a sigh of relief, his breath condensing and rolling out ahead of him.

It was colder down here. The front door was open and flurries of snow swirled in.

'Once we get outside,' said Dempsey. 'We'll need to keep moving. Stay close to me. I want you to count your steps. Every fiftieth step, I want you to turn and look behind you. These things can creep up on you pretty damn quick. You're going to be the eyes in the back of my head, Mr Garvey, okay?'

Jay nodded.

Abruptly, the quality of light in the shop changed. Jay couldn't see the doorway past Dempsey's considerable frame, but he knew someone, or something, was standing at the threshold. He moved a little to the left, peered around Dempsey.

Two hyenas.

Chapter Four

―――

Jay couldn't speak.

The hyenas looked like they'd crawled through a sewer. It was impossible to discern gender or age. They would have been indistinguishable from one another, in their filthy rags, painted-on grime and grease-shocked hair, if it wasn't for the fact that the nearest one of them was missing an eye. The socket was roaring with infection, seeping something that looked like engine oil.

Jay wasn't sure which Dempsey registered first, the look of queasy horror on his face or the putrid stink of the hyenas, but he turned on his heels and fired.

The harpoon passed clean through the one-eyed hyena's throat and neck and sank deep into the second hyena's shoulder. One Eye grasped its throat, blood bubbling out from between its scrabbling fingers. It staggered backwards into Two Eyes and the pair of them tumbled to the ground, thrashing against one another.

'There must be a fucking sale on,' said Dempsey and pointed to the large window to the right of the door. Out on Bold Street, beyond a display of crime novels stacked to resemble something like the Manhattan skyline, five more hyenas tramped through the snow toward Waterstones. 'Tell me there's a back door.'

'This way.' Jay ran toward the rear of the shop, past Fiction by Author, Horror, Science Fiction and Fantasy, Crime, Alternative Lifestyles and Classics, to a door with a narrow window of wired glass and a keypad sprouting something like a small metallic mushroom.

Behind him, he heard Dempsey reload the harpoon gun and, from further back, grunts, snarls, snorts of laughter and the sound of shelves being ransacked.

It occurred to Jay that lack of power might have caused the door to lock, like when the alarms all over Liverpool had automatically triggered when the electricity supply had failed not long after the Jolt They'd wailed into the night until their batteries ran dry and a weird, almost textured silence descended on the city.

He pinched the mushroom handle between thumb and forefinger and tried to twist it, but his hands were too sweaty, and he only succeeded in skimming around the crenulated perimeter of the mushroom.

'Come on, boy!' growled Dempsey.

Jay wiped his hand on his pants and tried again. Still too damp and his fingers slid off the mushroom once more.

'About now would be great, Jay!'

There was a clack and hiss and a hyena yelped.

Jay wiped his fingertips hard then gripped the metal mushroom so tightly that pain flared in his knuckles. He twisted. There was a click and the door swung inwards.

He rushed into what looked like a storeroom, books stacked on pallets, and Dempsey stumbled in behind him.

'A little help!'

Dempsey had dropped his harpoon gun and was leaning back against the door, heels pressed hard against the carpet tiles. A grimy rag-clad arm was swiping at him, preventing the door from closing.

The carpet tiles began to lift, and Dempsey moved forward an inch.

Jay shoulder-barged the door, throwing all his weight into it. There was a distinct snap as the hyena's arm broke. Howling, the thing withdrew its ruined limb and the door slammed back into place.

A second later, the door juddered as the hyenas shoved at it, but the latch held. Jay could just about make them out through the wire glass, furious, thrashing shadow things.

Dempsey picked up the harpoon gun and, reloading it, moved towards the back of the storeroom. Jay followed, the lantern held out in front of him. They stopped at a metal door, coated in thick, blistered, black paint. Panic punched Jay in the chest. If the steel slab was locked...

The hyenas were slamming into the door now, screeching with laughter.

'Maybe God's on our side, after all,' said Dempsey pointing to a bunch of fifteen or so keys dangling from the lock.

Dempsey went to work on the bolts, top and bottom,

turned the key, opened the door and let out an angry 'Fuck!'

A two-foot recess, then a roller shutter, bullet-locked to a steel footplate.

He thrust the keys into Jay's hand.

'Find it,' he said, turning to level the harpoon gun at the inner door.

Jay held the lantern to the bunch of keys. The keys all looked pretty much the same, and there were no labels or tags. He dropped to his knees and set the lantern down next to the bullet lock. He tried to insert the first key but managed to miss the barrel entirely.

'Christ!' He clenched his teeth so hard the hinge of his jaw ached and his ears felt like they were about to pop, but it seemed to go some way to steadying his hands.

He tried to insert the key again and this time it slotted in with no difficulty. He allowed himself a smile. But when he attempted to turn the key, it only shifted a couple of millimetres and no more.

'Shit.' He dragged the key out, selected another, shoved it in, but this one wouldn't even fit halfway down the barrel.

The third, fourth and fifth keys proved as deceptive as the first, slotting in with no difficulty then refusing to turn. The lock snubbed all but the tip of the sixth key.

From across the room, the thin, brittle sound of splitting wood.

'Apologies for stating the blindingly obvious,' said Dempsey, 'but we're in big trouble if those things get in here with us before you've got that fucking door open.'

A shriek of splintering wood.

'Get as far back as you can,' said Dempsey. 'And turn that lantern off.'

Jay did as he was told. Dempsey followed him into the recess and closed the metal door behind him. The darkness that filled the shallow alcove was substantial; Jay could almost feel it brushing against his eyeballs.

'You're going to have to go by touch, boy. And for God's sake, don't make a sound.'

From the far side of the storeroom, there was a crash as the inner door gave way. Then grunting and scurrying and crazed laughter.

Jay guided the next key into the barrel. The keys jingled a little, but Jay doubted the hyenas could hear much of anything over their own marauding hubbub. Books were being thrown around, shelves knocked over and all the while that harsh phlegm-threaded laughter.

The key slid all the way down the barrel but only moved a degree or two when Jay tried to turn it. Perspiration dribbled from his hairline, through his eyebrows, onto his lashes and into his eyes, stinging. Despite his predicament, Jay was suddenly acutely aware of his own acrid body odour, the result of weeks with nothing but a damp flannel and baby wipes to combat the forces of sweat and grime. He couldn't help noticing that Dempsey hadn't fared much better, although cigarette smoke and whiskey helped smother the worse aspect of the older man's defeat.

Something shuffled up to the metal door, sniffing and snuffling like a bloodhound.

Jay froze and sensed Dempsey do the same.

The clang as the hyena slammed into the door was almost deafening.

'You may as well put that lamp on, boy, they know we're here. And if they realise all they need to do is pull the handle to open the door, we're fucked because there's nothing to hold onto on this side.'

Jay thumbed the switch on the lantern and even though he'd been in darkness for less than a minute, the light that filled the recess jabbed at his eyes. Squinting, he swiped up the keys and started again, trying one key after another with a smooth efficiency that either belied or gave full credence to the fact that he was now certain that he was going to die.

The hyenas appeared to be taking it in turns to throw themselves against the door; every other second, there was a clang that hammered at Jay's eardrums.

The next key slipped into the barrel with such ease that Jay knew before he turned it that it was the one.

There was a satisfying *snip* as the barrel popped out of its sleeve. Jay hooked his fingers under the gap that had suddenly appeared between the bottom of the roller shutter and the footplate and lifted. The shutter rattled upward five or six inches then jammed; cool air and strangely muted daylight rushed in through the gap.

The hyenas were throwing themselves against the door with such force now that it was bouncing open a finger-width before the next hyena's assault slammed it shut again.

Jay tried to lift the shutter again, but it wouldn't budge.

Dempsey joined him.

'On 'one',' he said. 'One!'

They both lifted. The shutter moved another inch.

Behind them, the door bounced open, slammed shut again, bounced open, slammed shut again, and for each second it was ajar, the snarling and laughter of the hyenas flooded in and surrounded them.

'Again, on 'one'. One!'

Another inch.

'Go on, boy, you should be able to get under there.'

Jay shrugged off his backpack, set it down next to him and dropped down hard onto his back. For a couple of seconds, he saw the door snapping open and shut, and the savage faces of hyenas in strobe-light snapshots, then he wriggled headfirst under the shutter.

An instant later, his scalp struck a hard crust of frozen snowdrift and he understood why the light creeping in under the shutter was so muffled. He pressed his heels against the concrete and pushed, but the crust wouldn't give. He pushed harder. The vertebrae in his neck ground together and his chin was driven down against his collarbone.

'Come on, boy! Get moving!'

'I'm trying!'

The slamming of the door was like a manic drumbeat, punctuated by the snarling laughter of the hyenas.

Jay bent his legs, put his feet flat against the concrete and pushed once more, grunting with the strain, certain he was going to start crying and experiencing a ludicrous flush of pre-embarrassment at the prospect.

His neck felt like it was going to snap. The cold sent rods of pain burrowing into his skull.

There was a creak, a crack and the crust began to give way. He inched into the drift, shards of ice scratching his scalp, then forehead, then ears. Unable to focus on the ceiling of the tunnel he was slowly creating, it was as if he was immersed in a world of cool blue whiteness. He had to squint to fend off the snow crystals that were falling into his eyes.

He bent his legs again, dug his heels in and pushed himself further into the drift, moving a good foot or so this time. It felt like someone was driving a needle down through his skull and into his spinal column. His hands cleared the shutter and he tried to bring them up to his head to help with the tunnelling, but they were pinned to his sides. He bent his legs again but this time his thighs struck the bottom of the shutter. He angled his head upwards and tried to get in a sitting position with a view to pushing himself up out of the hardened snow.

The drift collapsed.

Cool blue whiteness became pitch blackness. The weight of the snow slammed Jay back to the ground and emptied his lungs. He gasped for air but only succeeded in taking in a mouthful of splintery snow. He thrust his arms upwards until his hands broke the surface and then scratched and scrabbled at the snow above his face until he could see the tops of the buildings bowing toward one another across the narrow width of Wood Street and, beyond that, a strip of heavy grey-brown cloud. He writhed and heaved himself up and out of the drift.

Alternately spitting snow and gasping in air, Jay stood swaying, almost embarrassed, to see that the snow drift only came up to an inch or so above his knees and was no more than four feet wide. He kicked at the remnant of the tunnel he had created, clearing the area around the doorway. He could see Dempsey's boot-clad feet, his fingertips as he tried to lift the shutter higher and the strap of his own backpack. He crouched down grabbing the pack and dragging it out, and then he noticed that the bottom corner of the shutter had popped out of the runner on one side, jamming it in place.

He looked up and down the street, scanning doorways, snow encrusted dumpsters and abandoned cars. He knew if he saw any hyenas, even a single hyena, loping towards him, he would turn and run, and even though it would sicken him, haunt him forever, he would abandon Dempsey to his fate. Because he was all fear now, his heartbeat the epicentre of his own personal earthquake. But there were no hyenas, just desolation and a constantly shifting polka dot fabric of falling snowflakes.

He kicked the corner of the shutter. It shifted a little but not enough to realign it with the runner. The slamming of the door continued unabated, accompanied by the slathering growls and laughter of the hyenas and Dempsey barking, 'Move for fuck's sake, you stubborn bastard! Fucking move!'

Jay kicked the corner of the shutter again. Then again, and again, and suddenly it jumped back into place. Dempsey lifted the shutter a couple of feet with a cry of, 'You beauty!' He dropped to his knees and crawled out, just as the slamming of the door ceased and a filthy arm swiped out after him, clawing with black fingernails. More grimy arms followed, then the top of a head, hair matted with blood and God alone knew what else. Dempsey stood, placed a foot on the lip of the shutter and stomped it back down. Hyenas shrieked. Blood, unexpectedly bright and clean, spattered the snow.

Dempsey turned to face him, grinning. The grin only lasted a second or two, replaced by a look that was equal parts embarrassment and panic.

'I hope you're good with your fists, boy,' he said. 'I've left the harpoon gun behind and I'm not that keen on going back for it.'

Chapter Five

'What? Oh, Christ.' Jay buried his face in his frozen hands.
Dempsey slapped Jay's arm and belly-laughed.
'Never mind, lad. Could be worse, eh?' He gestured back to the shutter which was shaking and buckling under a sustained hyena assault. 'Let's get moving.' He jogged to the middle of the road where the snow was only a foot or so deep. Weaving in between abandoned cars, he headed down Wood Street toward Hanover Street.

Jay followed. He passed an Italian restaurant, Villa Romana, on his left. The double doors beneath the round arch were ajar and the stench of rotten food leaked out into the cold air: ripe garlic, something like sulphur and other odours he just didn't want to think about. As they neared the bottom of the street, there was nothing but pubs and bars on either side. The smell of musty ale wafting out through broken windows was almost pleasant.

At the right-hand corner of the street, Dempsey came to a standstill, held a hand up, palm out, and Jay stopped. A second later, Dempsey moved off again and Jay followed. They ran diagonally across Hanover Street. A multiple fender bender meant they had to scuttle over the bonnets of abandoned cars. Jay was glad of the snow covering the windows of the cars. He didn't doubt for a second that there were bodies inside some of them. An Arriva double-decker bus, capped with snow, its turquoise paintwork slapped with bloody handprints, had mounted the pavement and almost ploughed into the Lloyds TSB. There was about a foot between bus and bank. Wading through a knee-high snowdrift, Dempsey and Jay slid through the gap sideways and followed the perimeter of the building round onto Church Street. Jay cast a glance back up Bold Street. There were nine or ten hyenas milling around the front of Waterstones, their attention utterly held by the bookshop and whatever it was they thought was in there.

Jay turned his attention back to Church Street. There were few vehicles on this wide pedestrianised thoroughfare — the odd van, a police car that appeared to have taken shelter under the glass-arched entrance to Clayton Square. But there were bodies. Most of them were under the snow, limbs protruding here and there. Jay thanked God for that, but the shop-window dead remained very much on display. In Oasis, a woman, her face a thick mask of dried blood bracketed by lank blonde hair, sat in the middle of a nest of clothes with what looked like a metal chair leg jutting from the top of her head. In Hallmark, a shaven-headed young man in a short-sleeved shirt that was now predominantly red knelt with his head bowed against the glass in what could have been an attitude of prayer; if only he'd had hands to clasp together. There were more, and worse, but Jay refused to allow his gaze to linger.

He forgot all about Dempsey's instruction to check

behind him every fifty paces or so and simply stumbled in the older man's wake, just trying to keep up.

They moved down the left of the street, keeping as close to the buildings as the drifts and debris would allow. At Primark, they had to arc round a tangle of mannequins and corpses that the snow had only half succeeded in concealing. The mannequins retained a rigid elegance and a healthy lustre which the dead — twisted, grey and doughy — couldn't hope to rival. Jay kept his eyes fixed on Dempsey's back and tried to ignore the feeling that the dead were fixing him with stares of their own.

They passed the high-walled, canyon-like Keys Court arcade, with its boutique stores, connecting Church Street to Liverpool One. As they approached the wide intersection with Whitechapel, the smell of rotten meat coming from McDonalds and Burger King thickened the air. They were about to cut across onto Lord Street when Dempsey stopped abruptly and backed into the doorway of Vero Moda and dropped down into a crouch. Jay did likewise, although he couldn't see anything. Then, from further along Whitechapel, out of sight, toward the Met Quarter, he heard sobbing. Then the unmistakeable cackle of hyenas. A lot of them.

Dempsey reached into his bag, pulled out a bowie knife and unsheathed it. Jay noticed dried blood speckling the otherwise gleaming blade.

'There's probably nothing we can do,' said Dempsey, his voice flat. 'Not without the harpoon gun, and probably even with it. Might be a good idea to avert your eyes, boy.'

He sighed, slumped a little.

Jay experienced a tremor in his gut, an inkling of what Dempsey was talking about and what was going to happen next.

Seconds later, an overweight, balding man in a duffle coat ran into view. His face was purple with exertion and his breath trailed behind him like the ghost of a scarf. Even at a distance of some sixty feet, Jay could see the tears glistening on his cheeks.

The man staggered, stumbled then fell face-first into the snow. He jerked back to his feet an instant later, as if someone had yanked on an invisible rope, then started running again. It was obvious to Jay that he was almost out of steam, struggling to lift his legs, his arms limp, head swaying from side to side, mouth hanging open.

'We should help him,' Jay whispered.

But then the hyenas appeared; six of them. The frontrunner, bounding along on all fours, had long hair — once blonde, now yellow as plaque — held back with a luminous pink Alice band. It leapt, the remnants of its flower-print dress flapping like an unravelling bandage. It landed on the running man, its feet striking hard against the small of his back.

In the split second before he went down, a blur of flailing limbs and a flash of snow, the man locked eyes with Jay.

'Help me!' he cried, spitting out bloodied snow and trying to rise to his feet despite the weight of Alice Band on his back. 'Jesus, you have to help me!'

The hyena brought both fists down on the back of the

man's head, driving him back down into the snow.

'Jesus!' His arms flailed. 'Christ!'

Again, both fists. This time there was a loud, wet crunch, a brief spurt of blood and the man went limp.

A second later, the other hyenas caught up, but Alice Band was already moving on, along Whitechapel. The rest of the pack followed. Except one. It was tall and gangly, with a face that was mostly nose counterbalanced by a stiff-looking ponytail. It looked down at the leaking mess that Alice Band had left behind. In one spindly hand it held a paperback *Collins English Dictionary* with most of the pages missing. It knelt next to the corpse and began poking a long index finger into the hole Alice Band had smashed into the man's skull.

Jay wanted to look away but couldn't. He felt as if something was about to be revealed, just as he had when the Waterstones hyena had begun eating pages from Byron.

The hyena pushed its finger in up to the last knuckle, all the while peering into the hole, as if looking for something hidden inside. It had the expression of a child trying to get a coin out of a drain. It wriggled its finger and the dead man's left arm twitched and flopped about for a few seconds.

When the hyena began breaking off pieces of cranium and throwing them aside, Jay had to look away. It had made a hole large enough to accommodate an entire hand now and was rummaging about, sifting through grey matter. Then, with a grunt of satisfaction, it pulled out a steaming chunk of brain and popped it into its mouth.

Hyenas

Jay's vision fogged at the edges and he slumped to his left, his head striking the glass of the Vero Moda door with a dull but resonant chime.

He heard Dempsey growl, 'Shite!' But the older man's voice sounded like it was coming from inside a tin can and down a length of string. Further off, hyena laughter. He knew the brain eater was coming but he could feel himself slipping deeper into darkness.

'Oh, for the love of God, don't fucking *swoon* on me, boy!'

It was the word 'swoon', with its humiliating aftertaste, that brought him round. The fog receded and he saw Dempsey standing his ground, one foot pointing forward, the other back and at a right angle to the first. He held the knife at his side, the arm swaying a little in readiness. The hyena was loping toward them, kicking up snow, its ponytail lashing about behind it. It was spitting out gobbets of brain; apparently, it *hadn't* found what it was looking for. Perhaps it thought it might have better luck rooting through the contents of Jay's and Dempsey's skulls.

Jay tried to stand but his legs failed him, and he flumped back down into the snow. The hyena was closing the distance. Jay noticed it was missing its right ear, and then it leapt. Dempsey brought the knife up in a smooth, taut arc. The blade sunk into the hyena's sternum and it gargled blood, its eyes rolling back into its skull. Momentum carried it into Dempsey and both he and the hyena went through the glass of the Vero Moda door.

Dempsey, his back arched over the aluminium door frame, tried to shove the writhing hyena off him but only succeeded in driving the knife further into its chest. Jay managed to stand, grabbed the hyena's shoulders and tried, unsuccessfully, to free Dempsey.

'Christ, for a lanky streak of piss, he's a heavy fucker!' said Dempsey. He relinquished the knife, planted both hands on its shoulders and pushed. Still twitching, the hyena lifted, and Jay grabbed the back of its collar and dragged it to one side, allowing Dempsey to clamber out from under its all-but-dead weight.

Dempsey was wincing as he stood, one hand planted on his lower back.

'Are you all right?' asked Jay. 'Did you pull something?'

'Pull something? You cheeky bastard.'

'Sorry, I didn't mean... you know.'

'That I'm an old cunt? I'm sure you didn't.' Dempsey took his hand from his back and showed the palm to Jay. It was slick with blood. 'I just went through a plate glass window. This isn't the films, boy. No sugar glass here.'

'Oh, Christ.'

'Please tell me you're not going to swoon again. I might be needing you.'

'No. Well... no, I don't think so. What do you want me to do?'

'Nothing just yet. I think there's a first aid kit on the boat. Now let's get moving and *do* try to stay conscious.'

Grimacing, his face pale and beaded with sweat, Dempsey bent down and drew the bowie knife from the hyena's chest. Not bothering to wipe the dripping blade, he set off across Whitechapel and up Lord Street.

Hyenas

As he followed, Jay couldn't help noticing that Dempsey wasn't moving at quite the pace he had when they'd first escaped Waterstones. And he couldn't help noticing the large slash in the back of the older man's black Crombie. The fabric surrounding the ragged hole glistened.

Chapter Six

———

At the top of Lord Street, Dempsey and Jay crossed over and followed the concave crescent of shops — Prêt A Manger, Blankstone Opticians and O2, with its proud display of halted technology — round onto Castle Street. They jogged past Mangetout, Blue Arrow Recruitment and Andrew Collinge, then, at the junction with Cook Street and Brunswick Street, they cut across the road, weaving in between snow-fattened abandoned vehicles.

As they passed the NatWest, Jay saw a severed hand sitting like a fat, pale crab on the keypad of one of two cash machines. There was something almost deliberate about the placement of the hand, and Jay had to repeat the word 'swoon' to himself, silently, until a sudden pulse of dizziness had passed.

At the corner of Water Street, Dempsey signalled for Jay to stop. Jay looked around, spinning on his heels, as he scanned for hyenas, certain Dempsey must have seen something. But Dempsey swept snow from an aluminium chair outside Starbucks and sat down.

'Just need to get my breath,' he said. His face was almost colourless despite his exertions.

'There was a Boots back there,' said Jay. 'They'll have bandages, antiseptic, pain killers.'

Hyenas

'I'll be okay,' said Dempsey. 'There's stuff on the boat. Getting there's the priority. Once we're in open water, where those bastard things can't get at us, we'll worry about my little flesh wound.'

Jay pulled up a chair, dusted it off and sat down, but continued scanning for hyenas.

'So,' said Dempsey, gazing up at the domed roof of the town hall. 'Where were you when it happened, this Jolt of yours?'

'Where you found me,' said Jay.

'What, in Waterstones? In a bookshop? What were you doing, looking at the pictures?'

Jay flushed. 'No. What? I was... What do you mean?

'Well, you weren't reading, that much I know.'

'I was... you know... I was...'

Dempsey caught the look of humiliation and confusion on Jay's face. He leaned forward and placed a hand on Jay's arm, squeezed it gently.

'It's okay, boy, there's no shame in it.'

'No shame in what?' said Jay, his voice lifeless and defeated.

'None of us could read, Jay. None of us survivors. We all had severe speech or literacy problems of one sort or another. Like me with my dyslexia or Campbell with his aphasia; that sort of thing. Stuttering, illiterate, inarticulate little fuck-ups, every one of us, until... bang!'

'Bang,' said Jay. A fat snowflake landed on his eyelash and when it refused to be blinked away, he wiped it off with the back of his hand. 'It was like something was trying to get out of my head, some massive thought making a break for it, but it couldn't escape. It was snagged on something. And then there was like... like a *tearing*.' He winced at the memory of not just the pain but the sheer disorientating *distress* of it. 'For a second, though, before I blacked out, before I fucking *swooned*, I felt... *wonderful*, like a strong, cold wind had blown through my brain and cleared out all the clutter and confusion, untangled all the knots that had been there since the day I was born. When I came to, I had Blake's *The Marriage of Heaven and Hell* in my hand. I'd had it in my hand the whole time, had never let go of it. I looked at it and... I looked at it and...' he realised he was on the verge of tears. 'I looked at it and I could *read* it. I could actually fucking read it. I could actually fucking *read*.' He laughed, 'And I wanted to tell everyone. But there was no *everyone* anymore, just hyenas.' Another fat snowflake came to rest on his eyelash, but he left it to melt in its own time. 'What the fuck happened, Dempsey?'

Dempsey shrugged. 'Campbell said it had something to do with NASA sending a signal into a black hole or something. Said it was on the news just before everything went pear-shaped. Me? I'll settle for the wrath of God or some such.' He got to his feet. A little colour had returned to his cheeks. 'Let's get moving. We're nearly home free, boy.'

Jay was relieved that Dempsey hadn't pursued the question of exactly what an illiterate fuck-up had been doing in a bookshop, clutching a copy of *The Marriage of Heaven and Hell*, no less. As he stood, he saw blood on Dempsey's recently vacated chair and red polka dots on the snow beneath. But Dempsey had already rounded the corner onto Water Street and Jay could only follow.

Before

―――

The egg custard was delicious, sweet with just the right amount of egginess. Jay was only five and he didn't know much, but he knew the difference between a good egg custard and a bad one. The good ones were sweet, a little eggy but not too much, and cold and creamy; they wobbled a bit when you tapped them with your spoon but, again, not too much. The bad ones were too eggy and were kind of slimy.

But this egg custard, the egg custard they served in Lewis's department store, was perfect.

Daddy wasn't eating his egg custard. He was just staring into his cup of coffee, drawing hard on a cigarette. He looked a little bit angry, like when he was marking schoolbooks, and Jason wondered if he was angry with him, because of what the doctor had said.

As if he'd read Jason's thoughts, Daddy looked up at him, smiled and said, 'Don't worry about it, son. Don't worry about what the doctor said. We'll figure something out. We'll beat this thing. Okay?'

Jason nodded. He wasn't sure what *this thing* was but he was fairly certain it had something to do with all the confusing stuff Doctor Leadbetter had said about how the way Jason's brain was put together meant he probably wouldn't be able to read or write. Ever.

Jason didn't really mind. None of his friends could read, yet. Well, some of them, but only a bit. And why would he want to read, anyway, when there was so much great telly, like *Count Duckula, Chuckle Vision* and *Rainbow*? Besides, if he did want a story book, Daddy could read it to him, like he did now. It just meant Daddy would have to do *all* the reading from now on. Which was fine because Daddy loved to read. All those poems, 'Tyger, tyger burning bright...'

He looked at Daddy. Daddy was staring into his coffee again. He'd even stopped smoking. He didn't look angry now. He had that look on his face — mostly blank but a little sad — that had appeared all the time after Mummy died.

'Daddy?'

Daddy looked up.

'Yes, son?'

'Can I have your egg custard?'

'Help yourself, kiddo.'

Daddy smiled.

Chapter Seven

―――

Water Street was a canyon of pale, mostly neoclassical buildings. The top of the Liver Building, with its verdigris birds, peered over Oriel Chambers and the white glazed brick of the Tower Buildings. Abandoned vehicles were scattered about with such randomness, it looked to Jay as if they had been dropped from the sky.

They had just passed the triple arched entrance to India Buildings, Jay catching a glimpse of the huge, vaulted arcade beyond the glass doors, when a horse bolted from Drury Lane to their left, cutting down and across Water Street to Tower Gardens and then was gone. The detonations of snow created by the horse's pounding hooves swirled about like miniature tornadoes. Jay couldn't help smiling. There was something about this huge, mahogany creature — a little undernourished and showing a few cuts and scrapes but otherwise in full command of itself — that charged him with an overwhelming sense of optimism.

'What the fuck was it running *from*?' said Dempsey.

He grabbed Jay by the arm and dragged him up the steps of India Buildings and out of sight behind the last arch.

A second later, hyenas, as many as ten of the things,

appeared in mad, cackling pursuit.

They waited for a full minute after the hyenas' clamour had faded before continuing down Water Street. They passed a burnt-out transit van, a few feet beyond which was a charcoal corpse, on its knees, head thrown back, open mouth filled with snow. Even now, presumably weeks later, the smell — bitter, sweet and rotten — was nauseating.

Water Street opened up onto the wide dual carriageway of The Strand, dominated by the Liver Building despite the best efforts of the neighbouring Cunard Building, the Liver Building's small albino sibling.

'We're exposed here, Jay,' said Dempsey. 'Keep to the vehicles and stay as low as you can.' He led by example, darting in a half-crouch toward an eighteen-wheeler that had overturned in front of the Tower Building, and Jay followed.

They skirted around the lorry, then in between a black cab and a National Express coach and onto the central reservation. There were very few vehicles on the far side of the carriageway, and they had to sprint. They stayed low, but Jay knew that if any hyenas in the vicinity happened to be looking in their general direction, they'd be spotted. They cut through a small car park to the right of the Liver Building, followed the curve of St Nicholas Place round the back of the large vacant site behind the Crowne Plaza Hotel and onto Princes Parade.

They were right by the Mersey now, the temperature dropping noticeably, and Jay could smell the distinctive and, to him, pleasant tang of its waters. It reminded him of ferry trips to see his Aunty Alison in Birkenhead, memories of Battenberg cake and Ben Shaw's Dandelion and Burdock.

They passed the long, covered jetty of the City of Liverpool Cruise Terminal, leading down to a narrow concrete docking area which ran parallel to Princes Parade for a few hundred feet.

Jay realised he was having to slow his pace a little to stop himself from overtaking Dempsey.

'Do you want to rest for a couple of minutes?' he said. 'Just until you get your breath?' He pointed to a bench, made cartoonish by snow.

'No, no. We're nearly there. A couple more minutes. The boat's moored up near that tower, there.' He jabbed a finger at the Alexandra Tower, three hundred feet of greenish-bluish grey and glass, cylindrical with its top lopped off at 45 degrees.

Despite his words, Dempsey stopped at the white bench and sat down anyway, not bothering to dust away the snow.

'Just for thirty seconds, then,' he said. 'Get my wind back.'

Jay remained standing, turning on the spot, looking out for hyenas. He had to squint as he turned toward the choppy waters of the Mersey: the wind seemed to be scraping ice crystals from the river's surface and flinging them in his face.

'Christ, it's cold,' said Dempsey, shivering violently. His face had lost its colour again. 'I was thinking we'd go south, where it's warmer. We'll sail through the Menai

Strait to Bardsey Island, then on to Ramsey Island, then Lundy and then the Isles of Scilly. Take it in little jaunts until we know what we're doing. Who knows, maybe we'll just keep going: Spain, Portugal, through the Strait of Gibraltar and on into the Mediterranean. What do you think, boy?'

'Sounds great. Pity I didn't pack any sun block; I burn like a ginger. You ready?'

Dempsey nodded, stood with a pained grunt. Wincing, he placed a hand flat on his sternum, moving it in a slow circle as if trying to alleviate indigestion.

'Let's be going, then,' he said in a bright, enthusiastic tone, as if he was about to set off at a brisk pace.

Jay stayed a step or so behind, as if some unspoken code was telling him it would be wrong to overtake. He wished he *could* overtake; then he wouldn't have to see the frequent drops of blood falling from the sodden hem of Dempsey's coat and patterning the snow.

It took them almost five minutes to reach the Alexandra Tower, with its small car park crammed with Mercedes, BMWs and Audis.

'There she is,' said Dempsey, each word punctuated by a harsh gasp. He pointed over the iron guard rail he was leaning against for support.

Jay peered over. About eight feet below, between a set of worn, stone steps and a decrepit wooden pier, was a sailing boat, moored to a rust-encrusted ring embedded in the promenade wall.

It was smaller than Jay had expected, about twenty-five feet from stern to prow, mostly white shell with occasional bursts of highly varnished pine and polished brass. The mast, wrapped in its snow-caked sail, lay folded flat across the length of the boat. There was an outboard motor, scorched and sooty; there were metal rings and pulleys, a spaghetti of guide ropes. He understood why Dempsey had visited Waterstones in search of *How to Sail a Boat if You're a Gobshite Who Knows Sweet Fuck All About Boats*. The name of the vessel, according to the flowery script painted on its side, was *Jerusalem*.

'And did those feet in ancient time...' said Jay and he wondered if it meant something, if it was a good omen. 'How come Pepper didn't get this one?'

'It wasn't here when our man Pepper went on his little scuppering spree,' said Dempsey. 'I watched it drift in over the last few days. Frustrating to put it mildly. It would almost make it to the promenade, and then a wave or a current or some such would drag it out again. I could have screamed, boy. Would have, if screaming hadn't been so very inadvisable. I knew it was only a matter of time before someone spotted it, one of those militia feckers. It's *still* only a matter of time. So, let's get our arses in gear, eh?'

He climbed over the rail, ignoring twin signs, one of which said 'Danger Deep Water', the other 'Warning Strong Currents'. During his first outing post-Jolt, Jay had been overwhelmed by the proliferation of signs and words. Everywhere he'd looked there had been a warning, an instruction or, on advertising billboards and bus shelters, ludicrous boasts. It was as if there was a mesh of language overlaying everything, most of it prosaic and useless. He wondered how the literate masses had been able to stand it, this daily barrage of patronising bullshit.

The moment Dempsey was on the other side, he let out a choking growl and his face, so pale only moments ago took on the vicious purple of a fresh bruise. His eyes rolled back in their sockets and a bloody foam oozed from between pursed lips. Both hands went to his chest and he began to fall, to *swoon* backwards.

'Dempsey!'

Jay lurched forward and managed to grab one of Dempsey's wrists in both hands. Dempsey was heavy, and Jay threw all his weight back away from the waters, hoping to drag Dempsey toward the rail. But Jay's palms were slick with sweat and numb with cold. It took three long seconds for Dempsey to slither from his grasp and then he and the older man were tumbling in opposite directions and Jay was on his back looking up at sandstone clouds and there was a crunch and Jay knew that Dempsey had struck the step and then a thick, oily approximation of a splash as the Mersey took him.

Jay jerked to his feet and lunged at the rail, as if Dempsey was still there, as if he could still save him. He leaned over the rail, looking like someone in the throes of severe seasickness. The snow on the stone steps was spattered with blood. Halfway down, it had been swept away completely, exposing thick brown and green weeds, glistening algae and weird growths that Jay assumed were barnacles but looked to him like grotesque, bony tumours. A faint ripple was swallowed up by heavy grey waves before it had travelled more than a few metres.

Jay clambered over the rail then dropped onto the steps.

'Dempsey!' He shouted down at the water, trying to project his voice through the undulating surface and into the depths where, in his mind's eye, he could see Dempsey, mouth agape, still clutching his chest, dropping like a stone.

He moved down to the second step, and then his feet flew out from under him. He managed to keep his head forward so his backpack absorbed the brunt of the impact, and then he was sliding down the steps on a conveyor belt of snow, ice and algae. He scrabbled at the promenade wall, his fingers skimming across the slimy surface. He struck the water feet first, the cold like an electric shock bolting up his legs and halfway up his spine. And then, just as he was in up to his knees, his fingers sunk into a barnacled fissure in the promenade wall. He felt the nails of his first and middle fingers torn from their beds and his arm snap-locked rigid, agony exploding in his elbow and arm socket. And then he was still.

Desperately trying to draw back the breath that had been knocked from him, Jay sat up. He dragged his legs from the water, surprised by the sudden weight of his own limbs. He held his trembling hands in front of him, as if seeing the physical manifestation of his shock might enable him to bring it under control, but the sight of his own blood pouring from his ruined nail beds didn't help at all.

It was a full minute before he was able to stand. Swaying a little, matching the motion of the waters that had taken Dempsey, he stepped onto the rocking deck of the *Jerusalem*. He stood there for a while, looking back at the steps, the waves, the promenade, the Alexandra Tower, until he was certain that Dempsey wouldn't suddenly surface, full of piss and vinegar and tales of his adventures on the murky bed of the Mersey.

And then Jay realised his brief companion wasn't the only thing he'd lost; he'd lost the sailing book, too.

Chapter Eight

His legs weighed down by the heavy, sodden fabric, Jay trudged across the small deck and ducked into the boat's cabin. It was cramped and gloomy, but it was dry and surprisingly warm. There were two small bunks and, further back, a sink, a stove and some cupboards. Jay sat on one of the bunks, elbows on knees, head in hands, and wondered just what he was going to do next.

The idea that occupied much of the foreground of his thought was this: cut the boat loose. Let it drift and see where he ended up, because anything would be better than Liverpool with its hyenas and militia. But what if he didn't arrive anywhere? What if he floated out into the Atlantic and died a slow, painful death from dehydration?

But what was the alternative? To return to Waterstones? What chance was there of finding another book that would enable him to sail the *Jerusalem*? And what about the hyenas? The place had been crawling with them when he and Dempsey had fled. What would it be like now? A nest?

He couldn't think. The pains in his fingers, elbow and shoulder joint were a constant distraction, and dread had settled in his belly like the beginnings of food poisoning. And what thoughts he *could* summon were swirling round his head like snowflakes, colliding with one another, no help at all.

He shook himself free of his backpack, brought it round in front of him and set it between his feet. He flipped open the lid and took out his Discman. He put in the earphones and pressed 'play'.

A man's voice, Liverpudlian, soft and deep:

'*What is the price of Experience? Do men buy it for a song or wisdom for a dance in the street? No, it is bought with the price of all that a man hath: his house, his wife, his children. Wisdom is sold in the desolate market where none come to buy and in the withered field where the farmer ploughs for bread in vain...*'

Jay listened for a few more minutes and felt his head begin to clear. And then he remembered there was *another* Waterstones, in Liverpool One, just a three-minute walk from where he'd been cooped up for five weeks. He wondered why it hadn't occurred to him sooner, but he knew the answer before the question was fully formed. He hadn't *liked* the new Waterstones. With its escalators and over-sized coffee shop and too many computer terminals, it hadn't felt right, hadn't felt like a bookshop at all. He'd been there once only and, unimpressed, had pledged his allegiance to the older Waterstones on Bold Street.

He stopped the Discman and took out the earphones.

He didn't want to go back to where the hyenas were skulking, but he knew he had no choice. Knowing he had no choice, he decided he wouldn't think about choices anymore, or consequences. He would just get on with it, because he imagined that was how Dempsey had survived. How Dempsey had survived before he'd had the misfortune of encountering Jay, anyway.

He searched the cupboards above the bunks until he found a first aid kit. He bandaged his bleeding fingers, cleaned his cuts and scrapes with cotton wool and witch hazel, then popped four ibuprofen. There were clothes in the cupboards, too: socks, boxer shorts, t-shirts, black canvas trousers and a thick, woollen, navy-blue jumper. He changed quickly, eager to be free of his icy, saturated pants. The borrowed clothes fit well enough, considering, and had been washed in some kind of floral conditioner, the soothing smell of which almost brought him to tears.

He rifled through a drawer near the stove and found two knives. One, a small paring knife, he put in a side pocket of his pack. The other, a good seven inches of stainless-steel blade and a heavy-duty rubber handle, he placed on one of the bunks.

He re-shouldered the pack, picked up the knife — trying to ignore the trembling of his hand, trying to attribute it to the cold — and left.

It wasn't until he was halfway back along Princes Parade, following his and Dempsey's backwards footprints, that he realised it had finally stopped snowing, and he wondered if things were looking up, perhaps.

He recalled Dempsey's instructions in Waterstones

and counted his steps, stopping at every fiftieth step to turn on the spot, scanning for hyenas.

He skirted round the Liver Building, crossed The Strand, weaving in between abandoned vehicles, and headed up Water Street. Every now and then, Jay spotted evidence that Dempsey had passed by — splashes of red — and each time, he wondered if he'd made the right decision, leaving the boat.

As he passed the NatWest on Castle Street, he noticed that the hand that had sat, crablike, on the keypad of one of the cash machines was gone. A hot pulse of nausea surged up from his gut and he realised that the thought of someone or something *taking* the hand was more disturbing than the severed hand itself. He scanned about for hyenas, without stopping or slowing, turning as he moved. He was convinced that whatever had claimed the hand was still around, quite possibly watching him right now from a doorway or from behind a snow-covered car. He was wondering if the hand had been taken by one of the seagulls, wheeling overhead, come out of hiding now that the snow had stopped falling, when he tripped over his own feet and fell. The knife jumped from his hand and skittered ten feet across the crust of frozen snow, spinning. Jay got up, dusted himself down and walked over to the knife. It was still spinning. He remembered an empty cider bottle doing the same thing toward the end of a party at Natalie Keegan's house when he was fifteen years old. He waited for the knife to stop spinning. At the party, the bottle had pointed at Jenny Lasseter and she'd kissed him hard, pushing her hot tongue deep into his mouth and running her fingers up the back of his neck and into his hair. She'd tasted of Cherry Bakewell. Excitement had risen in him so suddenly; he'd felt sick and dizzy, as if he was on an out-of-control rollercoaster. Here, now, the knife pointed across the road, at a newsagent. Behind the plate glass, between advertisements for Lotto and the Liverpool Echo, a hyena dropped the shredded remains of a magazine, spat a wad of pulp from its mouth and threw itself against the window. A dull chime rang out.

Jay scooped up the knife and ran.

Another dull chime. Then another. He was halfway down Castle Street, passing the old Cooperative Bank building, with alternating floors of red and yellow sandstone and its verdigrised onion dome, when he heard the newsagent's window shatter.

He couldn't help but look back. The hyena, clad all in black — black jeans, heavy black boots, black t-shirt — its face and hands bright with blood, was picking itself up off the pavement, mad eyes fixed on Jay. It cut diagonally across the street toward him, vaulting from the bonnet of a windowless, snow-filled Fiesta.

Jay crossed in the opposite direction, angling away from the hyena, toward Cook Street. He risked a backward glance. The hyena tried to change direction too abruptly, and it lost its footing. It fell back, its head hitting the ground with a crunch that might have been lethal had it not been for the relative softness of the snow. It lurched back to its feet almost immediately but appeared disorientated from the impact, scouring the vicinity for its quarry.

Jay, spurred on by this crumb of good fortune, picked up the pace and turned on to Cook Street. Halfway down, he threw a glance over his shoulder. The hyena was still coming. As Cook Street became Victoria Street at the junction with North John Street, Jay took a right then cut across toward Mathew Street, aiming to break the hyena's line of sight, just for a second or two, and give it the slip. A quick backward glance told him he had failed. A stitch like a brutal stab wound tore through his left side and he let out something very much like a whimper.

He considered going down Mathew Street, cutting through Cavern Walks, but what if that was a dead end? What if there were more hyenas in there, skulking amongst the Vivienne Westwoods, Roberto Calvallis and Diors? Then he remembered the next street along, Harrington Street, had a little side street breaking off it, about halfway down.

He passed the Hard Day's Night Hotel, with its gleaming granite pillars and huge Beatles faces in the windows, then turned onto Harrington Street. It wasn't much more than a glorified back alley, a place for deliveries and rubbish collections that sliced British Home Stores in two. Above the street, at first floor level, a glass walkway reconnected the two halves of the department store. Jay could see the side street on the right, about a hundred and fifty feet away.

The pain in his side was approaching unbearable, as if something hot and jagged was sinking deep into his muscle, rotating slowly as it went. He didn't look back now, despite the urge to do so. He could hear the hyena, its crunching footfalls and rasping breath. He willed his legs to move faster. His thigh and calf muscles burned, and a rusty blade seemed to saw into his shinbones, but he felt himself speed up.

He turned onto the side street so fast that he slammed into a shuttered door then pinballed diagonally into the opposite wall. But he didn't stop moving. Above him, pigeons clattered skyward. He knew the hyena would have seen him change direction, but he was praying that he would make it to the opening onto Lord Street, a hundred or so feet away, before it re-established its line of sight. Then — please, God — he could wrong-foot it and duck into a shop, stay quiet, stay still, be safe. And if he didn't manage to outsmart the hyena, he knew, knife or no knife, he'd have no energy left for the fight; he'd just fall to his knees, close his eyes and wait for the inevitable.

As he flew out onto Lord Street, he looked back. No hyena. He attempted a sharp right, but the manoeuvre was too ambitious by far and suddenly he was rolling across the snow, feeling like a cowboy who has just leapt from a moving train in some old western. As he rose to face the side street, he heard the hyena slam into the metal shutter at the other end, and he thanked God that his momentum had carried him over to the right and hadn't left him in full view of his pursuer.

He only had a few seconds to find a hiding place. Right in front of him was an open door and a narrow staircase leading up to a gloomy landing. A neatly scripted menu on a blackboard accompanied by cartoonish illustrations of sandwiches, bowls of soup and slices of quiche, told him that the stairs led up to a cafe. He darted in, turned to close the door, then saw the frozen drift of snow, about a foot deep, occupying the threshold and realised he wouldn't have time. He bolted up the stairs, but the pain in his side was too much and as soon as he reached the landing he fell onto all fours and crawled out of sight.

A few seconds later, he heard the hyena burst from the side street, snarling and panting. For what felt like a full minute, he heard it turning on the spot, then, unable to locate its prey, let out a strangled shriek of frustration and set off down Lord Street toward Whitechapel.

Jay waited until he couldn't hear its panting or snarling or crunching footfalls before getting to his feet. Even then, he peered around the newel post and down the stairs, a substantial part of him convinced he'd see the hyena framed by the doorway, laughing silently, its shoulders bouncing up and down. But there was no hyena.

He gave it another minute.

He was about to set off, when it occurred to him that he was planning to embark on a sea voyage that might, given his novice status, take a lot longer than it ought to and he wasn't sure how much, if any, food was squirreled away on the *Jerusalem*. He was almost certain that Dempsey would have taken care of that side of things, but still, here he was standing in a cafe. He could stock up on a few supplies and pretend it had nothing to do with the fact that he was more than a little reluctant to venture outside again.

He looked around. The landing where he stood formed a red-carpeted T with the stairs. There was a doorway at each end. The door to his right was open, revealing a dining lounge in some disarray. Cutlery, broken crockery and trampled food covered the floor. Some of the tables and chairs were overturned. A pair of bare legs, horribly bruised, extended out from beneath one of the fallen tables; nearby, a pair of shredded and bloodied jeans seemed eager to create a narrative that Jay refused to think about.

The door to his left, a plywood panelled affair, painted white, was closed. Shouldering his backpack, Jay walked to the door. He put an ear to it and held his breath, but all he could hear was his own speeding heartbeat. He grasped the brass-effect doorknob, at the same time tightening his grip on the rubberised handle of the knife, and pushed the door open a couple of inches with his foot. He braced himself to run at the slightest sound, at even a hint of growl or a giggle, but he heard nothing. He pushed the door open the rest of the way and stepped back, the knife held out in front of him in what he hoped was a threatening manner. Again, nothing.

In front of him was a serving counter, with a till, menus, napkins and a small wicker basket that contained a few pounds worth of tips. To his right was the dining area, windows overlooking Lord Street and the Barclays Bank opposite. To his left was a narrow corridor ending in a brick wall painted white. There were two doors set in the right-hand wall. A brass sign jutting out from the furthest door told him it was a toilet. The nearest door, Jay assumed, had to be the kitchen.

He repeated the same tentative two-part process with the kitchen door: tap it open a couple of inches, wait, then kick it wide and step back, knife at the ready. There were no hyenas but, in the middle of the floor, surrounded by pans, utensils, swags of kitchen towel and improbable quantities of various dried pastas, was a man lying flat on his back, milky eyes glaring up at the grease-spotted ceiling. His lower jaw had been ripped off and was sitting on his chest in precisely the spot where a paperback book might rest during a break in a beach read. One hand gripped a kitchen knife, streaked with dry blood.

Jay retched and turned away, pulling his scarf up over his mouth and nose. There was no real smell of decay — it was far too cold for that — but there *was* an insistent sour tang that wormed its way down the back of his throat.

'Okay, okay,' he said. Another dry retch. 'Just get some food and fuck off.'

He scuttled around the body to a counter on the far

side of the kitchen, with cupboards above and below. He stood his backpack on the counter and went through the cupboards as quickly as possible, just letting anything he didn't want fall to the floor and feeling like a lawbreaker about to be caught in the act. He grabbed crisps, a bag of sultanas, a packet of Rich Tea biscuits, bread sticks, a couple of tins of peaches and a jar of Marmite, stuffing them all into his backpack. Once it was full, he shouldered the pack and turned to the door.

The hyena, face and hands still bloody from its encounter with the plate glass window, was crouched at the threshold grinning, and Jay realised he'd left the knife on the counter behind him.

Chapter Nine

Still grinning, the hyena hopped forward, for all the world acting like a child pretending to be a frog. It didn't take its eyes off Jay for a second. It didn't even blink.

Jay shuffled backwards, toward the counter and the knife. The hyena approached until it was an inch away from the jawless corpse. It looked at the dead man, looked at Jay then barked laughter.

'Look,' said Jay, holding his hands up, palms out, like someone confronted by a mugger, a more rational stripe of violence. 'Look, just, I don't know, just, you know, don't.'

As he spoke, the hyena's eyes darted about, seeming to follow something that was moving around Jay's head, a fly perhaps, though Jay could hear no such thing. Or maybe it was simply fascinated by Jay's breath as it condensed in the cold air around him, a brief, crumbling white lace. Abruptly, it lost interest in water vapour or the flight of the silent whatever-it-was and leapt.

It struck Jay headfirst in the stomach. Winded, Jay staggered back until he felt the counter against his spine. He reached behind him, patting the worktop, in search of the knife but found only crumbs and grease. The hyena clawed at him with bloodied hands and

Jay raised his arms to fend off the assault, hearing his coat tear as long nails raked the fabric. He kicked out wildly and the hyena let out a yelp of pain and scuttled backwards.

Jay bolted for the door, but tripped on the jawless corpse, and flumped down beside it.

The hyena laughed.

Jay snatched the knife from the dead man's hand as he heard the hyena's grunt and sensed it hurtling through the air towards him. He flipped onto his back, his pack propping him up, and thrust the knife out above him in both hands.

The blade slipped into the hyena's chest, like a nail into soft pine. A mist of blood speckled Jay's face and then the hyena's dead weight hit him. His arms buckled and the thing was on top of him, gushing hot blood over his hands and down his wrists. He heaved it one way, and wriggled the other, until the eleven-stone blood sac was off him and he was able to slither back over to the counter.

He looked down at his hands. They were gloved in blood and shaking so badly they were almost a blur. A vivid red blur. His heart was beating fast, a tight rippling throughout his entire body.

The hyena was lying on its side. Now that it was dead, it didn't look like a hyena anymore. It looked like what it was: a dead person. And Jay realised for the first time that, prior to the Jolt, this particular hyena had been a girl, no older than nineteen or twenty. She was short and slight with close-cropped black hair. She wore a black t-shirt with the words 'It only hurts because it's true' printed in a bold, white san serif. Everything about her was small and delicate, except her jaw which was strong and jutted out in a way that, in life, might have made her seem confrontational even when she was just minding her own business. Jay felt certain that her smile would have been pretty spectacular, a light-up-the-room affair that would have made people realise they had her all wrong. She was fierce and honest and infuriatingly likeable. And she was just a little girl. And he had killed her.

Jay saw the Hello Kitty bracelet circling the skinny wrist of her limp left arm and started to cry.

He cried for fifteen minutes, his knees drawn up to his chin and his arms wrapped around his shins. As his sobs began to dry out, he found himself wondering what Dempsey would have made of him — a grown man crying — but what did it matter? He wiped his tears away with the back of his sleeve and got to his feet.

He washed most of the blood from his hands using the water that had been sitting in the pipe since the Jolt and had, thankfully, not frozen. He shook them dry. There was an apron hanging from a hook near the door; Jay fetched it and did his best to cover the dead girl. He thought about pulling the knife out, to make her look as normal, as unmurdered as possible, but he couldn't bring himself to do it. He considered saying a prayer but realised that, aside from about three quarters of the Lord's Prayer, he didn't actually know any. He only knew Blake.

So, he knelt down next to her, laid a hand flat against

the top of her head and said, 'In the age of gold, free from winter's cold, youth and maiden bright, to the holy light, naked in the sunny beams delight.'

He stood, trudged from the kitchen, onto the landing and down the stairs. As he was about to step out into the cold, a man wearing a combination of army fatigues and police riot gear, complete with visored helmet, stepped into view. He was holding a small, black assault rifle, which he was pointing directly at Jay's face.

Voice muffled by the visor, he said, 'What's your favourite Beatles song?'

Chapter Ten

———

'What?'

'Beatles song. Favourite. Which one?'

'Fuck off,' said Jay, surprising himself. He could feel anger forming inside him, a knot in his gut and a hot, red buzz in his brain. His fists were locked in a cycle of clenching and unclenching.

'Favourite. Beatles. Song.' With each word, the man jabbed the gun in Jay's direction.

'Octopus's Garden,' he said.

The rifle butt struck his right cheekbone and he dropped onto his backside.

'That's enough, Williams,' said a different voice. This voice wasn't muffled. It was deep, commanding Scouse.

'He said 'Octopus's Garden', sir.'

'He looks like he's had a bit of a rough time of it, Williams. Probably doesn't know what he's saying. Leave him to me.'

Jay sat up. The owner of the voice was wearing a similar uniform to Williams, military meets riot squad, but no helmet or visor. He was taller, a lot taller, about six foot four, with a heavyweight boxer's build — all shoulders and arms. His hair was cropped down to less

Hyenas

than half an inch. 'Fall in, Williams,' he said.

'Yes, sir,' said Williams and dropped back behind the man Jay felt certain was Sergeant Pepper. There were six other militiamen, all clad in the same motley fashion as Williams, all carrying assault rifles.

Sergeant Pepper had no assault rifle, just a pistol holstered at his side. Jay imagined this was intended to mark him out as 'officer class'.

'Looks like you've been in the wars, lad,' said Pepper, gesturing to Jay's blood-flecked face. 'Trouble with the jokers, eh?'

'Hyenas,' said Jay, getting to his feet. 'I call them hyenas.' He had liked it when Dempsey called him lad, but Pepper didn't look a day over forty and it seemed like too forced an attempt to establish seniority.

'Hyenas,' said Pepper, smiling a little. 'That's new. Like it.' He pointed at Jay's hands. 'So, I take it you killed one? One of these hyenas?'

'Suppose so,' said Jay looking down at his bloody hands.

'Suppose so? You weren't sure?'

'It was a hyena. Then I killed it and it wasn't a hyena anymore. It was just a kid. A girl.' He thought he might start crying again. The sorrow mixed with his growing anger and formed something that was almost unbearable.

'You did what you had to do. We need people who do what they have to do. But don't think because you've survived this long you've got what it takes. Not yet anyway. When the End happened, it was, what, eleven o'clock, Sunday morning? And you were here, in the city centre? Shops had just opened. A few hundred consumers milling about. The suburbs are where the real shit went down. And that's where you'll earn your stripes, lad. What's your name?'

'Jason Garvey. And you're Sergeant Pepper.'

'Yes. That's what they call me, Garvey.' A cold smile came and went. 'I prefer Vaughan, though.'

'Sergeant Vaughan?'

'Edward Vaughan. Just Vaughan to you.' Pepper — Jay couldn't think of him as Vaughan or anything else for that matter — took a step toward him. 'Are you with us, Garvey?'

'I don't have a choice, do I?'

'Of course you have a choice. You can choose to join us voluntarily or you can be drafted.'

'That's a choice?'

'Of sorts. But, one way or another, you *are* going to help me take this city back from the jokers.'

'Well, I suppose I don't have any choice but to choose to come with you, then, do I?'

Jay was suddenly aware of the sarcastic bite in his voice and realised he wasn't afraid, for the first time since the Jolt. He wasn't scared of these men with their guns, though he knew he had no choice but to do as he was told.

A commotion behind Pepper.

Williams said, 'Christ, would you look at that. A fucking horse.'

Hyenas

A horse — *the* horse — thick curls of steam rising from its back and flanks, had come from their right, from North John Street, showering the window of the Abbey National with chunks of white shrapnel. For a second, it looked as if it was going to plough right through them, and the militiamen began scuffling about, uncertain which way to move. A couple of them raised their weapons. Then, the horse veered away from them toward the middle of the street and thundered by. Jay could feel the percussion of its hoofs in his diaphragm, a slightly nauseating jitter that made him think of Jenny Lasseter again.

'Thanks,' he said.

'For what?' said Pepper, not looking at Jay, still watching the horse as it crossed Whitechapel and headed up Church Street.

'Not you,' said Jay. 'The horse.'

Pepper turned to look at him then, his expression somewhere between bewilderment and irritation. He took a pair of handcuffs from his belt and started toward Jay.

'Oh, bollocks!' blurted Williams.

The hyenas had arrived, just as Jay had known they would, eight of them so far and who knew how many more were still to come?

The militia began firing. Pepper dropped the handcuffs, pulled out his pistol and rushed forward to join his men.

Jay turned and ran, dipping back into the narrow side street from which he'd only recently emerged.

He thought he heard someone bark his surname, but it was impossible to be sure with the sound of gunfire bouncing off every surface, creating a painful mosquito whine in his ears.

Maybe it was the sight of the horse, its refusal to be brought down, but he was suddenly filled with a crackling, roaring energy. He felt strong, unstoppable.

As he neared the end of the side street, he was certain he heard his name called out. Then, a gunshot, this one qualitatively different from the others, and he knew someone — Pepper, almost certainly — was standing at the Lord Street entrance, shooting at him. Sparks flew from the wall to his left a few feet ahead of him. Another shot. Sparks to his right. Warning shots. But Jay didn't heed the warnings. At the end of the side street, he turned down Harrington Street, sprinting between the two halves of BHS, the walkway over his head. He didn't let the sight of too many bodies to count littering the floor and tables of the BHS restaurant slow him down or dent his sudden sense of strength and purpose. He didn't let the blood smeared windows or that thing that might have been coils of red rope hanging from one of the light fittings undermine his newfound energy and determination. He kept running. When he reached a side street branching off to his left, toward Mathew Street, he considered taking it, because it would lead him away from Pepper and his militia. But only for a second. This was the new Jay. He needed to get to Liverpool One, to Waterstones and the book he would need to sail the *Jerusalem* out into the Irish Sea; Mathew Street, though undoubtedly safer, was in the wrong direction. He continued down Harrington Street until it became Button Street — with its Bistro Pierre, Ted Baker and American Apparel — following it round onto Whitechapel.

He could still hear the sound of gunfire as the militia fought the hyenas. He risked a glance behind him. There was no sign of Pepper. He wondered how he was going to get to Waterstones without being seen. The quickest way would be straight along Whitechapel, onto Paradise Street and up College Lane, but that would mean running across the wide intersection with Lord Street, in plain view. But there were no other options. He'd just have to hope Pepper was otherwise engaged. He took three deep breaths, the freezing air cooling the inside of his lungs, and set off along Whitechapel.

At the intersection, he glanced up Lord Street, in time to see the last of the militiamen turn into the side street down which he'd fled, doubtless in full pursuit now. It was only because he'd witnessed the opening salvos of the skirmish that he was able to identify the dark, shapeless clumps lying about the snow as dead hyenas.

He was hoping Pepper and his men were heading toward Mathew Street, away from him — if they weren't, they'd emerge any moment now and spot him for sure — when he tripped on something and fell. He pushed himself up onto his knees and was about to spring to his feet, when he found himself looking into a fist-sized head wound. Alice Band's brutal handiwork. Blood was still leaking from the boned-edged hole, viscous now, moving like wax down the side of a burning candle, quick at first, then congealing to a standstill, reminding Jay of just how little time had passed since he'd crouched outside Vero Moda, swooned and brought about Dempsey's death.

He scuttled backwards, away from the body, and stood. He could feel the strength leaving his legs. Worse, he could feel his recently acquired determination and energy seeping away.

He ran, hoping it was simply the sight of the corpse that was leaching his resolve, that if he put it behind him, he'd be enervated once more. Ten paces later, a stitch began to hack at his side and needles of pain stabbed at his shins.

He tried to think of the horse, to summon it in his mind, a totem, but all he could visualise was the black hole in the dead man's skull, impossibly deep, with its steady and seemingly endless trickle of blood and grey matter.

As he turned up College Lane, his vision began to blur, a combination of sweat running into his eyes and sheer breathlessness. The smell of coffee from the Starbucks on the corner was so normal, so pre-Jolt, he almost began to cry. On the opposite corner, two stories of mannequins watched him through logo-plastered plate glass windows. And suddenly, the strength was draining from his legs and he was hardly running at all. The small set of granite steps halfway along the street did little to ease the effects of the steep incline and he had to stop, dropping first to one knee then the other.

From where he knelt, the cold drilling into his kneecaps, he could see Waterstones stretching off on his right, toward the corner of College Lane and Manesty's Lane; a great wedge of a building, too big to be a bookshop, the architecture somehow more appropriate to a cinema. Surrounded by clothes shops, it had always seemed lost to Jay, its days surely numbered.

Even before he'd wiped the sweat from his eyes and blinked everything back into focus, he knew something was wrong: the way the thick blanket of frozen snow seemed to have retreated from around the bookshop, drawn back several feet to reveal slate-grey paving stones. And then, confirming his worst fears, his nostrils prickled with the smell of ashes, and he noticed the thick, black scorch marks rising up the broken windows.

Chapter Eleven

———

Jay kicked his way through blackened books and couldn't help laughing.

'This is a fucking joke,' he muttered. 'A shit joke with a piss-poor excuse for a punch line.'

He looked around. Not all the books were destroyed. He could see a shelf labelled *Local Authors* that was mostly untouched. Niall Griffiths, Roger McGough, Nicholas Monsarrat, Brian Patten, Beryl Bainbridge, Ramsey Campbell, Adrian Henri. He felt unworthy. He was alive and they were gone, one way or another. It seemed wrong. It seemed like a colossal oversight. Maybe some cosmic intelligence would realise its gaffe and he and the hyenas would abruptly swap places, Jay the snuffling animal and the literate back in the driving seat once more.

He made his way over to a set of escalators on the far side of the shop. They seemed sturdy enough, despite being warped and soot encrusted; the rubber handrail had melted entirely.

Upstairs, things were worse. Very little made of paper had survived and most of the shelves had collapsed into jagged arrangements of metal and charcoal. The ceiling had been torched away in several places, revealing steel rafters and a confusion of ducts and drooping cabling. The floors groaned and squeaked under his weight. There were a number of blackened, grinning skeletons, contorted into all manner of impossible poses by the intensity of the heat.

He looked about half-heartedly for sailing books, knowing there was no chance. Some fiction had escaped harm and a shelf-load of graphic novels, but everything else was ash. There was an intact sofa in what used to be the shop's café. Jay leaned his backpack against it and slumped down. The smell of cinders rose up out of the fabric and foam.

His legs ached more now that he was sitting. When he was seventeen, he'd gone camping in Delamere Forest with his friend, Andy. They'd walked there from Liverpool, setting off in the early hours of the morning. They hadn't arrived until evening. Christ, it had been a slog. Neither of them had been camping without their parents before, so they'd never had to lug their own equipment. Naturally, they'd taken too much, thinking they were heading off into the wilds when in fact they were only ever a few miles from a supermarket. Once they'd passed Frodsham, it had started to get really hard. Jay's backpack straps had begun to cut into his shoulders and his legs had started to feel rubbery-numb and sore at the same time. For the last few miles, they'd had to stop and rest every half-hour. But every time they'd rested, it had been harder to get going again. It was as if the resting was somehow more exhausting than the walking. Jay could feel that now: inactivity draining the energy from him.

But he couldn't bring himself to stand up and ship out.

Andy. He hadn't thought about him for years. They'd been inseparable from sixteen through to eighteen. Andy had been a big reader, three or four paperbacks a week. But he'd never read in front of Jay, never even talked about books, never mentioned Jay's 'condition'. Jay only knew his friend was a voracious reader because Andy's dad had said so once, when they'd been watching *Bridge on the River Kwai* at Andy's house after Sunday dinner, almost too full to move.

'I don't mind talking about it,' Jay had said later. 'The reading thing.'

'But do you *want* to?' Andy had said.

'Not really.'

'Well, then.'

Andy had gone to university in Aberystwyth, to study archaeology. They'd kept in touch for the first year but had drifted apart after that.

Andy didn't deserve to be one of those things. Of course, Jay didn't think anybody *deserved* to be one of those things, but Andy had been one of the good guys. Other than his dad, Jay didn't think anybody had been as effortlessly, invisibly careful around him as Andy.

If his old friend was one of those things, a hyena, did he *know*? Was he in there somewhere, looking out, wrapped in a fog of illiteracy and incomprehension?

Hyenas

Was he somewhere pawing at books? Was he eating Byron or Blake or — *Jesus* — brains?

'Christ.' That propelled him up and off the sofa; the need to be active so as not to have to think, not to have to reflect on what had become of his friend, on what had become of *all* the good people.

He was about to head outside and back to the boat to take his chances with the open seas, hoping some genetic maritime instinct might kick in if backed into a corner, when he heard movement from the ground floor.

He froze for a second or two then began looking for somewhere to hide.

He heard a dull, gritty shriek and knew that whatever was downstairs had stepped onto the escalator.

He ducked behind the remnants of a counter, a blistered cash register the only clue to its original purpose. The till drawer was open, displaying blackened coins and ash. It wasn't until he crouched down that he realised he was sharing his hiding place with a corpse that was skeletal from the waist down but had retained flesh and even some clothing on its upper body. A metal hair slide in a Celtic cross design was fused to the corpse's scalp. The smell of burnt hair and skin was overwhelming here: bitter yet too sweet. It reminded him of a thick, black medicine he'd had to endure as a child, but he couldn't remember what ailment the medicine had been intended to treat. The floor beneath the corpse looked like it had been scorched to a black parchment on the verge of collapsing and dropping its burden of flesh and bone down to the ground floor.

The dull, gritty shrieks continued, getting louder, then stopped. Whatever it was had reached the top of the escalator. Jay realised he was close to the edge of the counter and shuffled further out of sight. The back of his hand touched the corpse's face, and something stuck to him, something tacky and still warm. He couldn't help but investigate and saw threads of semi-liquid flesh stretching between his hand and the dead woman's cheek. He snatched his hand away and clamped his other hand over his mouth, just managing to suppress a moan. His stomach seemed to shrink. Bile burned the back of his throat and his mouth filled with a salty fluid that told him he was going to vomit. He parted his fingers so he could take a deep breath and dry-heaved.

From somewhere out on the shop floor, there was a clatter and Jay realised that whilst he'd been distracted, the hyena had moved from the top of the escalator but Jay had no idea to where. He just knew it was up here with him, somewhere.

Slowly, painfully aware of every rustle he was making, he shrugged off his backpack and set it down between himself and the melted corpse. He unclipped a side pouch, reached in and brought out the small paring knife he'd taken from the galley of the *Jerusalem*.

Another clatter. This one louder, but Jay couldn't tell if that was because it was closer or because it had been more violently executed.

He remembered the hyena stuffing its mouth with

Hyenas

Byron, the hyena with its largely pageless dictionary that had killed Dempsey and Hello Kitty spitting out wads of pulped magazine before pitching herself at a plate glass window in her eagerness to do him harm. He wondered if she'd intended to punch a hole in his skull and rummage through his grey matter. He was certain it all meant something. Everything meant something once the world had come to an end. There was so little left that whatever remained inherited all meaning.

Then, from further off than the last clatter, the hyena said, 'Bingo. Tom Sawyer.'

Jay peered over the counter. On the far side of the shop floor in what — judging by the remnants of undersized tables and chairs — had been the children's section, was a tall man, at least six foot four, thin despite his winter padding, wearing a Peruvian-style bobble hat. He was dropping whatever minimally damaged books he could find into a large backpack. There was no sign of a weapon and none of the military and riot-gear motley of Pepper's militia.

Jay thought about the *Jerusalem*, the prospect of taking it out onto the Mersey and then the Irish Sea alone. And once he found a safe place, some little island, then what?

He stood and then cleared his throat to speak.

In a single fluid motion, the book hunter drew a small revolver from his pack, spun to face Jay and fired.

Chapter Twelve

The first bullet hit the blistered cash register, sending up a shower of carbon flakes.

'Jesus!' Before Jay could raise his hands to signal his surrender, the book hunter squeezed the trigger again.

The second bullet whined past Jay's left ear, hitting the wall behind him with a sound that was equal parts crack and thud. He didn't even realise he'd scrunched his eyes shut, every muscle in his body painfully tense, until the book hunter said, 'Christ, I could have shot you, you fucking bell-end!'

Jay opened his eyes. The book hunter had lowered his weapon, but not completely.

'I thought you were a fucking zombie,' said the book hunter. 'You're lucky I've got the eyesight of a mole with cataracts, or you'd have a bullet in you right now. I mean, it's only a .22, so at this distance, it's only slightly more dangerous than a hole punch, but still, you know, it'd fucking hurt, like being stabbed really hard with a blunt pencil. I'm Brian, Brian Hughes. Who the fuck are you? And could you put the knife down, please? It's making me want to shoot at you again.'

Jay lowered his hands and put the paring knife on the

counter in front of him. Carbon flakes were swirling around him, like black snow.

'I'm Jason Garvey. Jay.'

'Jay,' said Brian, seeming to weigh the situation on the basis of that one syllable. 'What are you doing here, Jay? You're obviously not one of Pepper's.' He lowered the gun a little more.

'I'm looking for a book.'

'Well, good luck with that. As you've no doubt noticed, this place has been visited by a little flame-related mishap. And the other Waterstones is overrun with fucking zombies. Anyway, all the best, mate. I'd better be getting back to the others. They start bickering when they run out of reading material. It was my turn to do the honours this time.' He shouldered his backpack but kept the gun in his hand.

'Others?' said Jay.

Brian flushed a little, realising he'd said too much.

'Look,' said Brian, 'I know it's not easy on your own, and I'm sorry, I really am, but we're not taking on any new personnel at the moment. Sorry, but you're on your own. You'd do the same if you were me. Maybe you'd be better off with Pepper.'

'I've already declined his offer,' said Jay.

'Don't blame you. I mean, don't get me wrong, I like The Beatles; I just don't fancy getting beaten to death by zombies during the Battle of Strawberry Fields, you know?'

Jay nodded.

'I'm off, then,' said Brian, shuffling his feet and

exuding awkwardness, like a guest trying to leave the world's dullest party without hurting anyone's feelings. He coughed twice, sighed, and then set off toward the escalators. 'Don't follow me, Jay. I'll shoot you in the leg if you do. And a blunt pencil wound is still going to be something of an impediment when you're being chased by a pack of those bastard things. Sorry, but life's a bit shit all round at the moment.'

As Brian started down the escalator, Jay shouted after him, 'I was looking for a book about sailing.'

'Keep looking,' said Brian, the top of his Peruvian bobble hat disappearing from view. 'But don't hold your breath.'

'An instruction manual, sort of thing.'

The escalator continued to squeak and groan. Then silence.

Jay waited.

A gritty shriek and the Peruvian bobble hat rose into view, followed by the rest of Brian.

'You've got a boat?'

'I've got a boat.'

Brian stuffed the gun into his coat pocket.

'What kind of boat? Where?'

'A sailing boat,' said Jay, coming out from behind the counter, scooping up the knife. 'And I don't think it would be very wise for me to tell you where it's docked, do you?'

'No, I suppose not. But how do I know you're not lying?'

Jay shrugged. 'You don't.'

'If you are, Jay, it's blunt pencil time. Seriously.'

'Fair enough.'

Brian's face underwent a series of contortions and he bobbed from foot to foot. Then he said, 'Christ, Dave's going to skin me alive. Come on. Follow me.'

They left the bitter stink of Waterstones behind, heading down the enclosed boutiqued canyon of Peter's Lane, then turned left onto School Lane, where the snow quickly reasserted itself, seeming to rise up around their calves. They passed Bluecoat Chambers. A large banner over the wrought iron gates advertised an exhibition by Peter Chang, with oversized images of Chang's jewellery; they looked like weird bioluminescent marine life or models designed to explain some elusive principal of quantum physics. They passed the Quaker Meeting House on their right. At the Old Post Office pub, with its inexplicable hedgerow, snow-capped now, running between the ground and first floors, they turned left down an alley crowded with dumpsters. One of the dumpsters had tipped over, spilling boxes of paperwork, toner cartridges and two human arms that were so physically different from one another they couldn't possibly have belonged to the same victim. A fat crow pecked at the limbs, hopping from one to the other, as if it couldn't decide which tasted better. It held its ground as Jay and Brian passed. The alley turned abruptly right, running parallel with School Lane, heading toward Hanover Street. When Brian stopped at a recessed loading bay with a steel roller shutter, not far from the end of the alley, Jay couldn't help laughing.

'What?' said Brian.

'Nothing. It was just that I was hiding out about a minute from here, in Waterstones. On Bold Street. We were neighbours.'

'Waterstones? Really?'

'Yeah. On the top floor. I set up camp in the old staff room.'

'We nipped in and out of there all the time, nicking books. Well, not 'nicking', exactly. I mean, they don't really belong to anyone anymore, do they? Anyway, we had to give up on the Bold Street branch after the zombies moved in.'

'Me too.'

Brian shrugged off his pack, rummaged about inside it, then produced a pink baby monitor. He gave Jay a sheepish grin and switched it on. It crackled to life, an arc of red LEDs lighting up.

'Anybody there?'

A pause, then, a man's voice, 'I'll be down in a second.'

'I've got company. Don't worry.'

'Oh, Christ, Brian, you know the rules on waifs and strays.'

'It's okay. He's cool.'

'And did you invite him to tag along on the basis of this 'coolness'? What precisely constitutes *cool* in Brianland? I mean, what, does he have great hair or something?'

'He's wearing a hat.'

'Is it as cool as your hat?'

'Not really. Sort of plain.'

'I was taking the piss, Brian.'

'Yeah, I know. Anyway, let us in, Dave. It's fucking freezing. I'm going to lose a nut if I stay out here much longer.'

'You're going to lose both fucking nuts when I get down there, Brian.'

'He says he's got a boat, Dave.'

The sound of breathing. A sigh so loud it produced a crunch of distortion.

'Hang on.'

Brian turned to Jay, putting the baby monitor back in his pack.

'See? What did I say? When they run out of reading material, they get all arsey. Me, too, though, if I'm being honest.'

Without making eye contact, instead looking up and down the side street, Jay said, 'So, what were you like before the... before whatever it was that happened?'

'We don't talk about that. First rule of Book Club: the past never happened. Better that way. Less painful.'

'Book Club?'

Brian grinned. 'That's what we call our little group. By the way, I'd put that away if I were you.' He nodded to Jay's hand.

Jay hadn't realised he was still clutching the paring knife. He put it into his jacket pocket.

There was a sharp click from the other side of the steel roller, then a rattling of chains. The roller began to rise.

When it was halfway up, the voice that had addressed them from the baby monitor said, 'Come on, stoop, you bastards.'

Brian did as instructed. Jay followed.

Dave — presumably — regarded Jay with undisguised suspicion and naked aggression. He wasn't much over five and a half feet tall, but he was considerably broader than Jay in the shoulders. Pushing fifty, he had the kind of face, lined and ruddy, that Jay couldn't imagine expressing anything other than distrust and hostility.

Brian dragged the Peruvian bobble hat from his head, revealing a thick scar running from his crown to just above his left ear. Jay felt certain Brian had been in some kind of accident, a car crash maybe, which had doubtless left him with the inability to read or write or both. That was why he was a survivor and not a hyena.

Dave caught him looking at Brian's scar and said, 'We don't talk about the past, so don't ask. And we aren't interested in yours, so don't tell. Are we clear on that?'

Jay nodded.

Without another word, Dave headed up a short staircase which opened up onto a small and weirdly angled reception area, as if a corridor had been ineptly reengineered for the purpose. There were a couple of leather armchairs and a small round table covered in magazines about cars, property and computers. About twenty feet to the left, a pair of tall glass doors presented a view of Hanover Street with its snow-covered abandoned cars. Between the Hanover Street entrance and the staircase from which they'd just emerged, there was a lift, the doors open a couple of inches. Dave headed right, down a narrow corridor and through a door marked *Stairs to All Floors*. Brian and Jay followed. On the fourth floor, they went through a fire door kept ajar by a bucket of sand and emerged into a small waiting room, all dark wood, leather armchairs and prints on the wall by Lucien Freud and George Stubbs. On the far side of the room was an open door, from beyond which Jay could hear men's voices raised in argument.

As Dave passed through the door, he said, presumably to the room's occupants, 'Brian's decided to bring a stray home with him. But don't worry, Brian says he's 'cool'. So that's alright, then, isn't it?'

Brian then Jay entered the room to a chorus of groans and a solo, 'Oh, for fuck's sake, Brian, lad, what are you doing to us?'

It was warm in the room, courtesy of two Calor gas heaters back-to-back at the centre of a rough circle composed of seven armchairs. All but three of the seats were occupied, and everybody — except Brian but including Dave — was looking at Jay as if he was the harbinger of a particularly irritating variety of doom.

The first to abandon his expression of guarded resentment was an Indian man in his early fifties. He wore a charcoal three-piece suit and a gleaming white turban. He was chewing on an unlit pipe. Taking it from his mouth, he produced a modest smile and said, 'I'm Kavi Singh. And you are?'

'Jason Garvey,' said Jay. He was embarrassed to hear a tremor in his voice and realised he felt intimidated by this room full of relatively ordinary people. But, at the same time, he was almost relieved to discover there were other sorts of fear, gentler than the outright panic and ground-in dread he'd been living with for the last five weeks. He couldn't help smiling. 'Jay. My friends call me Jay. *Called* me Jay.'

'What's so funny?' said Dave, as if he suspected he was the object of some private joke.

'Just nervous,' said Jay.

'Where'd the blood come from?' said a teenage boy, white but with straw-coloured dreadlocks that almost reached his waist. He was pointing at Jay with a paperback. *Ask the Parrot* by Richard Stark.

It took Jay a couple of seconds to realise he was still speckled with the evidence of his encounter with Hello Kitty.

'Hyena,' he said.

'Hyena?' said a man who was as tall and gangly as Brian, but with a substantial afro and deep, black skin.

'That's what I call them.'

'Zombies,' said the teenage boy. 'They're zombies.'

'Christ, Simon,' said Dave, 'we've no idea what the fuck they are.'

'Better than what Phil calls them,' said Simon, pointing at a man in his mid-thirties, with short hair and a neatly trimmed beard, both prematurely frosted. 'Fucking 'Twats'. I mean, you're a twat, Dave, doesn't mean you're going to beat me to death and try to eat my brain.'

'Yeah? Don't tempt me, Si,' said Dave.

Phil grinned, running a hand over his grey beard. 'Well, they are,' he said. 'A bunch of twats. I mean, they can't help it. Feel a bit sorry for them, myself.'

'But would you let your daughter marry one?' said the man with the afro.

'Now, if I'd said that, Joe,' said Dave, 'you'd be calling me a racist.'

'But you *are* a fucking racist,' said Joe.

Dave grinned. 'True. But an honest man.'

'I'll give you that, Dave,' said Joe, shaking his head but grinning a little.

'Jay's got a boat,' said Brian.

'*Says* he's got a boat,' said Dave.

All eyes were on Jay again.

'Is this true, Jay?' asked Kavi.

'Yeah. A sailing boat.'

'Where?' said Joe.

'Like he's going to tell us,' A woman's voice, from behind Jay.

He turned. Standing in the doorway was a woman of about twenty-five. Her brown mid-length hair was held up in a bun by two yellow pencils. She was holding an artist's paintbrush in one hand and an empty teacup in the other. She wore low-slung hipster jeans and a fitted blouse, both black and both splashed with various colours of paint. The last couple of buttons of the blouse were undone to allow for the fact that she was distinctly pregnant.

Chapter Thirteen

―――

'Where's the harm in telling us where the boat is?' said Simon. 'It's not as if we're going to kill him and take it off him, is it?'

'Depends how many people it can carry,' said Dave. 'Might *have* to take it off him. Christ, with any luck, we might have to leave you and Brian behind, Simon.'

'And who's going to sail the thing?' said the woman. 'You, Dave? Did you have many nautical themed away days while you were in Walton nick?'

Dave barked a laugh. 'Harsh as ever, Ellen. Anybody know how to sail a boat?' A chorus of negatives. To Jay, 'So how many people can this boat of yours handle, then?'

'All of us, probably,' said Jay but he was almost certain it would struggle to stay afloat with more than five bodies aboard.

'Anyway,' said Brian, 'even he doesn't know how to sail the fucking thing. He was in Waterstones looking for an instruction manual, weren't you, Jay?'

Ellen raised an eyebrow at Jay.

Jay nodded.

She rolled her eyes and then smiled.

'Well, I hereby declare you hopeless enough to join our

little club, Jay,' she said. 'We deserve each other.'

There was a half-hearted clatter of applause.

Dave smiled, shook his head and let out a long, sighing, 'Christ.'

'Fancy a cup of tea, Jay?' said Ellen.

'I'd love one,' said Jay.

'Well, put your bag down, take your coat off and I'll show you where the kitchen is. I like mine strong, just a splash of milk and no sugar.'

Jay dropped his pack, shed his coat and followed Ellen back into the waiting area and through a door opposite, into a small kitchen.

'Kettle's there,' said Ellen, pointing to a camping stove next to a couple of five-litre bottles of water, a few cartons of UHT milk and a box of Yorkshire Tea. She pointed to a piece of paper taped to the wall. Written on the sheet of paper in neat print was a list of everyone's names and how they liked their tea. 'There's your instructions. I'll leave you to it.'

As he watched her walk out of the kitchen and through a door that, before the Jolt, had probably led to someone's office, Jay realised he'd been hoping that she'd stay. Then Kavi appeared, holding a small wooden box with elephants carved into its surface.

'I'll make my own,' he said. 'You English don't have a bloody clue how to make a decent cup of tea.' He tapped the lid of the box. 'Cardamom, fennel and ginger. The secret to a really great cuppa. You should try it. You won't look back, I promise you.'

'Okay,' said Jay.

'Pass me your cup. I'll make ours, you can make that muck the rest of them drink.'

While Jay went about making the drinks, Simon appeared, moving into the corner of the kitchen, facing them, pale dreadlocks draped over folded arms.

'So, Jay, what do you think happened? You know, The End. What caused it?'

Jay shrugged. 'I don't know.'

'Most of them think it was either some kind of act of God sort of thing or something to do with that NASA malarkey, sending a signal into that black hole and whatnot. Dave thinks it was like a virus or something but that's bollocks because it happened to everyone at once and why would people who can't read or write be immune? Makes no sense. Act of God? Well, I don't believe in God for a start.'

'Doesn't mean it wasn't an act of God,' said Kavi. 'God doesn't require your belief in order to act, Simon. And if he decided the human race had run its course, well, that's that, then.'

'So, Jay,' said Simon, ignoring Kavi. 'Your theory, what is it?'

'I don't have one, but it has to mean something, doesn't it, none of us being able to read or write? I mean the fact that we've survived should tell us why everyone else died, shouldn't it?'

'Suppose so,' said Simon. 'I used to stutter like a bastard, words stuck somewhere between my brain and my lips and then *fuck*; suddenly it's like someone shook me until all the words came loose. Sometimes I just can't stop talking. Drives Dave mental.'

'Not just Dave,' said Kavi, a smile in his voice as he pounded fennel seeds and cardamom pods with a mortar and pestle.

When the coffee and teas were made, Simon and Kavi helped Jay take it through to the others. The books Brian had pillaged had been handed round. Dave was reading *The Adventures of Tom Sawyer*, and Jay found this surprising but couldn't say why.

'So,' said Phil, taking a sip of his tea. 'About this boat, then.'

'It's not far from the Pier Head,' said Jay. He took a sip of his own tea. His eyes widened a little at the barrage of flavours: the perfume of the cardamom, the sweetness of the fennel and the heat of the ginger. Then he realised he was still holding Ellen's tea in his other hand. 'I'll just take this through to, er...'

'Ellen,' said Brian.

Jay hadn't forgotten her name, but it had just seemed inappropriate somehow, a little silly even, that he should be seen to have remembered it.

'Yeah, Ellen,' he said.

As he made his way out of the room, Dave shouted after him, 'Tell her we need to make a decision about this boat of yours and I wouldn't want to be called sexist on top of everything else for leaving her out of the discussion.'

'Like you'd fucking dare,' said Joe.

Brian grinned. 'We're all a bit scared of Ellen,' he said to Jay. 'She takes no shit.'

Jay walked across the waiting area to the door he'd seen Ellen walk through after she'd taken him to the kitchen. The door was closed. He placed his own cup on a small side table next to an armchair and knocked gently on the door. There was no response so, a few seconds later, he knocked again, a little harder.

'Yeah.'

'Tea,' said Jay.

'Come in.'

Jay pushed open the door. Ellen was mostly hidden behind a large canvas that was balanced on a makeshift easel cobbled together from a random collection of wood. The window behind her offered a view of the back alley where Jay and Brian had waited for Dave to let them in. There were canvases all around the room, at least fifteen of them. About half were turned away, the rest displayed permutations on the same subject: a hyena in a variety of poses rendered in violent strokes of thick, black oil paint; the images looked less painted onto the surface of the canvas than the canvas had been clawed and shredded to reveal a rich, almost liquid blackness beneath. Swarming around the head of a hyena in one painting was a cloud of words that the hyena appeared to be swiping at, as if trying to dispel or capture the swirling characters. It was impossible to say which. As Jay peered closer, he saw that the swarming words were composed from no alphabet he recognised.

'Is that what they see when we talk, do you think?' said Jay walking over to Ellen and handing her the tea.

Ellen took the tea and said nothing, just continued to jab at the canvas.

'There was this hyena,' said Jay. 'A couple of hours ago. When I shouted at her — at *it* I mean — to get back, its eyes were darting all over the place and I thought it was my breath it was looking at because it was so cold, you know, but maybe it wasn't; maybe it was the words she — I mean *it* — was looking at. Like in your painting. Is that what you think? Have you seen them do that?'

Ellen levelled a stare at Jay, took a sip of tea, then said, 'Fuck's sake, you talk more than Brian and Simon put together. But you make a fairly decent cup of tea.'

'Thanks. Were you an artist before the Jolt, before this all kicked off?'

'Was. Still am. This shit changes nothing. And when someone tells you that you talk too much, it can be taken pretty much as read that they want you to be quiet.'

'Sorry.'

'Don't take it personally. I love painting, and people generally get right on my tits, so when a person interrupts the painting, well, you know, it's like a double whammy of annoyingness.'

'Fair enough.' Jay smiled.

Ellen took another sip of tea, jabbed the painting a few more times, then glanced at Jay.

'You're still here. I mean, you're not talking so that's a point in your favour, but you're still, you know, here.'

'Erm, Dave, is it? He said we were going to discuss the boat situation and you'd be pissed off if you weren't invited.'

'Well, he's not wrong. I would be. Tell them I'll be in when I'm done here.'

Jay nodded. 'I'll leave you to it, then.'

'Yeah,' Ellen pointed at the door and made a little shooing gesture with her finger.

Back in what Jay had already come to think of as the reading room, a silence had descended, interrupted only by the occasional susurrus of pages being turned.

Dave glanced up from *The Adventures of Tom Sawyer*. 'What she say?' he asked.

'She'll be in when she's done,' said Jay.

'Artists,' said Dave with a roll of his eyes, and returned to his book.

Jay went to his bag, fished out *Fearful Symmetry* and sat in the empty armchair.

There was a collective intake of breath.

'Ellen's chair?' said Jay.

'Ellen's chair,' said Joe over the top of *Devil in a Blue Dress* by Walter Mosley. 'Just make sure you're out of it before she comes in. And I mean a good five minutes before she comes in. If that seat's still warm from your arse… she won't be best pleased.'

'What you reading?' asked Phil, scratching his beard with the corner of a battered paperback. Jay couldn't see the title or author, just the cover art. A tyrannosaurus rex looming over two men in pith helmets.

'It's a critical study of William Blake,' said Jay. He immediately felt embarrassed. A few months ago, he hadn't been able to read at all. None of them had. Who was he to be reading Blake, let alone a 'critical study' of the man? He felt like a scavenger, gnawing on literature's corpse and, at the same time, like a little boy trying to walk in grown-up shoes. But mostly he felt like a pretentious dickhead.

'Blimey,' said Phil. 'Bit heavy, that. I had to ease myself into it. Reading.' He turned the book he was holding so Jay could see the cover clearly. *The Lost World* by Sir Arthur Conan Doyle. 'I used to work on a building site. Just lifting and shifting. My gaffer, Dennis Cattrall, lovely man, used to always have a book tucked into his back pocket. He used to read them on his lunchbreak. I used to be a bit jealous, the way he'd just pull the book out, sit down and start reading. His face would change. He'd just go into this whole other world for twenty minutes, half an hour. It was like a magic trick.' He cracked the book open. 'Anyway, this was the sort of thing he'd read. Adventure stories. Old ones. Tarzan and that. Doc Savage. Don't think I'd be able to get more than a page into a… a 'critical study' of William Wordsworth or whoever.'

Jay wanted to tell him that he'd struggled too. He wanted to tell him that he'd set Blake aside on any number of occasions. But he'd always picked him up again. He wanted to tell him it *had* to be Blake. But then he'd have to explain why, and that he didn't want to do.

'Richard Stark for me,' said Simon, pushing his straw-coloured dreadlocks back. He held up his book. *Ask the Parrot*. The cover depicted a wooded North American backroad, with a single car approaching, headlights illuminating the misty rain. 'The Parker books. Crime capers. This is my fifth one. They always start the same. Parker's in the middle of a job or just finished one, and something goes wrong. Usually, someone's fucked him over.' He laughed. 'Been there. Me, Wezzy and Macca were turning over this cash and carry in Warrington. The busies showed up, blue lights flashing. They got to the car before me and the bastards drove off. I was left standing there coughing on burnt-rubber fumes. Did the better part of four months in Altcourse. Fucking shit, that was.'

'We're in danger of breaking rule number one, lads,' said Dave, without looking up from *The Adventures of Tom Sawyer*. 'No talking about the past.'

'We're not talking about the past,' said Simon. 'We're talking about books.'

'Anyway,' said Joe. 'The main reason you don't like talking about the past is because yours is dodgy as fuck.'

Dave grinned. 'True. But also, remember that time Phil started talking about his nan's Sunday dinners and then had a full-on crying fit because he was never going to eat roast potatoes and partridge again.'

'Partridge!' said Joe, slapping his thigh with his

novel. 'I'd forgotten about that. Who has *partridge* in Liverpool?'

'He's from the posh bit, our Phil,' said Brian, putting his copy of *The Hobbit* on the arm of his chair. 'Calderstones. They have partridge every other day there. Partridge and chips. Partridge and mash. Partridge and roast potatoes. They're partridge mad in Calderstones.'

'Fucking hell,' said Phil. 'I only had it the once. Wish I'd never mentioned it. And I *didn't* fucking cry.'

'Well, you were doing a convincing impression of it,' said Dave.

'I miss good food,' said Kavi. He closed Spike Milligan's *Adolf Hitler: My Part in his Downfall* over his finger. 'Rajma, bhindi, karela. Proper food. Indian food. Not your boiled peas and soggy cauliflower. The only thing you English do well is comedy.' He waved the book. 'And Spike Milligan was born in India. Technically, he's one of us. But I have to give you credit, you *Angrezee*, you have a talent for being daft.'

'That we do,' said Dave. 'Especially now it's just us. Or people like us. Dregs. Daft fucking dregs.'

Joe was nodding. 'How can we be it? How can we be what's left? The survivors. It's mental.' He held up his book. 'This guy, Walter Mosley, his writing's so... I don't know... so fucking great. I'm not a critic. It's just great. When you're reading it, you're just... there. With Easy Rawlins and Mouse. You're with them. In their world. And now, I'm here, reading this book and hardly able to string the words together to describe it, and the guy who *wrote* the book? He's probably eating junk mail or beating someone to death with a fucking chair leg. Christ.'

'And this is why we don't talk about the past,' said Dave. 'It always ends up with one of us punching ourselves in the face with the present. Or Phil crying about his nan's partridge.'

'So,' said Ellen, stepping into the reading room.

Jay practically jumped out of Ellen's chair, much to everyone's amusement, including Ellen's. As Ellen took his place, she gave him a nod that reminded him of Dempsey. *Good lad*, that nod said. And he was surprised to find he didn't mind that much.

He put *Fearful Symmetry* back into his pack and sat on the arm of Ellen's chair.

'What did you want to talk about?' said Ellen.

'The boat,' said Dave, putting his book down. 'What should we do about it?'

'Do about it?' said Phil. 'What can we do? It's a sailing boat and none of us, including the boat's current owner know how to sail. What's to discuss? It's a nonstarter.'

'Agreed,' said Simon.

'We could get a book,' said Brian. 'That's what Jay was doing.'

'From where?' said Dave. 'Waterstones, Liverpool One, is just a scorched carcass and the Bold Street branch is full of those fucking...'

'Hyenas.'

'Zombies.'

'Twats.'

'Whatever you want to call them,' Dave finished.

'There must be other book shops,' said Kavi. 'What about Blackwells, up by the University?'

'Mostly for students,' said Joe. 'If it isn't on some syllabus or other, you won't find it there.'

'And how would you fucking know?' said Dave. 'You were functionally illiterate up until a few weeks ago. Just like the rest of us.'

'Mate of mine was studying architecture at John Moores. Functionally illiterate I may have been back in the real world, but I used to associate with a better class of person than you fucking dunderheads.'

'What about second-hand book shops?' said Brian. 'There's a few of them. Oxfam further up Bold Street.'

'There was only one sailing book in Waterstones,' said Jay. 'I don't fancy our chances in a second-hand book shop.'

'What about,' Kavi began. Then, 'No, it closed down a couple of years ago.'

'They all closed down except for Waterstones,' said Phil. 'All the little independents went to the wall.'

'What about W.H.Smiths?' said Brian.

'Great,' said Joe. 'If you want a magazine, a pen or a fucking toner cartridge.'

'They had some books,' said Brian. Then very doubtfully, 'Didn't they?'

'They had Toblerones,' said Simon, and Jay couldn't tell if he was being derisive or wistful.

Jay saw Ellen shake her head in mock despair.

'What?' he said.

'The library?' she said. 'William Brown Street. I imagine there's quite a few books in there. One or two about sailing, even.'

'The library,' said Brian. 'Fucking hell, yeah. Why didn't I think of that?'

'I could answer that, Brian, but I wouldn't want to shit all over your feelings,' said Ellen.

Phil huffed and rolled his eyes, childlike despite the whiteness of his beard and hair.

'Boat or no boat, book or no book, I don't see why we'd want to leave here, anyway,' he said. 'We just need to wait out the winter. The cold will kill off the Twats but hopefully not before they've killed off Pepper and his pals, or at least drastically thinned their numbers.'

'I'm with Phil,' said Simon.

'Come the spring it'll be a new beginning for all of us,' Phil continued. 'Until then, we just need to sit tight. Use your heads, people, for fuck's sake.'

Jay didn't realise he'd emitted a little snort until all eyes were on him.

'You don't agree,' said Phil

Jay licked suddenly dry lips.

'Well,' he said, his voice a little high and uneven. He coughed to steady his nerves.

'Do you want to wash that blood off your face before you carry on?' said Phil.

Jay wasn't sure whether Phil was being sarcastic or

patronising, or which of the two was worse. But the thought of the blood on his face and how it had got there, of Hello Kitty, seemed to fill him with something like resolve. He wondered at first if it was the fact that he had killed that was making him feel as if he didn't have to take being talked down to; that he had proved himself. But then he realised it was precisely the opposite: he didn't want to have to kill again and whilst he was in Liverpool with its hyenas and militia, he would very likely have no choice in the matter if he wanted to survive.

'I'll wash it off in a minute,' he said. 'When I've said what I need to say.' He paused as he tried to recall Dempsey's words. 'If you think you can stay in your foxhole and wait for the cold to kill off all the hyenas or jokers or zombies or whatever you want to call them, you can think again because it isn't going to happen. The cold will only kill off the weak ones, leaving you with the really strong, vicious fuckers once spring comes. And think of the disease that's going to arrive along with the warm weather, all those dead bodies starting to rot; the rats'll having a fucking field day. It's going to be like something out of the middle ages. We have to get out of the city. Find somewhere less populated, somewhere open. Somewhere we can fish and grow food. There really isn't any alternative. Well, not one that isn't suicide of one form or another.'

'Where did you have in mind?' said Ellen.

'I was thinking we could go south, where it's warmer.

Through the Menai Strait to Bardsey Island, then on to Ramsey Island, then Lundy and then the Scilly Isles. Take it in little steps until we've got the hang of it. We could even keep going: Spain, Portugal, through the Strait of Gibraltar and into the Med. I don't know. I haven't really thought that far ahead.'

Nobody spoke for a few seconds but it felt like longer to Jay. He was almost certain he was about to be assailed by waves of laughter and accusations of having appropriated someone else's ideas and rhetoric.

'Well, I'm with you,' said Ellen. 'I've always said, the first chance I get, I'm gone. Can't have my baby here. And in a couple of months, I won't be able to fucking move, so it's now or never.'

'I'm with you,' said Brian, to Jay or Ellen, it wasn't clear.

'And me,' said Joe.

'Alright,' said Dave with a reluctance that Jay thought was largely for show. 'Count me in. I can't leave you in the hands of this bunch of inepts, can I, Ellen?'

'True,' said Ellen, and Jay really couldn't tell if she was joking or not.

Simon rolled his eyes, 'You've got to be having a laugh,' he said. 'Just because he says it'll be worse after the thaw doesn't mean it will be. What makes him such a fucking expert. I say we sit tight. Right, Phil?'

Phil had been looking up at the ceiling throughout Jay's speech and since. He let loose a long sigh.

'No, Simon,' he said, turning his attention to Jay. 'He's

right. I mean, the cold hasn't killed them off yet, has it? And survival of the fittest? Well, there's no arguing with that, is there? I might not believe every word this lad says but there's no arguing with basic Darwinism.'

'Well, I'm not staying here on my own, am I?' muttered Simon. 'But don't blame me if we all get drowned.'

'After we've drowned, Simon,' said Dave, 'we promise to keep our opinions to ourselves.' He stood up. 'Right. Me, Simon and Kavi will take a trip to Tesco, stock up on dried foodstuffs and bottled water. Phil and Joe, you're doing Boots, Castle Street. Baby stuff. Formula, nappies, bottles, clothes. Fill a couple of bin bags. Plus medicines, anything you can grab, especially pain killers and antibiotics. Ellen, Jay and Brian can do the library, get that book. Don't mean to patronise you on the basis of you being pregnant, Ellen, but the library's the soft option and, well, you know, you *are* pregnant, aren't you? Jay, you have to go to the library. You're the only one who knows what the boat looks like.'

'Fine by me,' said Ellen. 'I'm not looking to prove anything.'

'Why am I going to the library?' said Brian.

'You'll be keeping an eye on our newest member, making sure he doesn't pull a fast one. Besides, you can't shoot for shit and you fight even worse. Just watch out for paper cuts, eh?'

'Cheeky bastard,' said Brian. 'I can handle myself.'

There was an outbreak of undisguised mirth.

'We leave here in thirty,' Dave continued, 'and meet up

at the boat one hour later. That should be more than enough time to get our respective shit together.' He turned to Jay. 'So, where's this boat of yours, then?'

'We'll meet by the Liver Building,' said Jay. 'I'll take you from there.'

'Fuck sake,' said Simon. 'He still doesn't trust us.'

'He's got his head screwed on, that's all,' said Dave. 'I wouldn't fucking tell us, either. I mean, look at us, a right bunch of shady bastards. Alright, Jay, Liver Building it is.' He clapped his hands. 'Get your tea down your necks folks. Pee if you have to. We need to arm up and fuck off. Thirty minutes. Let's go!'

Jay drained the remainder of his tea and took his cup to the kitchen. He didn't even realise Brian had followed him until he turned around to leave.

'To be honest, I was a bit relieved to get library duty,' he said.

'Me too,' said Jay but something felt like a cold dead weight in his gut and he had no idea why.

Chapter Fourteen

———

Jay just nodded when Dave handed him the pistol. He didn't want to admit that he didn't like the feel of it in his hand. It was only a small gun, identical to the one Brian had tried to shoot him with an hour ago, and perhaps that was why it didn't feel right: it was too small to feel so heavy, so dense.

Dave handed them out, one each, from a wooden crate as they stood around a boardroom table, coats on, packs on and ready to go.

'You've got five bullets each. That's all we had left. I've divvied them up evenly, except for Ellen. You've got six.'

'Sexist little get,' said Ellen, as she shoved *Childbirth Without Fear* and *Ina May's Guide to Natural Childbirth* into her backpack.

Dave smiled and carried on. 'Don't pull the trigger unless you know it's going to count. Five bullets will be gone in no time. Don't go for the head, go for the chest. It's easier to hit and it'll stop whatever you're shooting at in its tracks. Probably.'

'Where did they come from?' said Jay.

'The guns?' said Dave. 'Pepper. I grabbed a load before I got the fuck out of there.'

Hyenas

'You were in the militia?'

'Yeah. Anyway, shut the fuck up. The past is just that and of no fucking use to anyone.' He tucked his gun in the waistband of his pants and zipped up his coat. 'Simon, Kavi, let's go. I'll see the rest of you in one hour. Best of luck. And if anyone doesn't make it, don't worry about it. They were probably too stupid to live.'

Dave, Simon and Kavi left. Everyone else busied themselves donning gloves, hats and scarves. Jay tried to mimic Dave and put his gun down the waistband of his pants but found it was more difficult than it looked. Instead, he put it in his coat pocket, wondering if Dave's stint in Walton prison had been for armed robbery; he certainly seemed at ease with firearms.

Ellen and Brian seemed content to keep their guns in their hands.

Phil and Joe were next to leave.

'No matter how tempting it may be,' Joe said to Ellen as he passed through the door, 'try not to shoot Brian.'

Ellen laughed and Brian rolled his eyes and flicked two fingers at him.

'Why don't we all just stick together?' asked Jay, once Phil and Joe had left. 'You know, safety in numbers?'

'You'd think,' said Ellen. 'But it doesn't work out that way.'

'Yeah,' said Brian, trying and failing to spin his revolver like a gunslinger. 'Big numbers attract attention, from zombies and the militia both, but mostly the zombies. Don't know why, but it's like they can sense larger groups. They just home in, like flies to shit.'

'Come on,' said Ellen. 'Let's get this over with.'

By the time they dipped under the half open roller shutter and out into the alley, there was no sign of the others.

'Best route?' said Jay.

'Hanover Street,' said Ellen, pointing up the alley.

'What?' said Brian. 'That'll take us past the bottom of Bold Street. You know, Bold Street? Waterstones? More zombies than you can shake a bloody stick at?'

'It's quicker than going back down School Lane and round. We haven't got time to piss about. Christ, we don't even know how long it's going to take us to get into the library. As for finding the book? Well, none of us has got much experience of the Dewey fucking Decimal System, have we? One hour, Brian. I want to be on that boat in one hour. We just need to keep low, use the cars and buses for cover.'

Ellen set off before Brian could formulate a counter argument. Jay followed.

'Fucking great,' said Brian. 'Nice to see British democracy is still a joke, post-apocalypse.' He threw his arms in the air, spun around a couple of times as if seeking agreement from an imaginary audience, then trotted after them.

They emerged onto Hanover Street and moved in close to the wall of abandoned vehicles. Single file and stooped, they advanced with some difficulty through the knee-high snow that had drifted up against the cars and buses. As they reached the junction of Bold Street and Church Street, where Hanover Street became Ranelagh Street, Ellen raised a hand, indicating they should stop. She pointed to a gap between the people carrier they were crouched against and the next vehicle in the dead procession, a battered Cavalier that looked as if it had been ready for the scrap yard long before the Jolt. The gap was about seven or eight feet across, and Jay could hear the snarling laughter of the hyenas in Waterstones.

'We go back,' said Brian. 'School Lane. Late's better than dead. They're not going to go without us.'

'And what if Pepper finds the boat? Torches it?' said Ellen.

'The chances of that,' Brian began.

But Ellen was already peering round the edge of the people carrier. A second later she was up and running across the gap, then dipping down behind the Cavalier.

Jay shuffled forward and took a peek at Bold Street. There were six hyenas outside Waterstones, less than fifty feet away, fighting over the half-mangled books that were strewn across the snow. He could make out the indistinct shapes of more hyenas through the shop window.

He made a break for the Cavalier. He was halfway across the gap when one of the hyenas turned toward him as it tracked the trajectory of a flying paperback. Jay froze. The book hit the ground with a puff of snow. The hyena darted toward the book, scuttling across the snow like a dog closing in on a tossed stick. A couple of feet before it reached the book, it stopped. It reared back up on to two feet, revealing the shredded, filth-caked remnants of a police uniform. It grinned at Jay.

'Bollocks,' he managed to whisper.

The hyena barked a laugh and tensed for the chase.

Jay managed to summon the word 'run' from his panic-fogged mind, but his mouth and throat were too dry to put it out into the world.

And then Constable Hyena was slammed down into the snow with such force he all but vanished in a cloud of white. Alice Band let out a triumphant snarl and grabbed the book. She began tearing pages from it immediately, stuffing them into her mouth, at the same time returning to the rest of the hyenas, her back now to Jay.

Jay turned to Brian, who was looking at him with something very much like stark terror, certain they'd been spotted and Ellen's decision was going to end in death for all of them.

Jay signalled for Brian to follow him.

'Quick,' he said when Brian appeared unable to move. 'Now or never, Brian. Come on, lad.'

When Brian still remained frozen in place, Jay lunged at him grabbed his wrist and dragged him to his feet.

'Now!' he growled.

Brian stumbled after him and they both fell to the ground beside Ellen.

'What happened?' she said.

'One of them saw me,' said Jay. He risked a glance round the edge of the Cavalier's rust scarred boot. Constable Hyena was lying motionless in the settling snow and Alice Band was beating another prone hyena about the head with such brutality blood was flying from her fists. 'It's okay now, though.'

Ellen set off up Ranelagh Street, staying in a half-crouch behind the trail of vehicles until she was out of the hyenas' line of sight.

They were next to a shattered shop window, spectacles and sunglasses scattered across the snow — the entrance to the Clayton Square shopping centre approaching on their left — when, from somewhere to their right, the sound of hyenas came at them with the suddenness of a radio surging to life following a power cut.

Despite the fact that the sound was almost certainly coming from ahead of them, Jay looked back the way they had come, convinced he was about to see Alice Band and her pack bearing down on them, spitting out pulped paper. But all he saw was Brian's terrified face.

Ellen rose up a little and looked over the bonnet of the Ford Fusion they were hiding behind. She dropped back again a second later and Jay saw fear on her face for the first time. She jabbed a thumb over her shoulder, indicating that Jay should take a look. After a few seconds' hesitation, Jay did so.

Across the road, filling the downward-sloping entrance to Central Station, were about twenty hyenas, more than Jay had ever seen in one place before. They appeared to be unable to decide what to do next. Some were turning on the spot and sniffing at the air, as if trying to catch a scent of prey.

'Fuckshit,' he blurted.

'What?' Brian demanded. 'Christ, will one of you say something.'

'Hyenas, zombies,' said Jay. 'Twenty. Maybe more.'

'Well, we can't carry on this way, can we?' said Brian. 'We have to go back.'

Jay turned to Ellen who nodded.

'Back onto Church Street,' she said. 'Then through Clayton Square.'

'Clayton Square?' said Brian. 'Indoors? I fucking hate indoors. After what happened last time. Don't fucking do this to me, Ellen.'

'What happened last time?' said Jay, remembering his own encounter with Hello Kitty, that horrible sense of no escape, of being penned-in by fear and death, and what he had to do to get away.

'Don't like to talk about it,' said Brian.

'Except when he does,' said Ellen. 'Which is *all the fucking time*. Sometimes I have to give him a toffee to make him stop.' And then she was up and off. She paused for a second at the gap, glancing toward Waterstones, then moving on. She stayed low and close to the cars until the buildings began to curve away. Then she moved closer to the shop fronts, following their arc — a chip shop, an opticians, a betting shop, a travel agent — round onto Church Street.

Jay and Brian struggled to keep up, pausing for longer at the gap, despite the fact that the hyenas were all fully occupied shredding and eating books, and attacking one another. But even without the longer pause, they'd have had trouble keeping up. Jay wondered if what separated Ellen from Brian and himself was the fact that she didn't just have herself to think about; Ellen was determined to survive whereas they just didn't want to die.

Ellen was waiting for them under the glass archway of the Church Street entrance to Clayton Square, by the shattered plate glass doors which had once slid dutifully back and forth, consuming eager shoppers. Jay tried to ignore the carnage that had caught his eye as he'd made his way down the other side of the thoroughfare with Dempsey earlier. He was determined not to register such things, particularly in close-up.

'Come on, before we're seen,' said Ellen.

Jay followed her over broken glass and then they were in Clayton Square.

'I fucking hate being indoors,' said Brian.

'You said,' Ellen reminded him.

There was an immediate hike in temperature as they stepped out of the reach of the bitter wind that Jay hadn't really noticed whilst he was outside; sweat erupted all over his face, scalp and across the back of his neck. There was a subdued brown quality to the light that strained through the snow-patched glass of the arched roof. The smell hit him next. The acrid stench of the dead that had yet to start rotting but had begun a process of inward, secretive corruption. The originators of this meaty sourness were everywhere. Steel stairs disappeared through a door-sized rectangular hole in the ceiling, and an old man was sprawled on them, arms and legs impossibly positioned. A traffic warden sat slumped against a photo booth, the blue curtain clutched in his bloody fist. Amidst toppled buckets and crushed flowers was the body of what Jay was reasonably certain had been a woman; the head was so comprehensively smashed it was impossible to be sure. There were more, at least another eight, but Jay tried his best to avoid looking at them. When they forced themselves into his line of sight, he tried to trick his eyes into throwing them out of focus. But even then, his attention snagged on the most horrific details. A gristly hole where a nose should have been; an empty eye socket; a sheet of flesh ripped from an arm, complete with flaps of finger and painted nails; a ragged-edged face, like a mask, slapped onto a window between disinterested mannequins.

Jay wanted to take a deep breath to quell his surging nausea but didn't dare; a mouthful of that abattoir stink would have emptied his belly in a second. He was relieved when Ellen said, 'No time for window shopping' and set off. At the junction where twin escalators rose up between concessions that had once sold mobile phone accessories and offered watch repairs, they turned left, following a shop front filled with kitchen gadgets and household appliances. A transit van had crashed through the Parker Street entrance and filled most of the corridor, side on. The windscreen of the van was mostly frosted from the impact and those areas that weren't frosted were coated on the inside with something treacly and reddish. There was a limp arm dangling from the roof of the van and Jay assumed it must be attached to a body, otherwise the weight of the hand would have dragged it slithering down to the ground. It was missing most of its third finger, but a blood-dulled wedding ring clung to the tatty stump. Jay tried to blur the image by throwing it out of focus and in doing so created the impression that the hand had twitched, an optical illusion his rattling heartbeat could have done without.

He could taste the almost fresh air coming in from the ruined entrance, could feel the breeze easing the relative but unbearable warmth inside the shopping centre. Out in the middle of Parker Street, twenty or more crows undulated about something raw and scarecrowish.

Ellen was passing the transit van when the arm snaked up and out of sight. Jay couldn't speak as the small, stocky hyena reared up, its long comb-over dangling over its right ear.

Chapter Fifteen

———

'Jesus!' Brian shouted, but Jay could hardly hear over the blood pumping in his eardrums. The blanket of crows flew apart, black rags clattering skyward, exposing something that didn't really look like a scarecrow at all.

The hyena dropped down toward Ellen before she'd even had time to wonder what Brian was squawking about. It misjudged her speed and instead of landing on her, pinning her down, it glanced off her back and sent her sprawling across shards of glass and scattered greetings cards from a toppled concession. As Ellen hit the ground, her pistol jumped from her hand and skidded out into the snow.

Jay struggled to unzip his pocket and draw his own gun. He could feel the weight and shape of the thing through the slippery fabric of his coat, abstract and useless.

The hyena looked at Ellen, then Brian, then Jay, its eyes wide with delight. It lunged at Ellen.

She had seen it coming, though, and had managed to roll onto her back, bringing her legs up. When it struck her, she kicked it away, sending it flying back against the transit van.

Jay struggled with his pocket and tried to pull the gun

through the too small hole.

Ellen got to her feet and started towards her own gun. The crows were still in disarray but refused to stray more than a few yards from their meal. The hyena grunted as it lurched after Ellen, its greasy comb-over trailing behind it.

Jay tore at his pocket which still refused to release the gun.

'Fuck, Jay!' he said, 'What in the name of all that's fuck is fucking wrong with you?'

The hyena stopped dead and turned toward Jay, its eyes even wider than before.

'What the fuck are you looking at?' said Jay.

The hyena's eyes darted about as Jay spoke, as if it was attempting to follow the erratic paths of several bluebottles, reminding Jay of Hello Kitty.

'What?' he shouted. 'What the fuck are you looking at, Bobby fucking Charlton?'

The hyena grinned, dipped its head a little, and sped toward him.

A firework exploded somewhere behind Jay or something very much like a firework. At the same time, a penny-sized hole appeared in the side of the van. Jay looked back to see Brian, smoking gun in hand.

'Get the fuck down, Jay!' he shouted, although his voice was muffled behind a high-pitched whine which had taken up residence at the centre of Jay's head. 'You know I can't see for shit!'

Jay dropped to the ground. The hyena was still coming,

undeterred by the gun shot. A string of drool almost as long as its rancid comb-over trailed from its mouth and over its shoulder.

Another firework exploded.

Another penny-sized hole appeared in the side of the van a couple of inches to the left of the first hole.

'Jesus, Brian, the van's already dead!'

The hyena pressed on, only a few feet from Jay now. He scuttled back on his buttocks, broken glass slashing at the back of his pants.

Another firework.

A penny-sized hole appeared above the hyena's left eye.

But it kept coming. The bullet appeared to have done nothing. Maybe there was so little going on inside its skull that it could take a bullet to the brain and still function.

Another firework exploded. The van manifested a third hole.

'Fuck's sake, Brian!'

Then the hyena's legs folded as if some internal switch had been thrown. It hit the ground face first, arms limp at its side and slid the remaining few inches until its hairless scalp touched the soles of Jay's shoes.

All this in the few seconds it took Ellen to retrieve her gun from the snow and turn, ready to fire.

Jay got to his feet. His legs felt slightly anaesthetised.

Brian was grinning and nodding his head, as if in enthusiastic agreement with some amusing remark. He still had the gun trained on the dead hyena, his arm shaking so much it looked as if he was trying to flick something disgusting from the barrel of the gun.

'Bloody hell,' he said, voice tremulous. 'I thought it was too stupid to die for a second there.'

Jay was about to concur when he was distracted by a small lifeless chime and saw that the wedding ring had fallen from the angry stump of the hyena's third finger. He watched as it rolled in a loose circle then fell on its side an inch from the hand it had slipped from, as if it had been trying to find its way back home. Without knowing why, Jay found himself reaching for it, wanting to put it in his pocket, keep it as a symbol or reminder of something he couldn't even begin to define. Then he realised Brian was speaking to him.

'What?'

'I said keep it in your hand, Zippy,' said Brian with the exasperation of someone who's had to repeat themselves several times.

'Keep what in my hand?' said Jay, thinking that Brian might be referring to the wedding ring.

'Your gun. You had it zipped up in your pocket, for fuck's sake. Some fucking gunslinger you'd make.'

'I'm not a gunslinger,' said Jay. 'And neither are you.'

Brian's face flushed. 'Yeah. I know. Sorry.' He took off his bobble hat and used it to wipe a sheen of sweat from his face. 'Scared makes me snappy.'

'It's alright,' said Jay. 'I haven't stopped being scared since this whole palaver started.' He wasn't sure why he'd opted for 'palaver'. He couldn't think of a less appropriate word for what was, essentially, the Apocalypse. Maybe he was just trying to take the sting out of it all.

'I was scared before, though,' said Brian. 'Before all this. I lived in a scary house.'

Jay couldn't help glancing at Brian's scar.

'Not like that,' said Brian, tugging his hat back on. 'It was a quiet house. Dad left when I was eight. And Mum stopped speaking. I mean, she *spoke* but she didn't talk. I knew it was my fault, my dad going. It was because of the way I was. And I knew that my mum wanted to go too, that my dad had just beaten her to it. Whenever I heard a floorboard creak in the night, I didn't think it was the bogeyman or a werewolf or a fucking *zombie*, like most kids. I thought it was my mum, with a suitcase, sneaking away. I was scared to go out, in case I came back to an empty house, or found another family living there, looking at me like *who the fuck are you*? I remember, once, I told my mum how my mate's mum was weird because she was always hugging him. She just looked past me, at the door.' He laughed, a cold bark. 'I thought she was going to make a run for it, there and then!'

'Brian, Jay, we need to get moving,' said Ellen. 'They'll be coming.'

A second later, there was a high, warped thud from the Ranelagh Street entrance. Jay recognised the sound from his first encounter with Hello Kitty on Castle Street: the sound of a hyena throwing itself at a plate glass window. The short interval between each distorted thud was too brief to be the work of just one.

'Now,' said Ellen.

Brian set off at a brisk walk. Jay unzipped his jacket pocket — with no difficulty now, of course — and took out his gun. It still felt like it was constructed from some impossibly dense alien material; cold, hard but with a muted kind of life humming at its centre. The next warped thud was accompanied by a sharp crack of breaking glass. Jay took one last glance at the ring, decided against taking it, still uncertain as to why he would want to do so in the first place, and followed Brian and Ellen out onto Parker Street.

The crows had taken up residence on the BBC Big Screen that, pre-Jolt, had broadcast football matches and the local news down onto throngs of shoppers, like the instrument of some science fiction tyrant. Now the deadness of its screen reminded Jay of the thick, liquid blackness that had seemed to lurk beneath Ellen's canvases. Ahead of them, the Radio City Tower sprouted upwards, looking to Jay like a pale, apocalyptic fungus, dwarfing the surrounding structures.

They turned right, away from the lifeless television, and a steep quarter-circle of steps took them up to Great Charlotte Street and a convoy of abandoned buses, windows shattered and blood-smeared. Jay glanced right. A couple of hundred feet away, where Charlotte Street branched off from Ranelagh Street, two, three, four, five hyenas flew round the corner and into one another as if pursued or in pursuit of something that had slipped from view and gone to ground. Jay didn't think the hyenas possessed the necessary intelligence to attempt to trap them; nonetheless, he felt as if he was being surrounded.

Jay didn't have to say anything: Ellen and Brian were already running in the opposite direction, up Elliot Street, past Saint John's Precinct with its Argos and All You Can Eat Chinese Buffet tucked beneath the Holiday Inn, toward Lime Street. Opposite them, across what used to be a busy intersection and a potential death trap to the distracted, the Victorian colonnaded arch of Lime Street Station was preternaturally still now that it had been stripped of its perpetual skirt of luggage-dragging commuters. There appeared to be some activity within, visible through the glazed gable end, but Jay was certain that was just an effect of the intricate mesh of sickle girders that supported the structure's sweeping roof.

They followed Elliot Street round to their left and the neoclassical mass of Saint George's Hall heaved into view, beyond the wide, downward-sloping bus lanes of Saint George's Place.

Jay could hear the sound of hyenas from behind him somewhere. They were muffled by distance and confused as a consequence of being bounced from building to building, until he really couldn't tell how far away they were; he couldn't even be entirely certain they were coming from behind him. He threw a glance over his shoulder but there was no sign of any hyenas. As he returned his attention to Saint George's Place, it was snared by the illusion of more movement from Lime Street Station, a moiré of criss-crossing girders. The illusion was more vivid this time, as if the station was seething with activity.

And then the illusion spilled out of the station onto the broad, low steps that swept up to meet the glass gable. Fifty, sixty, seventy hyenas, swarmed from the station with a sudden roar of noise, tendrils of steam rising from their scalps to create a tattered haze above them.

Ellen and Brian turned; their faces seemed to be attempting in vain to express what Jay was feeling. His legs felt weak, almost numb. He felt as if he was on the verge of waking, of struggling up from the depths of a nightmare into a tangle of damp bed sheets and a long sigh of relief. But, no, he wasn't dreaming. They were coming. And something inside him wanted to say 'enough', wanted to lie down in the snow, curl up in a little ball and just wait for it all to be over. But still he kept running.

Ellen vaulted the barrier with surprising ease. Brian followed, a little less gracefully. Ellen was already springing over the low railings that were designed to keep pedestrians from wandering from the pavement into oncoming buses as Jay all but fell over the central barrier, only just managing to stay on his feet and keep moving forward. His balance was completely off by the time he reached the railings and he had to flop over, landing on his back then lurching up again.

They were moving down Saint George's Place now, along the high-walled plinth-like structure the hall appeared to sit upon. There were two doors. The furthest, which if Jay remembered correctly led under the hall itself, was closed. The nearest, leading down to the Northern and Wirral lines and back to Lime Street Station, was open and broadcasting the snarling laughter of hyenas.

As they neared the corner of the hall and the steps on their right leading up into Saint John's Garden, Jay chanced a look back. The hyenas had already halved the distance.

Ellen had cleared the steps and Jay was about to set foot on the first of them when Brian, halfway up, slipped. His legs whipped out from beneath him and he fell backward, arms flailing, gun flying from his hand. The back of his head hit the stone steps with a noise that was almost identical to the one Jay had heard when Alice Band had punched a hole in her victim's skull. Upon impact, the Peruvian bobble hat jumped from Brian's head and flopped down to the pavement; Brian slithered down after it, a brief moan escaping his mouth, his eyes showing only whites past fluttering eyelids.

Jay knelt down next to him, shoving his gun into his pocket but not zipping it this time. The cold bit at his knees, icy teeth drilling into the bone. He reached behind Brian's neck to lift his head and felt hot blood wrap around his hand, a liquid glove. Brian's eyes had stopped flickering now. His face looked waxy, suddenly unreal.

Chapter Sixteen

———

Jay looped his arms under Brian's armpits. He pivoted Brian round and began dragging him up the steps.

'Ellen!' he shouted back over his shoulder. 'Lanky streak of piss weighs a ton!'

He heard Ellen's crunching footfalls as she came up behind him.

'Jesus,' she said. 'What happened?'

'Fell. He just fell.'

Ellen reached around him and tried to help but only succeeded in getting her feet tangled with Jay's. Jay fell, just managing to get himself clear of Brian.

He got back on his feet and was reaching down for Brian when the first hyena appeared at the bottom of the steps, drooling bloody saliva almost as long as the wire from the iPod earphones still pressed into its filthy ears. Jay thought it couldn't possibly have moved so fast as to catch up with them already. Then he realised it hadn't been part of the Lime Street pack. It must have come from under Saint George's Hall, and how many more were behind it?

He grabbed the shoulders of Brian's coat and began dragging him backwards through the snow. The hyena bounded up the steps and launched itself at him, its feet landing squarely on Brian's chest. Jay lost his grip and lurched backwards, landing on his backside. The hyena reared up.

Behind Jay, a gunshot. He recognised the sound now, would never mistake it for an exploding firework again; it was a sound Jay couldn't help but think of as somehow *absorbent*, as if it drew in all other sound around it. The hyena flopped to the left, eyes wide and unblinking. Jay couldn't even see where it had been shot. He turned and saw Ellen, revolver in hand, behind a haze of blue gun smoke. Her face was pale and slack, He wondered if it was the first time she'd fired a gun, maybe even the first time she'd killed. Jay turned back to Brian, stooping to grab his shoulders again, and realised Ellen's expression had nothing to do with guns and killing and everything to do with the horde of hyenas coming up the steps.

Ellen fired again, then again. Two hyenas fell, taking five or six more down with them in a tangle of limbs.

'Run!' she shouted. 'Just run. Brian's dead. Look.' She pointed to the widening red stain spreading out through the snow around Brian's head, a dark halo. 'He's fucking dead!' She looked like she was about to start crying, then her face hardened and she fired again. A hyena that had clambered over its fallen pack mates fell backwards, gargling blood, hands grasping its throat as if it was trying to choke the life from itself. 'Now!' She turned and ran, toward the library, its columns and dome visible now across the breadth of the gardens, and next to it the museum, looking like its own perfectly preserved exhibit.

Jay took one last look at Brian — he looked like a very poor waxwork — tried to convince himself he wasn't relieved, and followed Ellen. They moved between the back of Saint George's Hall on their right and the low balustraded wall on their left, guarding an eight-foot drop before flowerbeds and lawns swept down to the road and the entrance to the Queensway tunnel. Behind him, the hyenas' din seemed to be swelling by the second. He fumbled the gun from his coat pocket and, ignoring the stitch that was beginning to gnaw at his side, forced himself to move faster and catch up with Ellen. He wondered how she was doing it, moving so fast whilst pregnant, then realised he'd answered his own question.

As they bolted from the gardens, Jay glanced left, down William Brown Street. He had a clear view of the tunnel now and thought he saw movement in the darkness of its downturned mouth, movement that made him think of fish darting about the bottom of a murky pond, half-shapes, shadows in shadow.

'Oh shit,' he heard Ellen all but whisper.

He turned his attention away from the tunnel and saw Ellen pointing at the library. The large folding wooden doors were closed.

'Fuck the library,' said Ellen. She started to turn down William Brown Street, then stopped dead. 'Shitshitshit!'

The half-shapes and shadows had resolved themselves into a chaotic regiment of hyenas.

Hyenas

Jay and Ellen turned back to head toward Lime Street. But there were hyenas that way, too, coming around the side of Saint George's Hall, beyond the dead fountain and the statue of Wellington, almost indiscernible on top of his comically high column.

'Dead,' said Jay. It was all he could say, all he could think. 'Dead. Dead.'

Ellen had the gun held out in front of her and was backing toward the library; there was really nowhere else to go. The hyenas were bursting from Saint John's Garden now, slamming into one another in their eagerness to get at their prey. Jay didn't even want to think about how many there were. More than the eight bullets they had between them.

Ellen fired. The lead hyena lost a piece of its temple and dropped to the snow. Four hyenas tripped on the body, sprawling forward, and more tripped on them.

Jay and Ellen were backing up the steps now, toward the closed doors. Ellen fired again. A hyena that had been climbing over the low stone wall, sagged, as if abruptly drained of all energy, then flopped to the ground face first.

'Start shooting, for fuck's sake!' she shouted. Jay trained his gun on the nearest hyena, almost at the wall, one of four frontrunners. He pulled the trigger. It surprised him how little effort was required. He'd expected there to be some resistance but there was none. The report didn't seem as loud with the gun held out ahead of him and, instead of the vicious recoil he'd been anticipating, the barrel just lifted an inch or so, as if a brief but firm wind had got under it. A small black hole that put Jay in mind of the opening of a pencil sharpener appeared beneath the hyena's left eye and something like dark powder puffed out from behind its head. It slowed, took another two steps, limp and uncertain, as if they were its first, then dropped onto all fours before falling flat, its arms trapped beneath its body, its legs still pedalling weakly, kicking up decreasing quantities of snow.

Two of the other frontrunners tripped over the dying hyena and pitched forward into the snow. The fourth, bearded and scrawny, glibly sidestepped its fallen packmates and closed in on Jay.

He fired, aiming at its head. He wasn't sure if he'd missed or hit the thing but it kept coming, less than ten feet away now. He fired again, lowering his aim to its chest this time. He couldn't see where he'd hit it, but it stopped advancing, performed a brief, jerky dance and fell.

The rest of the pack had caught up now.

Ellen fired her last bullet. Somewhere near the centre of the mass of steaming bodies, a hyena dropped from sight and several more went down with it.

A hyena that looked like it had been a professional rugby player pre-Jolt bounded over the low wall. Jay shot at it whilst it was in mid-air. A blackish spray told him he'd hit the top of its lowered head. It continued to travel through the air, landing at the foot of the steps and immediately staining the snow a vivid red.

Three hyenas jumped up onto the wall, one after the other.

They panted through grins that looked painfully wide.

Jay shot the tallest of the three in the chest, and it fell back off the wall, landing on the advancing horde and taking down as many as eight of its pack mates.

He carried on pulling the trigger three, four, five times, hoping that the useless click would miraculously transform into a deafening crack but knowing it wouldn't; knowing that it was over and he was dead. That Ellen was dead and the *Jerusalem* was going nowhere. He suddenly found himself wishing he'd told the others where the boat was moored and hoping they'd find it anyway.

Before

―――

'It's Alan Bates,' said Jason's dad.

They were sat on a bench in Sefton Park. The water sparkled, as if bioluminescent fish were playing close to the surface. Swans, geese, ducks, moorhens and coots were fighting over the chunks of bread father and son had half-heartedly cast onto the water.

'Who?' said Jason, although the name was familiar. He turned the cassette over in his hands and mustered the most dismissive expression his fourteen-year-old face could accommodate.

The painting on the card insert was Blake's *God Judging Adam*. God on his throne of fire pointing an accusing finger at a submissive Adam, whose straggly hair and beard draped from his stooping head. Jason had seen it before in one of his dad's books. He used to look at his dad's books all the time, thinking, hoping, that somehow the tangle of tiny shapes on the page would spontaneously lose their similarity to dense, twisted hawthorn and resolve themselves into words. They never did, though, and he always ended up just looking at the pictures.

'It's William Blake,' said his dad. 'Alan Bates reads the

poems. He's an actor. Great voice. *Whistle Down the Wind*? No?'

Jason shrugged, although he'd seen the film only six or seven months ago. He'd enjoyed it and the girl in it (he couldn't remember her name) had reminded him of a girl he liked in school, and when the man had said 'Why are you helping me?' and she'd said. 'Because we love you,' he'd had to fight back tears and was relieved his dad had been busy marking school books in the kitchen.

'Never mind,' said his dad, in his best. 'Kids, these days' voice. 'Anyway, I thought you might like to listen to them. Remember when I used to read them to you when you were a kid? You used to love the *Songs of Innocence*. But then you got a bit old for, you know, bedtime stories. So, I thought you deserved to hear them read by a professional instead of a bad cover version by a dreary, old Scouser like me.'

Jason shrugged, but when his dad flinched a little, he said, 'Okay, I'll give it a go.'

'Great. You won't regret it. How's things at school?'

It was Jason's turn to flinch. His dad was about to tell him to forget he'd asked when Jason said, 'The same. Surrounded by freaks and zombies.'

His dad was about to give him *The Importance of Kindness* lecture when he saw a look on his son's face that indicated a hardened weariness that, for a moment, made him feel *like* he was the child and Jason the battle-scarred veteran of life. He didn't like that feeling, didn't really know what to make of it.

'I don't know what to say to you, son. Just keep going and something will turn up. I wish I could offer you more than that, I really do. Christ, I'm your dad, I'm supposed to heft you up onto my shoulders and carry you to safety. But this *thing*... it's everywhere. Nowhere's safe.'

Jason could see that his dad was close to tears and he wished there was something he could say, something he could do, but there was nothing.

'Something'll turn up,' he said.

'Yeah. Something.'

'When you least expect it and you've given up hope.'

Chapter Seventeen

Jay's heart was beating so hard he almost didn't hear the clunk behind him. He turned to the source of the sound, keeping the empty pistol pointed at the advancing hyenas, still pulling the trigger. He saw that the door had slid open a couple of feet and Darth Vader was stepping out onto the snow. Except it wasn't Darth Vader, it was a samurai. Or someone wearing a samurai helmet and, from the waist up, armour. Below the waist were grubby jeans and Converse boots. The half-samurai was holding a Japanese sword in two hands above his head. He rushed past Ellen and Jay, shouting, 'Get in for fuck's sake!'

Ellen didn't need to be told twice; she plunged through the gap. Jay followed, still clicking the gun even though it was no longer pointed at the hyenas. As soon as he was through the door, he turned in time to see the half-samurai backing toward him, sword sweeping out ahead of him in blurred arcs, accompanied by a high, thin swoosh that pricked painfully at Jay's ear drums. There were four hyenas at the half-samurai's feet, all pumping improbable quantities of blood from gaping wounds. The rest of the hyenas, whilst still advancing, were doing so with noticeable hesitancy. And Jay thought, they don't understand the gun, it's too complex, too far removed from the injuries it inflicts, but the sword is simple; they know what it is, what it can do, cause and effect. One hyena in school ma'am-ish attire and still sporting, against all the odds, a reasonably neat bun, lunged toward the samurai. The sword blurred and the hyena's left arm was hanging on by threads; of flesh or fabric, it was impossible to tell which. It let out a shriek that still had something of laughter about it and folded down into an expanding pool of its own blood. And then Jay had to step back as the samurai reversed through the gap. He let his sword clatter to the floor, slid the heavy door shut and rammed brass bolts down into the stone floor and into the brass-plated beam above. The door began to rattle immediately as several hyenas slammed against it, now that the sword was out of sight and doubtless out of mind.

'What the fuck was I thinking, saving you?' said the samurai. 'I could have been killed.'

He took off his helmet with a grunt of relief. He looked about fifty, with black hair that was losing the battle against the grey and a beard that had surrendered long ago. Small round spectacles slightly magnified pale blue eyes.

'I'm Robert, by the way. Not Rob, Bob, Robbie or Bobby. Robert. I saved your lives, so don't piss about with my name. You owe me that much.' He took off his spectacles and rubbed at the lenses with a paper tissue.

'Jay.'

'Ellen.' She looked at a Jay. 'Brian. Fuck.'

Jay shook his head, shrugged, grimaced. He didn't know what to say.

'He was mine,' said Ellen. 'My stray. I rescued him, brought him back to the Book Club. Found him tucked between two dumpsters on Wood Street. I thought *I* was scared until I saw his face. He was out of his mind with fear. I think if one of the others had found him, Dave or Phil, they'd have killed him. Would have thought he was one of those things. Is it horrible that I found his terror reassuring? It made me feel like I had some measure of my shit together.'

Ellen winced, put a hand to her belly.

'You all right?' said Jay.

Ellen nodded.

'He didn't talk for about two weeks,' she said. 'Brian. Not a peep out of him. Unless you tried to take his hat off him. Then he shrieked like fucking monkey. Then, one morning, he woke up and he was just... Brian. Daft and annoying Brian. He was—' A sharp intake of breath. A hiss of pain.

She bent as double as her pregnancy would allow, both hands flat against the sides of her belly.

'Are you *sure* you're okay?' said Jay.

'Oh, please don't tell me you've gone into labour,' said Robert. 'I've seen enough blood and snot to last me a fucking lifetime.' He took a deep breath, blew it out as if he was demonstrating the correct breathing method for Ellen's benefit, then stepped forward and put a blood-spattered hand on Ellen's arm. 'Are you okay?' he asked, voice suddenly low and full of concern.

'Just a twinge,' said Ellen. 'I don't *think* it's labour, but I didn't go to any of the classes, just thought I'd cross that bridge when I came to it. Anyway, we haven't got time for a fucking nativity. Those things'll figure some way to get in here.'

'You better have a sit down,' said Robert.

Jay grabbed a chair from behind the booking desk and slid it behind Ellen, who sat down in three distinct stages.

'And don't worry about the mouth-breathers,' said Robert. 'Out of sight, out of mind. Give them half an hour and they'll forget why they're there.'

'Let's hope so,' said Ellen. 'Anyway, I should be okay in a minute. Probably just the baby trying to kill me from the inside out.' She produced a grin that comprehensively failed to hide something close to horror.

'I don't think you've got anything to worry about,' said Robert.

'What do you mean?' Ellen half-snapped. 'What am I worried about?'

Robert looked embarrassed. 'Sorry. None of my business.'

'No, really, what makes you think I've got nothing to worry about?' said Ellen, aggression giving way to muted optimism.

Robert sighed.

'Your baby,' he said. 'I thought you might be worried that it might be one of, you know, them. A mouth-breather. But it won't be. At least I don't think so. Not if my theory's right.'

'And what's your theory?' asked Jay and realised he was still holding his revolver. He shoved it into his pocket.

'I was an academic proofreader, *before* the Spasm. I had a degree in History but, you know, good luck finding a job with that. And I fucking hate kids.' He turned to Ellen. 'No offense. So, teaching was pretty much out of the question.

'A couple of years ago, a few days after I turned fifty, I had a stroke. A big one. It was like God shitting lightning all over me. After that, no reading or writing. Aphasia.

'Then, bang! God shits lightning on the entire fucking planet! And, at the same time, it's like all the gridlocked traffic in my brain is suddenly rerouted and everything's flowing like it used to. I can read, write. No more aphasia and good fucking riddance. But I can't celebrate with anyone because the whole world's gone completely insane. Not that I had anyone to celebrate with before the Spasm. Not so much a loner as intensely unlikable.'

Jay found himself taking a breath on Robert's behalf.

'Anyway,' Robert continued. 'What the fuck happened? Assuming it *wasn't* God shitting lightning.

'When I was a proofreader, I read all kinds of scientific papers, books, articles, dissertations. Some stuff about linguistics, philology, that kind of thing. And I knew all about NASA's *Chandra* X-ray observatory, the *Sagittarius A* black hole, the transmission. So, I had the tiniest inkling but nothing I could bring into focus. And I just *had* to know. Something like this, you can't just shrug and say, 'Ah well, one of those things.' So, I came here. To the library. Books, man. Fucking fabulous. You can tap into the knowledge of these incredibly intelligent and brilliant people without having to come into direct contact with the egotistical and socially inept individuals themselves.'

There was a series of thuds from the library's front door, almost rhythmic. Jay imagined a cluster of hyenas slamming their palms and fists against the thick timber. He hoped Robert was right; he hoped, given half an hour, they'd forget why they were there.

'There were three of us originally,' said Robert. 'We were in speech therapy on Rodney Street, when the Spasm happened. We picked up two more strays en route. But I was the only one who finished the journey. On any other day, it wouldn't have taken more than twenty minutes. Took me four hours. Anyway, never really liked the stuttering buggers to be honest. Liked them even less when they could finally fucking annunciate.

'So, I entrenched myself in the library and I start reading.

'Did you know that no-one really understands how or why or when language started? I mean, there are lots of theories, but nothing that can be argued with any certainty. Maybe it started with us imitating animal noises, or maybe it developed from involuntary expressions of surprise or rage. Whatever, nobody really knows. All I know for certain is it *went*. Language left.

I mean, didn't you feel it? That horrible pulling, like all your thoughts were being dragged out through your fucking follicles?'

'I felt it,' said Ellen.

Jay nodded.

'So, language left. It vacated the premises. Except for *those* people with twisted grey matter or fucked up neural pathways. It kind of got snagged up in the deformed loops and whorls of all that shit-over-by-God brain tissue. In fact, those people, by whom I mean, of course, *us*, the neurologically deformed, seemed to benefit from the linguistic equivalent of some sadistic physiotherapist violently cracking and popping something back into alignment, back into usefulness.

'Anyway, I'm not particularly imaginative. I've always been a facts and figures sort of person. But the way it tried to drag itself free and left a piece of itself behind, I couldn't help thinking of language as a lizard fleeing from the grasp of some predator or a trap, sacrificing a limb in order to escape. I couldn't help thinking of language as a *thing*, a thing with purpose.

'And if language *left*, this 'thing with a purpose', pissed right off like some self-serving, eat-fuck-survive lizard, then it must have *arrived* at some point.'

Robert paused. He seemed unable to look at Jay and Ellen, turning his attention to the high ceiling. What he said next came out in a rush, as if he was hoping to blur his words until they were unintelligible.

He said: 'I think language is an extra-terrestrial entity.'

Hyenas

He looked to Ellen, then Jay. 'Cue laughter,' he said. 'I'm saying language came from outer space. That it's a sentient being. Feel free to laugh your arses off.'

When they didn't as much as smirk, he continued.

'I think it came to earth during mankind's infancy and it kind of *infected* us, like a parasite. Or, more accurately, a symbiotic organism. We used it as a tool to advance our progress toward civilisation and it used us to move around, to reproduce itself, to develop and grow. What we think of as language acquisition is just this thing's means of transmission.

'When NASA projected that broadcast into the wormhole, thinking 'I wonder what will happen if...' language, fully developed now and with no further use for its host, hopped aboard and left. *2001: a Space Odyssey* in reverse. Bye-bye black monolith, hello ape man.'

There was another eruption of thuds and bangs from the library door, but Jay thought it lacked the intensity of the previous outburst. Perhaps some of the hyenas had already sloped off. He hoped so.

Robert seemed to be oblivious to the racket.

'And when language left *them*, the pre-Spasm literate and articulate, it plunged them into savagery, had a sort of atavistic effect, it drove them insane. I mean, Christ, it would, wouldn't it? Language is all over the brain, it isn't all housed in one part. The frontal lobe controls expressive language. Damage to the parietal lobe can result in problems with reading and writing: anomia, agraphia and alexia. If the occipital lobe is damaged, the victim can suffer from word blindness. Temporal lobe trauma can lead to Wernicke's Aphasia, characterised by difficulty understanding spoken words. Language is *threaded through* the brain. Rip it out and what the fuck's left?'

'Mouth-breathers,' said Jay.

'Mouth-breathers. That's right.'

'But why didn't they just end up like, I don't know, *vegetables*?' said Ellen. 'I mean, why *murderous* animals?'

'I don't know. Maybe there was some other damage, to the amygdala, perhaps, or the prefrontal cortex. But, like with language, aggression is associated with lots of different parts of the brain. Christ, I don't know. It's just a theory. We'll never know. All the great minds are gone now. As we speak, Richard Dawkins is probably eating his own shit.'

He turned to Ellen. 'Whatever the finer details, your baby, I think it'll be normal. I think it will pick up language in exactly the same way we did. There was no language in its brain to be torn out. I don't think you've got anything to worry about.

'But I could be, you know, wrong. It's only a theory. And now that I've said it out loud for the first time, I sound like a complete fucking nutter.'

'I've heard worse,' said Ellen.

'But not much worse,' said Jay. And yet there was something in what Robert had said that had set off little sparks in Jay's mind. He could almost feel connections forming.

'Anyway, we better get looking for that book,' Ellen said to Jay.

'Book? You're kidding? You actually came here on purpose, looking for a *book*?'

Ellen nodded.

'Christ, I just assumed you got *corralled* toward the library. What book would be worth that kind of risk?'

Ellen turned to Jay, eyebrows raised. Jay sighed, then nodded.

'A sailing book,' he said.

'You've got a boat.'

'Yes. We have a boat. But no clue how to sail the thing.'

A window to the right of the main entrance shattered behind its iron security bars and, a second later, there were hyenas pressing up against them, their filthy arms stretching in.

'Weird,' said Robert. 'Usually, they lose interest and fuck off. Maybe they want to borrow a book, too.'

More connections formed in Jay's mind. He found himself recalling that as they'd left Saint John's Garden, emerging onto William Brown Street, there had been hyenas at the top of the road near the Wellington monument and at the bottom of the road, spewing from the Queensway Tunnel. He'd noticed it at the time, of course, but he'd been all fear then. Now, he was calm enough to reflect upon what it meant. And then all the other little inklings, suspicions and what-the-fucks that had been rattling around Jay's mind since he'd witnessed the Byron-eating incident from beneath a table in Waterstones abruptly adhered to

Robert's outlandish theory.

'They weren't following us,' he said.

'What?' said Robert.

'The hyenas. Mouth-breathers. They were coming here, to the library. They want the books.'

Robert offered Jay a patronising smile.

'I really don't think so, Jay,' he said. 'Books? Really? What are they going to do with them, exactly?'

'Eat them,' said Jay. 'I was holed up in Waterstones. A hyena got in. It started eating the pages from a book. Poetry. Byron. I saw more, later, eating books, magazines, a fucking dictionary. I think, they... Christ, what's the word? Crave. That's it. I think they crave language. They can sense it. You must have seen the way they follow your words when you speak, like they can see them coming out of your mouth. It's like they're mesmerised. Like in your paintings, Ellen.' Like Hello Kitty, he thought. 'It didn't happen right away. It took a few weeks for them to become... attuned? They weren't following us at all. They were coming here. All of them. They can sense the books, the words, the language. Christ, we're in the middle of a fucking *beacon*. The biggest language beacon in the North West.'

Robert's patronising smile held but he looked pale, sick, and his voice wavered. 'I'm hardly in a position to dispute your theory on the basis that it sounds insane, given my own little treatise. But if they want books, they can have them. Let's get out of here and leave them to it. They can choke on the fucking things.'

Hyenas

Another window shattered but it was impossible to tell where, the sound echoing off the ornate wooden panelling that had doubtless, pre-Jolt, created an air of cosy, Victorian studiousness.

'Fuck! Let's get moving,' said Robert. 'Sport section's this way.' He started toward a staircase that zigzagged back on itself, beyond which ranks of bookcases faded into the gloom. 'No offense, but I imagine neither of you are that well-acquainted with the Dewey-Decimal System. Did I mention that I'm coming with you on this boat of yours?'

There was a prolonged crash from some indefinable point in the library, the kind of sound a toppling bookcase might make.

'Oh, Jesus, I think they're in,' said Robert. He headed up the stairs. 'Come on.'

Ellen took a deep breath and rose slowly.

'You going to be okay?' said Jay.

'I have to be, don't I? Unless you fancy giving me a piggyback.'

'You must be bloody joking,' said Jay, forcing a smile. 'My spine would snap like a fucking Twiglet.'

'Cheeky little bastard. I'm not that heavy. Anyway, I'm all baby.'

'If you say so.'

Ellen flicked him the 'v' and set off after Robert.

From somewhere within the library, possibly from the same location as the crashing bookcase, there was the shrill, cracked laughter of hyenas. Jay hurried after Ellen.

Chapter Eighteen

―――

Robert, Ellen then Jay emerged onto a mezzanine with windows overlooking Saint John's Garden. On a counter running beneath the window, there was a scattering of books, papers, empty Evian bottles and crisp packets. It looked like the aftermath of an all-night study session. Jay was pretty sure the library had to have been shut on the Sunday of the Jolt, so he surmised that the materials were Robert's.

There was no time to ask. Robert was already making his way up to the first floor. From down below there were more crashes and a sudden surge of grunts and shrieks.

'They're in,' said Robert. 'They're definitely fucking in. *Jesus*.'

When he reached the first floor, Jay hoped Robert knew his way round the library. There were at least forty wide bookcases running in parallel ranks down the length of a space that was far too big to be called a room. The walls were lined with books too, from floor to ceiling. About eight feet up, a sort of balcony, accessible by four small spiral staircases, skirted the entire perimeter, containing more bookcases with just enough room between them for two people to stand back-to-back and scan the spines.

'Over here,' said Robert, moving off to their right and stopping at one of the wall shelves about halfway along. A rectangular red plaque above the top shelf said Sport. The plaque was duplicated above the next five shelves.

Jay didn't even want to think about how many books they had to search through.

'You start at this end,' Robert said to Jay and moved down to the fifth shelf. 'And I'll start at this one.'

Jay went to the first shelf, tipped his head and began inspecting the titles.

Robert leaned his sword up against the sixth shelf then began sweeping armfuls of books onto the floor.

'If you see a boat, shout out,' he said to Ellen.

Jay immediately adopted Robert's irreverent but undeniably expedient technique. The floor was soon awash with footballers, tennis players, snooker champions and formula one racing drivers. The next cascade produced a couple of books with images of rock climbers on their covers and Jay knew he was in the right vicinity. He began dragging out books in smaller numbers now, threes and fours. More rock climbers. A scuba diver. Then, a boat. Not a yacht; a speed boat. He stopped dragging the books out now, instead flipping the books down into the space left by his earlier excavations and glancing at the cover of the next book revealed.

And suddenly, there it was, on the back cover of the seventh or eighth book Jay slapped down onto its face, the *Jerusalem* or a sailing boat very much like it. He lifted it out with both hands, turned it over and started flipping through the pages. It was the same book that had followed Dempsey down to the bottom of the Mersey. A different edition, older, but the same book.

When Robert stopped littering the floor with books, Jay assumed he'd noticed Jay holding *the* book. But then he saw Robert reach for the sword. Then Ellen pointed her empty revolver somewhere past Jay and began pulling the trigger, her face rigid with panic.

Jay turned. They'd made so much noise knocking the books onto the floor, had been so focussed on the task in hand, they hadn't heard the hyenas approaching. Five of them. Four were at the top of the stairs about twenty feet away, one was advancing quickly, less than ten feet away, and one was reaching toward Jay, close enough that when Jay gasped, he inhaled a lungful of its rancid stink.

As Jay staggered back, the hyena, tall and skinny, filth and ruined clothing almost obscuring the fact that it had once been a woman, snatched the book from his hand.

In the time it took the hyena to take the book, the second hyena had closed the gap and Robert lunged at it, sword arcing out ahead of him. The blade tore across the hyena's chest and blood leapt from the wound in fat droplets that rained down on the cream-coloured tiles of the library floor. The hyena's mask of mindless savagery was replaced by one of almost innocent stupidity. It crumpled as if boneless.

Something about that look of dumb acceptance, the ease with which the blood had been released, the sound it had made when it had hit the floor, like sweaty applause, threw a switch somewhere deep in Jay's exhausted and desperate brain. As he launched himself at the book-stealing hyena, a detached, clinical aspect of his consciousness supposed there was a psychological term for what was happening to him.

He planted both hands on the hyena's shoulders and slammed it to the ground. Its head cracked against the floor with a sound that could have been tile, skull or both breaking. Then he began punching its face over and over. He heard its nose break, felt its lips tear and its teeth give way beneath the weight of his fist. He punched until his knuckles, wrists and shoulders ached, until the hyena's face was slick with blood and didn't look much like a face at all anymore. Even then he carried on punching until he was grabbed by the hood of his coat and dragged to his feet.

'It's dead,' said Robert from behind him. 'And we will be too, unless we get out of here right fucking now.'

Jay couldn't take his eyes from the mess on the floor at his feet. His heart felt as if it was trying to hammer its way through his sternum and his mind was wrapped in a hot fog of rage. He couldn't think. There were no words. There was just the pain in his hands and arms, and a fury that felt like it was in his blood, propelled through his body by bomb-blast heartbeats.

'No words,' he heard himself say. Then, his first thought in what felt like an age: *Is this what it's like to be one of them; to be a hyena?*

'And when I say right fucking now, I mean right fucking now, Jay,' said Robert.

Jay dragged his eyes from the dead hyena, catalogued briefly the five other corpses strewn about the floor and turned to see Robert's irritated face. Beyond that, Ellen, staring at him with something between horror and, if not quite admiration, a kind of grudging approval. He shook his head to dislodge the thought and bent down to pick up the book. The plastic protective cover was slippery with blood.

'Which way?' said Ellen. 'They're everywhere.'

And Jay noticed for the first time that the library had been comprehensively breached. The sound of hyenas and crashing bookcases came from every direction.

'Up,' said Robert.

'Up?' said Jay, the word emerging as a coarse whisper.

'Yeah, up. The roof. We can cut across to the museum. There's a broken skylight, drops you on the top floor. Where do you think I got this samurai stuff? Debenhams?'

Jay nodded, shook his head, nodded again. He had no idea what Robert was talking about. He could hear the words, he understood them individually, but they seemed to have been thrown together with little consideration given to coherence.

'What?' he managed.

'Jay,' said Ellen, placing a hand on his elbow. 'You're

going to have to pull yourself together, okay?'

'Okay. What? Oh, pull myself together, yeah.' He gave his head a shake, felt his thoughts clear. Not much, but enough. He shrugged off his pack, shoved the book inside, then shouldered it once more. 'I'm fine. Let's go.'

Robert headed back toward the stairs that lead down to the mezzanine but, before he reached them, swerved left through an open doorway. Ellen, then Jay, followed. They were on a landing with a green marble floor. To their left, windows provided a view of bookcases and desks. Ahead, closed doors, staff only. To their right, a zigzagging stairway, from the bottom of which rose a chorus of shrieks, grunts and giggles.

That sound finished the job that thoughts of Dempsey and Lucozade had started, and Jay experienced a kind of drawing together of all the pieces of his mind that had broken off and drifted away. He sprinted after Ellen and Robert as they all but threw themselves up the stairs. Jay wasn't sure if he could only imagine the collective heat of the hyenas below.

Something about the high magnolia walls, the dimness and the way their slapping footfalls echoed sharply took Jay back to school for a few seconds and he couldn't help smiling as he thought *I never imagined I'd ever find myself wishing I was back in that sadistic little shitehole.* Time heals all wounds. Time and Armageddon.

Jay wasn't sure how many flights they had covered when they arrived on the top floor. It was even more school-like up here. There was something that looked very much like a classroom ahead of them, off the narrow corridor which formed a T-junction with the top of the staircase.

'This way,' said Robert, breaking left. The corridor ended in shadow, less than ten feet later, and Robert went through a door on the far left near the corridor's end.

Before following Robert and Ellen through the door, Jay glanced back.

The first few hyenas were at the top of the stairs already, fighting with each other to get at their prey.

Robert dragged Jay the remaining few inches over the threshold and slammed the door shut. Ellen had a chair ready and passed it to Robert who wedged it under the brass doorknob.

Jay looked around. They were in a small room, containing only the chair, a scratched and battered desk and a metal filing cabinet from which the beige paint was peeling. There was a large sash window opposite the door. The pane was wire-glass, murky daylight straining through.

Robert put his sword aside and gripped the bottom of the sash.

'I thought they wanted the books,' he said. 'Why the fuck are they chasing us?'

'I don't know,' said Jay. But he thought maybe he *did* know and in his mind's eye he saw a hyena sinking its fingers into a shattered skull, rummaging about in search of... *something*.

There was a thud from behind them as the first of the

hyenas slammed into the door. The chair shifted half an inch, its feet screeching briefly against the tiled floor.

Robert grunted and the sash juddered upward in a shower of paint flakes.

'You first,' Robert said to Ellen.

Another screech from the chair and the door was open wide enough for filthy fingers to worm into view.

Jay watched as Ellen clambered out into a high-walled well which sprouted various pipes and ducts. There was a cast iron ladder, rust blistered, attached to the far wall.

Another screech. Hands grasped and clawed at nothing and the small room was assaulted by the sound of the pack. From somewhere beyond the hyenas, somewhere deep down in the library, Jay thought he heard a gunshot, then another.

Robert followed Ellen, who was already halfway up the ladder.

Another screech. The chair moved a couple of inches this time then dropped to the floor. The door flew open. Three hyenas were wedged in the frame, grinding against one another to be the first to claim a victim.

Jay plunged headfirst out onto the roof.

As he got to his feet and looked up, he saw Ellen looking down from the top of the well and Robert completing the last few rungs before scrabbling from view.

Jay stumbled over to the ladder.

The way the walls seemed to lean in toward the grey-brown rectangle of sky above, disorientated him and threw him off balance. He leapt onto the highest rung he could reach, dragging himself up, his feet scuffling for purchase. Below him, a hyena grunted laughter. The ladder shook. He didn't look down, didn't dare, didn't have time. His feet found a rung and he scuttled up.

He was close to the top, Ellen and Robert reaching down to him, when the hand seized his ankle, its heat pouring immediately through the fabric of his trousers. He tried to shake his leg free, but the hyena's grip was fast, its fingers striving to sink into flesh and down to the bone. He lifted his other foot from the rung, letting his hands and arms take the strain, and stomped down on where he hoped the hyena's head would be. He connected with nothing.

The hyena dragged at him and he felt his fingers begin to lose their grip on the rung. Ellen and Robert were on their knees now, straining toward him but he was still a good foot or so out of reach. He knew that if the hyena got hold with its other hand, it would all be over. And there was a part of him that wanted it to be over, that wanted to let go, the way he imagined a vertigo suffer experiences that strange compulsion to make real their fear and plunge headlong into space. But he didn't let go, he stomped again. And this time he struck something. The hyena's grasp loosened a little. He stomped again and as his heel ground into what he thought and hoped was the hyena's scalp, and as the hand relinquished its grip entirely, there was a metallic snap from somewhere above him and his face and hands were showered in rust particles and brick dust.

At first, he thought it was an optical illusion, a trick of perspective like before, when he'd lurched toward the ladder, but no, the bolts holding the ladder to the wall really had broken or come lose and the ladder really was tipping backwards.

He could hear more hyenas below him now, could feel their grasping hands snagging at his feet and ankles, and he knew it was only the fact that they were fighting amongst themselves to get to him that was preventing him from being dragged down to his death.

Chapter Nineteen

Feeling ridiculous in spite of everything, Jay continued to scuttle up the ladder, knowing it was too late and his arcing trajectory would deliver him into the snickering mob below any second now. And then he saw Robert lunge for the ladder and manage, just, to curl the ends of the index and third finger of his right hand over the top rung.

But he had over-reached. Too much of his body was stretched out across the gap and Jay could see the panic on Robert's face as he waved his free arm back to grab the edge of the roof, flailing at thin air. The ladder continued to tip, dragging Robert with it.

Collective hysteria erupted from the hyenas below, accompanied by reeking clouds of rotten breath.

Then Ellen grabbed Robert's wrist with both hands. She dug in her heals and leaned back.

The ladder stopped tipping.

Ellen leaned back further, her teeth bared, and managed a first then a second step backwards. And Robert's flapping hand found the edge of the roof and latched onto it. His face turned purple with the strain and the ladder began to move back toward the wall. Jay continued to crawl up it. By the time it was against the wall, he was at the top. He scrambled off it and onto the roof, half submerging himself in deep snow.

He got to his knees, then to his feet and turned back to see Robert plant a heel in the face of a thick-bearded, dreadlocked hyena. The ladder and the hyena, spitting blood, tipped back then fell from view. There were shrieks of fury from the pack. Struggling to catch his breath, Jay looked out across the city. Saint John's Beacon dominated the view, front and centre, and only Saint George's Hall and the Holiday Inn offered anything like resistance. Beyond this disparate trio was a patchwork of rooftops, then, off to the South West, the gauzy outlines of Moel Famau and the Welsh hills. Looking down at Saint John's Gardens, Jay saw fifty or more hyenas scurrying amongst the statues and memorials, looking, at this distance, like children at play. On the far side of the gardens, near the steps, Brian's body, arms and legs all wrong, lay at the centre of a disc of blood. At this distance, it looked to Jay like a red badge with an esoteric symbol printed on it, a character from an alien alphabet. Crows like scraps of black cloth, ten or so of the things, had formed a rough perimeter around the symbol and were closing in.

And then he realised that Ellen and Robert were already on the move, across the roof toward another ladder which, along with various aluminium ducts, led up to a higher level. Before Jay could catch up, Ellen was already at the top of the ladder and Robert was close behind.

Jay was relieved to find this ladder was relatively new, doubtless used regularly for maintenance work. Robert had made it to the top and gestured to Jay to hurry up. Then his face seemed to go limp as he looked past Jay in the direction from which they'd just come. Jay thought he saw Robert mouth 'Jesus'.

He didn't want to look back, didn't want to see what had caught Robert's eye and drained the colour from his face. He wanted to get up the ladder, to keep moving, to waste no time. But he had to look.

He turned to see a hyena, a giant of a thing, dragging itself up onto the roof where the rusty old ladder had been. The remains of its clothing (all black, including its shiny bomber jacket) and close-cropped hair — doubtless shaved down to the follicle pre-Jolt — told Jay it had once been a bouncer or private security storm trooper.

It glared at Jay, grinned — a gold incisor gleamed amidst brown and yellow — and then it charged.

Jay darted up the ladder, noting that Robert had done the sensible thing and made himself scarce.

The hyena let loose a roar that narrowed to a hiss.

From the top of the ladder, Jay saw Ellen lowering herself backwards through a broken skylight next to a submerged pyramid of verdigris-stained roof. Robert, sword in hand, spun on his heels, communicating equal parts impatience and stark terror. As Jay was stepping off the ladder, he felt it thrum through the sole of the foot that remained on the top rung. This time, he didn't look back. He sprinted across the roof toward the

Hyenas

skylight, where Robert had just dropped from view.

Behind him, the hyena roared again.

Jay threw his backpack through the skylight, dropped to his knees and scuttled backwards after it. As he slithered down, nubs of broken glass lacerating the front of his coat, he locked eyes with the hyena. Steam huffed from its gaping mouth, trailing behind it like cobwebs. Hands grabbed Jay's legs and waist as he dangled down, and he could only hope it was Ellen and Robert.

'Let go, for fuck's sake,' said Ellen.

Jay did so and dropped an embarrassing couple of inches.

'It's coming,' he said, taking in a square-ish corridor, poorly illuminated by the murky glow falling from the skylight and Robert's sweeping torch. To his right, against the wall, was a display case containing a brass sextant and theodolite. Behind him, two doors led to ladies' and gents' toilets. Ahead, was another display case containing antique navigation equipment and then the corridor curved left into an open space.

'What's coming?' said Ellen.

'Christ,' said Robert. 'It saw you? It saw you come down here?'

'What saw you?' said Ellen.

'Hyena,' Jay gasped. 'Biggest fucking hyena I ever saw.'

'It saw you come down here?' Robert repeated.

'Yeah.'

'Shit,' said Robert, swiping his sword down at nothing.

Jay could hear its pounding footfalls beyond the

ceiling, thought he could even hear it panting.

'This way,' said Robert. He ran to the end of the short corridor, torchlight whipping out ahead of him. Jay and Ellen followed.

They were in an open space. In front was a set of five stairs leading up between a wheelchair lift and, in a large display case, a Victorian gentleman, one hand on a brass projector, frozen in the middle of an astronomy lecture. A few feet beyond the top of the stairs, past a display of grandfather clocks, double doors opened onto a cafe swimming in turgid daylight.

Behind them, closed lift doors. To their right, an opening to a room, along the ceiling of which was suspended a space rocket fuselage about twenty feet long. To the right of the entrance was some kind of rocket booster, a metal dome big enough to hide a grown man, sprouting a confusion of pipes and canisters. Everything else was shadows, shapes and darkness.

Robert went into the dark, running beneath the space rocket to the back of the room, torchlight bouncing.

'Don't worry,' he said over his shoulder. 'There's a door. I've used it before. The mouth-breather will go the other way. Toward the light.'

Ellen followed and, as Jay did likewise, he felt a thud as the hyena dropped through the skylight and into the museum.

At the far end of the room, beneath a wall-mounted television screen, was a large cuboid desk covered with pencils and activity sheets with pictures of astronauts, meteors and re-entry vehicles. Past the desk, set into the far wall and painted black, was a door.

Robert ran over to the door and made an elaborate display of running his hands around the edge of the door frame. Jay was wondering what this desperate mime was all about when he saw that there was no handle on the door. At the same time, Robert turned to them, his face somehow both apologetic and terrified.

'It's closed,' he said. 'Last time I was here, it was open. But now it's closed and there's no fucking handle on this side. Shit. Shit, shit, shit!'

'Behind the desk,' said Ellen, her voice a harsh whisper. 'And turn off that fucking torch.'

Ellen, Jay then Robert dropped behind the desk. Robert switched off the torch.

The darkness seemed to collapse onto Jay; it had weight and texture.

The hyena roared and the sound seemed to thicken the darkness, to add to its weight. Then there was a shattering of glass, and Jay was almost certain that the Victorian gentleman's astronomy lecture had been permanently interrupted. There were a few crashes and clatterings, then silence.

Jay strained to detect any hint of what the hyena was doing and, more to the point, where it was doing it. But all he could hear was his own heartbeat. What felt like a full minute passed but Jay suspected it was only half that. He could only surmise that the hyena had moved on, doubtless toward the dishwater light of the cafe, just as Robert had predicted. He couldn't imagine it simply waiting in the dark, waiting for them to give themselves away. They were savage things, the hyenas; they couldn't strategise. It wouldn't be laying in wait, surely, like some animal.

Robert must have been thinking along the same lines because Jay heard him shift position, as if he was getting ready to stand.

And then Jay thought, *like some animal* and realised that was precisely what the hyenas were, animals, and laying in wait was precisely what just such an animal would do. And then the stink of it unfurled through the darkness. But it was too late, because Robert was already rising.

Despite the fact that they had been in darkness for less than a minute, when Robert thumbed the torch into life, the sudden flare of light was momentarily blinding.

The hyena leapt first onto the desk, then down onto Robert. It was little more than a blur, a dark smudge staining the afterglow. The torch leapt from Robert's hand, spinning through the air, throwing its disk of light from wall to ceiling to floor to wall to ceiling, before hitting the floor with a crack that submerged them in darkness once again.

Robert let out a hollow gasp as the hyena drove him into the floor. His arms and legs lashed out. A grasping hand seized Jay's ankle then let go and slapped about his foot like a wrestler signalling submission. And Jay realised that Robert was trying to find the sword. He began feeling for it himself, sweeping his palms across the coarse carpet tiles.

There was a grunt from the hyena, then a gristly thud. Robert let out a groan. Another grunt, another gristly thud. This time, Robert responded with something closer to a whimper.

Jay extended his search, sending his hands out in all directions, turning on his knees. His fingertips struck something hard. He snatched at it. But it wasn't the sword, it was the torch. He turned it in his hands until he'd worked out where the button was. He jabbed the button with his thumb. Nothing. It was dead.

Another grunt from the hyena. Another gristly thud.

Jay thought he heard Robert whisper, 'Jesus.'

He began his search for the sword again and this time his hand fell upon it almost immediately. He ran his fingers down the blade until he felt the cord-wrapped handle. He stood and lifted the sword above his head.

'Ellen, get as far away as you can,' he said.

He heard movement and didn't know if it was Ellen moving away, Robert thrashing to free himself or the hyena turning toward him.

He brought the sword down where he thought the hyena was and could only hope he didn't hit Robert.

There was a kind of wet crunch, like a spade sinking into damp, gritty earth, and a violent tremor whipped down the blade and wrenched the sword from Jay's hand. His eyes had begun to adjust to the dark. What little light had struggled through from the cafe and the broken skylight created shapes in front of him, abstract outlines that he couldn't identify. One such shape dominated. It reared up and at the same time there was a shriek-roar from the hyena.

He had wounded it. He tried to grab the sword's handle but only snatched at thin air.

'Run, Ellen! Robert? Can you run?'

The outline of what he assumed was the hyena seemed to swell and Jay realised it was lurching toward him. A slab of a hand struck his left shoulder. All feeling left the arm as he staggered sideways from the force of the blow, only just managing to stay on his feet.

The hyena roared again and Jay could make it out a little more clearly now, its arms lashing out as it turned on the spot. He looked toward the exit, a rectangle of dingy grey, and thought he saw someone stagger right and out of view. Jay made for the exit. Behind him, the hyena had ceased shrieking and roaring and was grunting to a slow steady rhythm.

Jay was nearly at the exit when his feet struck something, and he almost fell to the floor.

'Jesus, which way's up?' It was Robert, his voice thick and slurred.

The hyena stopped its rhythmic grunting and charged toward the voice. Glass shattered as it collided with a display case.

In the dim grey light, Jay could make out Robert, crawling on all fours. He reached down, grabbed his arms and tried to lift him. But he was too heavy.

'Robert, you've got to stand. I can't carry you.'

The hyena roared, then another display case met its end. Jay could see it now, getting closer, lurching and staggering. And he was certain, with the exit behind them, that it could see them.

'Now, Robert!' With a hiss off effort, he dragged Robert up onto his feet. But, almost immediately, he began to fold again, and Jay could feel himself being dragged down.

The hyena lumbered closer. Jay knew he was going to have to leave Robert, knew he couldn't possibly carry him, that it was Brian all over again. And then there was a movement next to Robert and Ellen was grabbing Robert's other arm and helping Jay guide him toward the exit. But even with Ellen's support, Robert was too heavy, and Jay knew they'd be lucky if they got more than twenty feet before the hyena caught up.

As if sensing Jay's doubt, the hyena barked laughter.

Broken glass cracked and crunched beneath their feet as they worked their way around the Victorian lecturer, headless now, and the remains of his projector and orrery.

'Just get him to the stairs,' said Jay.

'What? That thing's still coming.'

'Get him to the stairs. Try and bring him round. I'm going to...'

What was he going to do?

Jay and Ellen lowered Robert onto the stairs, then Jay began walking back toward the astronomy exhibit and the hyena. As he walked, he reached into his pocket, took out the empty revolver and held it by the barrel. The hyena had almost made it into the grey smudge of light. Jay could see the samurai sword embedded in its right side.

Even though he knew he was acting under his own volition, every step he took toward the hyena was a surprise.

He raised the pistol above his head and, when he was less than an arm's length away from the hyena, he brought the butt down on its skull. The sound of scalp splitting and of wood on bone seemed to send a signal to his hitherto uninformed logical self and the urge to run was almost overwhelming.

The hyena reached out for him but, at the same time, its legs buckled and it dropped to its knees. Jay brought the gun down one more time. Something hot peppered his face. The hyena fell flat. He stood there for a couple of seconds not feeling anything, then, pushing the sticky gun back into his coat pocket, he returned to Ellen and Robert.

They were at the top of the stairs now, surrounded by antique clocks — brass, silver and gold managing to gleam despite the dingy light — and Robert was standing, swaying a little but resolutely on his own two feet.

'Christ, he's a mess,' said Ellen.

But Jay didn't really need to be told. He could see the veil of red that seemed to cling to Robert's face from the bridge of his nose down, with what looked like glistening beads cascading from it.

Robert said something that might have been, 'Let's just get the fuck out of here,' but the words were soupy and half-formed.

As they moved through to the cafe, a window to their left offering the same view as the rooftop, Jay said, 'Where did you get the sword? We need more.'

Robert spat out a thick wad of phlegmy blood and Jay tried not to linger on the fact that he thought he'd seen a tooth amidst the tangle of glossy threads.

Robert turned to him and Jay saw properly for the first time what the hyena had done to his face. His nose was split open, his lower lip was torn and hanging from a near-toothless mouth. His left eye was already swelling shut beneath a lacerated brow.

Jay tried not to react. Robert seemed dazed, half-asleep.

'Downstairs,' Robert managed, spitting blood again. 'Third floor. World cultures.'

'Hang on,' said Ellen. She jogged further into the cafe, toward an L-shaped service counter. She went behind the counter, opened a lightless fridge and pulled out a bottle of water. Then she grabbed a handful of serviettes from next to the cash register and came back, opening the bottle.

'Close your eyes, Bob,' she said.

'Robert,' he managed but did as he was told.

Ellen poured water over his brow, nose and mouth. The floor at his feet was immediately awash with a solution that was two parts blood to one-part water.

She handed him the serviettes and he held them to his mouth and nose.

'Do you want to rest for a bit?' said Jay.

Robert shook his head and walked to the exit. There was something in his determined but slightly listing gait that made Jay think of a drunk trying to prove he was anything but.

Before they set off after him, Ellen turned to Jay and whispered, 'I hope they got that first aid stuff. He's a fucking mess. He's going to need stitching up and who the hell's going to do that? And before you ask, no, I can't fucking sew.'

They emerged at the top of a small flight of stairs, at the bottom of which was a glass-doored lift; to the right of that, stairs zigzagging downwards. Robert was already halfway down the first flight by the time Ellen and Jay caught up, his route marked by what looked like a scattering of bright red coins. Another staircase mirrored their own ahead of them. To the left of the stairs, through a fine wire mesh they could look down five stories into what had once been a courtyard before an arching glass roof had turned the outside in. Two walkways crossed over the courtyard, one on the fourth floor, the other on the third. A Sputnik hung from wires above the fourth-floor walkway and, between the ground floor and the third-floor walkway a skeletal Pteranodon hung, its bones the colour of tobacco-stained teeth. A totem pole of blackened wood, standing against the left-hand wall between twin exits, reached almost to the fourth floor. Jay hadn't been to the museum since he was a child, and it had changed completely.

They passed the fourth floor, its walls covered floor to ceiling in dusky-orange images of fossils and strange rock formations. Robert was waiting for them on the third floor. The wall here displayed red duotone images of a South American tribesman and, in sweeping, almost calligraphic brushstrokes, a top-knotted Japanese nobleman.

Robert took them left across the landing, past three small glass display cases containing Greek and Roman statuettes, and through glass double doors. The wall immediately ahead of them was filled with a photographic image created from five vertical panels showing a throng of crimson-robed Buddhist monks meditating. The small space opened up to the left. What little light had followed them through the glass doors began to fail a few feet in.

Jay shrugged off his backpack and rummaged through it, pushing aside various Blakes and the Northrop Frye that had ultimately brought him here, until he found the battery-powered lantern. He flicked it on and passed it to Ellen. As soon as he'd re-shouldered his pack, they went left, into the gloom.

They passed displays of Chinese vases and a spread-eagled Tibetan robe, its yellow silk catching the torchlight and gleaming like gold. The layout steered them left, past oriental ceramics and elaborate lacquered furniture. Ahead and to their left, the display cases were shattered, shards of glass littering the floor, creating an impression of a frozen pond that some unfortunate had plunged through. The display — samurai armour, swords and bows and arrows — had been ransacked with little concern for the artefacts' preservation. Jay, Ellen and, still unsteady on his feet, Robert reached past threatening shards like some crude attempt at a theft deterrent and each took a sword from a rack from which one weapon, presumably still buried in the hyena upstairs, was already missing.

Armed, they began to head back the way they had come but the sound of shattering glass from that direction stopped them dead. They about-faced, ran past the plundered samurai display and a collection of netsuke. The exhibition space narrowed to a corridor. Exhibits scrolled by. Bronze Tibetan tigers the size of terriers guarded the entrance to a room off to the right containing paintings on silk of the Buddha; to their left more Tibetan silks, swords and a red-faced mask with hemispherical eyes decorated with mesmeric concentric circles. The corridor opened up into a square-ish room dominated by an intricately carved ivory chair; around the sides of the room, carvings from some kind of volcanic rock of Indian deities, and shadow puppets frozen in melodramatic poses. The room opened up ahead and swept off to the left in a broad curve. Behind them, the museum's acoustics making it impossible to tell how far, there was another shattering of glass. They passed totem poles, decorative woven rugs, furs and skins, a canoe and an improbably vast and elaborate Native American head dress. As the curve persisted, taking them into a room filled with African masks, Jay began to suspect they were turning in a steady circle. Another crash behind them told him they had no choice but to push on. They dodged round a central display cabinet containing four carved elephant tusks, curving up toward one another, tips almost meeting; then another cabinet of downward-pointing spears hanging from threads like a prop from an illusionist's repertoire. And then they passed through double doors and were out on the landing by the stairs spotted with Robert's blood. The sound of hyenas flooded down. It sounded like the upper floors were filled with them and the detour to fetch the swords seemed like an exercise in futility.

There was something else, too. Burning. Jay was certain he could smell burning.

Robert almost fell down the stairs in his eagerness to put as great a distance as possible between himself and the descending pack but managed, just, to seize the banister and steady himself. The wad of serviettes, still pressed to his face, were entirely red now.

Jay and Ellen exchanged a look of concern, not realising that Robert was looking over his shoulder at them.

'I'll make it,' he slurred. 'I'll fucking make it. I'm fine. I fell off a first-floor balcony when I was sixteen.' He spat blood onto the floor. 'Spent five weeks in the Royal eating food that I'm pretty sure someone else had already had a go at before me. This isn't going to beat me.' But he was breathless following his tirade, his eyes distant and swimming. 'Lead on.'

They passed the second floor, bright green walls printed with images of insects and a sign saying 'Special Exhibition Coming Soon!' And even though he hadn't visited the museum since he was a child, the thought that there would be no more exhibitions, special or otherwise, here or anywhere else, filled Jay with a sadness so sudden and intense that his heart ached like the strained and tired muscle it was.

A stench of rotten fish and stagnant water hit them as they passed the aquarium on the first floor. Jay tried not to imagine the tanks, cloudy and filled with belly-up fish swollen and bursting with decomposition. He held his breath until he made it to the foyer, the outside-in courtyard, with its turquoise- and gold-mosaiced Lambanana beneath the swooping skeletal Pteranodon.

To their left, beyond sliding glass doors, the main exit was closed and shuttered. The shutters were made of a kind of steel mesh and Jay could discern movement beyond. Ahead, to the right of a huge wall-mounted spider crab, the windows of closed double doors provided a view of a gift shop and cafe.

Robert shoulder-barged open the doors and stepped into the gloom of the gift shop cafe. Ellen then Jay followed, Ellen carrying the lantern. The room was split in two. On the right, tables and chairs and a counter, behind which was a glass-fronted fridge and a cappuccino machine. On the left were shelves containing stuffed dinosaurs, figurines of Tutankhamen and Anubis, model space shuttles and various rubber insects. In the far-left corner, was a curved counter with a cash register.

Robert marched directly over to a set of doors opposite, identical to the ones they had just come through and leading to a corridor which was only half-illuminated by grey light seeping through the windows of another set of doors at its far end. As he pushed open the doors with a jab of his foot, there was a flash, not like a camera flash, more like a brief distress flare. Then, at the same time, Robert seemed to toss back his head, hand and serviettes dropping from his face, and there was a crack that Jay immediately identified as a gunshot, and Robert was arching backwards, a thick rope of blood whiplashing out from his forehead in the opposite direction. The sword dropped from Robert's hand and clattered to the floor.

Chapter Twenty

Jay dropped down onto all fours and, still gripping his sword, scuttled to the left, past shelves of toys and replica antiquities, over to and then behind the counter. He hoped Ellen had followed him but as he lay there trying to control his breathing, he realised she hadn't. He had no idea where she was.

Then, voices from the corridor.

'Shit, I don't think that was a joker.'

'Course it was. Didn't you see the state of it?'

Footsteps crossed the room.

'Fuck. It was just some bloke.'

'Fuck. How was I supposed to know? It's dark, he was moving fast, blood all over his face. Fuck.'

'Boss isn't going to be happy. We're supposed to be recruiting, not reducing the human population any more than it already has been.'

'Fuck off. Tell me something I don't know. Shit.'

'Come on. Let's see if we can find the other two. Pepper said there were three of them. Assuming the jokers haven't done for them already.'

'Fucking hell. Don't let him hear you calling him that. *Pepper*. He'll have your—'

There was a sudden flurry of movement, a clatter of weaponry.

'Don't fucking move!'

Jay froze, wondering how the hell they could have seen him. Then, from somewhere across the room, he heard Ellen say, 'All right boys, you can put the toys down now. I'm not armed. The only thing I'm carrying is a highly developed foetus and I promise I won't let it hurt you.'

'Where are the rest of you?'

'Lying on the floor at your feet. One of you halfwits shot him.'

'Who are you calling a halfwit?'

'She's got a point, Pete. You are a few chips short of a butty.'

'Fuck off, Colin.'

'Just saying.'

'Well don't 'just say'. Got feelings, you know.'

'Yeah, I was forgetting. You and your feelings. It always slips my mind when I see you shooting anything with a fucking pulse.'

'Piss off, you sarcastic get. Anyway, are you going to come quietly or what, love?'

'Don't 'love' me, you patronising twat. And no, I'm not coming quietly. I'm not coming at all. I've got other plans. So, piss off and play soldier somewhere else.'

'No can do, love. Orders. Put the cuffs on her, Colin. And if you put up a fuss, *love*, I'll knock you out and drag you through the fucking streets. And if my arms get tired I'll leave you for the jokers.'

'Speaking of which, Pete, we'd better get a wiggle on. Sounds like the place is filling up with them.'

'Good. We'll burn this one down, too.'

Jay slipped the revolver from his pocket and rose slowly until he could see over the top of the counter, between a wicker basket of ammonite key rings and another of Fair Trade chocolate bars.

The two militiamen were facing away from him. Ellen was facing toward him. She gave no indication that she'd noticed him, though Jay thought it very unlikely that she hadn't. One of the militiamen — Colin, presumably — slung his assault rifle over his shoulder and began walking toward Ellen. The other tried to keep his gun trained on Ellen but his attention kept drifting toward the door leading to the foyer and the growing sound of hyena activity. When Colin was a couple of feet away from Ellen, she reached into her coat pocket. Colin was looking down, struggling to free a pair of handcuffs from his belt and failed to notice the movement. Pete was glancing at the door and also failed to notice. Jay stepped out from behind the counter and began moving, as quickly and as quietly as he could, toward Pete.

Colin freed the cuffs and looked up at Ellen in time to see her pull the pistol from her pocket and point it at his face. He stopped dead and dropped the cuffs. At the sound of the cuffs hitting the floor, Pete looked away from the door.

'Jesus!' He tried to level his rifle at Ellen, but Colin was in his line of sight. 'Colin! Get out of the fucking way!'

'Don't listen to the halfwit, Colin,' said Ellen.

'She won't shoot,' said Pete. 'She hasn't got it in—'

Jay pressed the barrel of his revolver against the base of Pete's skull. Pete jerked, as if he'd been jabbed with a cattle prod.

'Don't move,' he said.

'That could be a bit of pipe for all I know,' said Pete but there was a distinctly clenched quality to his voice.

'Why don't you turn around and see if my colleague's holding a length of pipe, Colin?' said Ellen.

Colin turned slowly.

'No,' he said. 'He isn't holding a length of pipe, Pete.'

'Now that we've cleared that up,' said Ellen, 'why don't you boys place your toys on the floor, then kick them away?'

Colin and Pete did as they were told.

Jay, still keeping his empty gun trained on Pete, picked up the assault rifle. Ellen did likewise.

'Okay,' said Ellen. 'We're not completely without compassion, so we're going to leave one of these rifles outside on the street where you can see it. We'll take the other one. Give us a two-minute head start.'

'Two minutes?' said Pete. 'In case you haven't noticed this place is going to be crawling with jokers in about a minute and a half, probably less.'

'I said we're not completely without compassion but that doesn't mean we entirely give a shit, either,' said Ellen. 'There's a sword on the floor over there. Robert used to put it to good use before you shot him in the face.'

Ellen and Jay began backing toward the corridor. The sound of hyenas was getting louder all the time. The smell of burning was getting stronger too.

'I'll kill you for this!' snarled Pete. 'I'll fucking kill you! Shoot *you* in the fucking face, you pair of gobshites!'

Ellen and Jay ignored his ranting and continued to back down the marble-floored corridor, grey light becoming brighter, but no less grey, as they got nearer to the exit. They passed gleaming marble pillars and a leather sofa; it was less a corridor than a long and absurdly lavish waiting room. Ellen backheeled the door and they stepped outside.

Jay turned to get his bearings. They were between two sets of stone steps running down about five feet to the street below, left and right. Ahead was a balustraded balcony. Twin flyovers — vast serpents of jaundiced concrete — swept down from behind to their right and over a wide dual carriageway that Jay remembered as always being gridlocked with growling traffic but was now more snow than cars. One flyover snaked away from them coming to earth a couple of hundred feet ahead, at the start of Dale Street, the pale-yellow gothic spire of the Municipal Building visible a little further on. The other curved off to their right, seeking out the bottom of Tithebarn Street. Between the two was the old Blackburn Assurance Building, an Art Deco block, its decorative spandrel panelling stained with verdigris.

Jay could smell burning, could see black smuts drifting on the air like polluted snow.

'They set fire to it,' he said.

'Set fire to what?' said Ellen, throwing the assault rifle down into the snow at the foot of the left-hand staircase. It dropped out of sight, leaving a distinct rifle-shaped hole behind. Jay had been hoping Ellen would keep her rifle and his would be the one left in the snow. He didn't like the feel of it, the sense that some internal mechanism was so tightly wound that he might be able to trigger it with a cough or an aggressive thought.

'Sergeant Pepper. The militia. They set fire to the library.'

'Seems like a good plan. Maybe they're not *all* halfwits. Come on. They'll come out looking for their toy in a minute and we don't want to be in their line of fire when that happens.'

Ellen went down the right-hand staircase then turned right, around the back of the museum. A boxy staircase, the low walls of which were decorated with small white tiles, zigzagged up to a walkway that stretched out over the wide main road and under the Churchill Way flyovers toward John Moores University's science building with its cluster of steel exhaust pipes sprouting from the roof. Halfway along, the walkway branched off to the left, following the underbelly of the Tithebarn-bound flyover before sweeping steeply left toward Dale Street.

As they reached this intersection and turned left, a loft of pigeons taking flight at their approach, Jay said, 'I don't think burning the library was a good idea.'

'Why not?'

'I don't know. I mean, if that's why they came, for the books, for the words, what are they going to do when it's all turned to ash?' He thought about Alice Band punching a hole through someone's head to get at the language inside. He thought about Hello Kitty's eyes darting about as she watched the words emerge from his mouth. He thought about Ellen's paintings. He thought about Brian saying that the hyenas could sense survivors in big numbers — *Big numbers attract attention, from zombies and the militia both, but mostly the zombies. Don't know why, but it's like they can sense larger groups. They just home in, like flies to shit.* 'I think they're going to go even more crazy. And I think they're going to come looking for the only place where language is left. Us.'

They followed the walkway down to the pavement. Jay glanced over toward the library. From this angle, it was hidden by the bulk of the museum, but he could tell that the black smoke that was billowing out onto the street and across Saint John's Gardens was coming from the library's windows. The smoke was so thick it looked solid, like the tentacles of some vast sea creature.

'I think we're going to be like fucking beacons now,' he said as they turned right onto the bottom of Dale Street, moving uphill, parallel to the last fifty feet or so of the flyover. 'It's like the library was a honey pot and me and you are a couple of half-eaten, half-melted ice lollies. Once the honey pot's gone, the wasps are going to come after the ice lollies.'

'I'm not a half-melted ice lolly,' said Ellen. 'Not so sure about you, though.' She stopped, turning to face him. 'We just need to keep moving, Jay. We're on the home straight now. If burning the library has fucked them up in some way, then maybe it'll buy us some time. While they're still reeling, we can get down to the river. By the time they realise what a feast your sticky, melting hide represents, we'll be on the water and fuck them.'

Jay was about to say he didn't think the hyenas would be reeling for very long at all, but then he saw the weariness on Ellen's face and realised it was only pure will that was driving her forward and if he told her they probably weren't going to make it, then that might be enough to stop her in her tracks and bring her to her knees.

'Yeah,' said Jay. 'Fuck them. Let's get moving.'

They headed down Dale Street, Ellen setting the pace a few feet ahead of him. Outside the magistrate's court, they had to circumvent two tangled, snow-encrusted corpses. It was impossible to say whether either of them had been hyenas or the victims of hyenas or just victims of the cold.

They were about sixty feet from where Moorfields branched off to the right and rose up toward Tithebarn Street, when Jay experienced a sense of dread so intense, he thought he might throw up. Something was wrong, or was about to go wrong. He had no idea what.

He was about to call out to Ellen when she came to an abrupt halt. He wondered if she had experienced it too, this vague but powerful premonition. But then she turned, one hand pressed to the side of her belly, her face scrunched with pain.

'Just need a minute.' The words were expelled from between clenched teeth. 'Don't worry, not about to give birth. At least, I don't think so. Just need a minute.'

'Okay. No problem.' Jay pointed to the doorway of an office furniture shop. 'You want to sit down?'

'No. Better standing.'

'Okay.' Jay smiled but the sense of dread, the premonition, was growing, beginning to coalesce. He could almost articulate it.

Looking down at Ellen, seeing the lines of pain grooved into her forehead, Jay said, 'The boat's along from the Liver Buildings. Just follow Prince's Parade until you're almost at the Alexandra Tower. There are stone steps leading down. Be careful, they're slippy as fuck. You know, in case I don't make it.'

Ellen managed a smile. 'Thanks, Jay. But you'll make it.' She grinned. 'Probably.'

'Yeah, probably,' said Jay. 'Funny thing is, I didn't think I was going to make it *before* all this. Back when everything was normal. Normal for everybody else, anyway. Every day was too hard. Sometimes, I just wanted to go to sleep and not wake up. Not kill myself. I never thought of it like that. And I don't think I would have done that. I didn't have the will or the courage. Because it must take courage, mustn't it? To do a thing like that? To just stop? I could never do that. I don't think so, anyway. But, if there'd been some way I could have just drifted in and out of sleep for the rest of my life, some pill I could have taken, I think I'd have jumped at the chance.'

'Booze,' said Ellen. 'That pill. It's called booze. I drifted in and out of sleep for the better part of three years thanks to booze. And I'm going to be honest with you now, Jay, because there are no social workers or therapists around to contradict me, to *frown* at me, but it worked pretty damn well. I wasn't happy but I wasn't… desolate? Alcohol exists in nature for a reason. Feeling numb in all the right places and buzzing in the all the others isn't such a terrible arrangement. It just isn't sustainable. So, I started painting instead. Not as therapy. Not as a way of busying idle hands, but because it was a way of saying 'fuck you' to words and books and all the horrible shit I'd felt and endured for years because I couldn't fucking read. A picture paints a thousand words, but sometimes it's just the same words over and over again. And those words are 'fuck you, books.'

'Well,' said Jay. 'I can't draw for shit. Played Pictionary a few Christmases ago and it was one of the few times my dad lost his temper with me. He was pulling his hair out. I can't even remember what it was I was supposed to be drawing but he said it looked like a cross between a pig, a worm and an internal combustion engine.'

Ellen laughed.

Jay laughed, too. Then stopped. The premonition, that growing sense of dread, had crystallised.

Moorfields.

Moorfields Station.

The hyenas were flooding into Liverpool via the railway lines, via the tunnels. He and Ellen were running across the surface of a wasps' nest, its intricate network of tunnels thrumming beneath their feet. And now that the library was burning, now that the honey pot was gone, the wasps were going to go crazy and spill from the nest and come looking for something sweet to eat.

'Ellen, we have—'

But it was too late. The hyenas were already appearing, surging onto Dale Street from around the corner of Moorfields, some still shielding their eyes against a grey-brown light that, compared to the darkness of the tunnels from which they'd recently emerged, must have been like looking directly into the sun.

Chapter Twenty-One

Ellen looked over her shoulder.

'Oh, for fuck's sake.' She took a couple of steps forward, stopped, grimacing and gripping her side. 'Fuck!'

Some of the hyenas had spied them and were already bounding in their direction. Jay raised the assault rifle. Looked down the length of the barrel and trained the sight on the nearest hyena.

'Don't waste the bullets. We're going to need them.' Ellen headed back the way they had come, at a considerably slower pace. A few feet later, she turned left up a narrow alley between an office building and a Spa. As he made the turn, Jay looked back. The hyenas were already gaining. He returned his attention to Ellen, who was already at the top of a small set of steps, between boarded windows and high graffiti-bedraggled walls. Jay caught up with her easily before she'd reached a road which curved right toward a side street dominated by a Premier Inn. Ahead of them was a four-storey car park — a box of red brick and, on the upper storeys, green-barred glassless windows.

'Ellen, they're—'

'Catching up. I know. I can't run much further. We're

going to have to hide. Or I am. You can keep running if you like.'

'I'll stick with you,' said Jay.

'I'm touched.' She pointed to the car park. 'In there.'

They jogged through the wide main entrance, dipping under the red and white barrier. Darkness and more than a hint of piss closed around them. They made their way to the back, the darkness and the stench thickening. There were a few cars parked-up in the bays and one car, a Vauxhall Meriva with *In the Night Garden* sun blinds on the back windows, was abandoned across two bays, one door gaping open and a man's patent leather shoe on the roof. They reached the far wall and slid behind a white Fiat mini-van with a decal of a cartoon painter and decorator on the side.

Putting down the assault rifle, Jay dropped onto all fours and lay flat on his belly so he could see under the van. He could hear the hyenas, a tangle of snarls and shrieking laughter, funnelled through the narrow alley and into the car park where it echoed from the bare brick walls. The sound alone felt like the first wave of an attack. And then the hyenas began to appear. Framed by the car park exit, there was something cinematic about the parade of hyenas as they stumbled, staggered and bounded past. Fifteen or more went by and Jay was beginning to feel hopeful, until one stopped, extracted itself from the pack and shuffled toward the car park. It had been some kind of builder or labourer before the Jolt. It still wore overalls — once pale blue, now filthy and torn — and heavy work boots. The inner framework of a hard hat was clamped to its head, greasy fronds of dirty-blond hair sprouting through the gaps. Blackened eyes and a beard matted with dried blood spoke of a broken nose. Jay hadn't thought it possible, but it looked somehow wilder than any of the hyenas he had seen before, and he thought of the library in flames. For a moment, he wasn't sure what it was that made the hyena seem more savage, what visual tic was sending that particular message, and then he realised there were threads of panic and desperation running through the usual tangle of rage and hysteria that were the hallmarks of the hyena face, and he thought of the library again, soon to be ashes.

He looked up at Ellen. The pain-induced lines were no longer scored into her forehead. She nodded and produced a small, tight smile as if to say, I'm okay.

Jay returned his attention to the builder/hyena he had unconsciously named Bob. It was standing at the threshold of the car park now, where the snow sloped down to the tarmac, whiteness fading through grimy grey to black. A look of excitement took over its face for a moment, briefly eliminating the rage, hysteria and panic, and Jay suspected — no, not suspected, he knew — it could sense all those currents of language swirling through and between the various components of his brain. He tried not to think, but knew it wasn't possible; he could only think about not thinking, and words, language, were the building blocks that this thought was made of.

As if to underscore Jay's concern, Bob let out a little giggle of delight that turned into a low, steady moan. It stepped into the car park, its heavy boots clomping on the tarmac. Behind it, the rest of the hyenas streamed by, apparently oblivious to Bob's piqued interest. Jay wondered if some of them were more sensitive to language than others, craved it more. And then he tried to stop wondering and wondered if it was possible to empty his mind but that just made him think of Zen, the word pulsing through his brain: Zen, Zen, Zen, Zen, Zen Zen ZenZenZen.

Bob took a few more steps, its clomping boots making Jay think, Fee, Fi, Fo, Fum. A few more steps. It was about twenty feet away now. Jay reached for the rifle, knowing he couldn't risk using it — the gunshot would bring more hyenas than there were rounds in the curved magazine — but wanting the comfort of it, all thoughts of its hair-trigger lethality swept aside.

Grunting, Bob dropped into a crouch, then slowly tipped its head to one side until the position of its eyes matched Jay's.

Jay stopped breathing and, without even trying, emptied his mind of words until his skull was just an echo chamber for his ranting heartbeat. His hand tightened round the rifle, but there was still a steady, staggering Cinemascope parade of hyenas passing behind Bob.

Bob stood, as slowly as it had crouched, like an

old man rising from an afternoon spent in a low, soft armchair. Then, with an abruptness that caught Jay completely off guard, the hyena was charging toward them. Jay scrabbled to his feet.

'Ellen, fuck, it's...'

Bob slammed into the side of the van with a sound like someone trying to destroy a kettledrum, and the van actually lurched on its suspension, as if it was flying at high speed round a hairpin bend.

Another kettledrum assault and there was Bob, on the roof of the van, glaring down at them, from Jay to Ellen, Ellen to Jay, as if it couldn't make its mind up which one to make its victim.

Ellen darted right, heading to the back of the van. Jay went left, toward the front.

Bob made up its mind. Jay.

It stepped from the roof onto the slope of the windscreen, towering above Jay. Its legs bent as it prepared to leap. Jay ran further off to the left, but, just as in Waterstones, he tensed with a premonition of the hyena landing on his back and driving him down to the oil-stained tarmac, acutely aware that he couldn't outdistance it. And then there was a crack, like a frozen pond giving way and Bob let out a strangled growl. Jay turned and saw that the hyena's right foot had plunged through the windscreen, its leg sunk in up to the knee. He looked back at the exit. Hyenas were still passing by. He scanned for Ellen and saw her disappear up one of two parallel ramps that led to the upper levels.

Hyenas

Jay had taken only a couple of steps in Ellen's direction when Bob let out a long shriek. Jay wanted to keep moving but he couldn't help turning. Bob had dragged its legs free of the windscreen and in so doing had lost shoe, sock and most of the skin from its foot. Blood spilled onto the bonnet, running down to the floor. Still shrieking, Bob leapt from the van, lurched toward Jay, then dropped to its knees. It tried to get back to its feet but only managed to rise halfway before falling again. It looked back at its wounded leg, drawing Jay's eye to what looked like a stub of gristly cable protruding just above the heel. It had severed its Achilles tendon, Jay realised. Unable to walk, its shrieking dropping to a low, steady moan, it began crawling toward him.

Jay was about to give thanks to Whoever for this nugget of good fortune when he noticed the collective silhouette of the hyenas filling the main exit and growing as they moved toward him. He couldn't follow Ellen; even if he could make it to the ramp before they caught up with him, they'd follow him up the stairs and, once they were on the roof, where would they go? They'd be trapped. He looked around for another exit but there was nothing, not even a window. He raised the rifle, ready to begin firing, knowing he'd run out of ammunition long before all the hyenas had fallen, and even if he did have enough bullets, how long before more hyenas came, attracted by the sound of gunfire?

Then he registered the Meriva for the second time, a shoe on its roof and one door open.

The mini people-carrier was equidistant between Jay and the hyenas. But they were advancing, and he had yet to take a step toward the vehicle. If there were keys, he could get the Meriva moving, plough through the hyenas. If not, it wouldn't take long for them to break the windows; Christ, Bob had done it without even trying. But what other choices were there?

He sprinted toward the Meriva. As one, the hyenas surged in his direction, there cacophony filling the car park, sounding like a riot.

Halfway to the Meriva, his heel skidded on a patch of diesel. He managed to stay on his feet, but the assault rifle flew from his hand. It hit the ground ahead of him, bouncing on its stock. He continued toward the car, stooping for the rifle at the same time. He grabbed it by the strap, but in so doing overbalanced and spilled to the floor, rolling the last few feet toward the Meriva. He succeeded, just, in keeping hold of the gun. The hyenas shrieked with something like joy as they saw their prey go down. It was all over in their eyes.

Jay reached up and grabbed the inner handle of the open door and dragged himself up and into the vehicle. There was a thud as a hyena slammed into the other side of the car. Then another. Another. And another, this one from the roof. Jay dragged the door closed as a dirt-encrusted hand swiped down from above. Filthy fingers were momentarily caught then dragged away with a shriek.

The vehicle began to rock and a collage of hyena

hands and faces filled every available inch of window.

Jay was in the passenger seat. He squirmed out of his backpack and over to the driver's side, slapped a hand against the ignition, thinking, please, please, please let there be keys.

He felt nothing but the cold, metal slot.

Chapter Twenty-Two

'Fuck!'

Jay slammed the heels of his hands against the steering wheel. 'Fuck! Fuck! Fuck!'

Ahead of him, kneeling on the bonnet, a hyena that had cultivated an elaborate Mohawk pre-Jolt, wilted now, appeared to be mimicking him, slamming its own hands into the windscreen. It grinned as it beat its palms against the glass, revealing toothless, bleeding gums.

Jay sat back in his seat and wiped the sweat from his face. He looked down at the gun, his heartbeat thrumming down into his stomach, churning its contents, and thought... He wasn't sure what he was thinking. Try and shoot his way out, even though he knew that was hopeless? Or put the barrel of the gun under his chin and pull the trigger, quick and painless?

For a few seconds, the Meriva rocking and booming, he considered the latter option. It would be over in an instant. He wouldn't even feel it. The last sensation would be the trigger passing the point of no return, then a slow-motion awareness of the rifle's mechanism taking over, unstoppable, as he seceded power to the gun. It sounded so easy. The easy way out. The coward's way out. But he knew it was neither of these things. It would require an act of near-superhuman will and he knew he just didn't have it in him.

So. Option one. Start shooting. Keep shooting until the rifle runs dry. He tried to raise the gun, to point it at Mohawk, who was still grinning, still pounding against the windscreen, but he was too close to the steering wheel. He reached under the seat, groped around until he found the metal bar, lifted it up then pushed the chair back.

There was a handbag in the foot well, black with mother-of-pearl sequins.

Jay propped the gun up next to his backpack and snatched the bag.

Amidst all the howling and banging, Jay thought he heard the click-creak of glass beginning to give. Mohawk was licking the windscreen, slathering it with blood-threaded saliva.

Jay began scooping out the bag's contents and dropping them on his lap. A mobile phone, a packet of tissues, a purse, lipstick, compact, a packet of Airwaves and — last, of course last — a bunch of keys. There were eight or nine keys on the *Mama Mia* key ring, but Jay knew immediately that not one of them would start the car. They were house keys; Jay could tell at a glance. Still, he worked his way through the bunch because there was nothing else to do.

Another click-creak of glass under strain, and still the car rocked from side to side like an amusement park ride. Jay threw the bag back into the foot well and was about to sweep the bag's contents from his lap when he realised he'd seen something on the floor an instant before the bag had landed.

He kicked the bag aside.

A key. A car key.

As he reached down for it, there was another click-creak but this time the creak was more protracted. He glanced up as his fingertips found the key, flipping it into his palm, and saw that the windscreen was beginning to sag as the seals started to give way. As if sensing this slight shift, Mohawk stopped his licking and hammered against the glass with renewed enthusiasm.

Jay tried to slot the key into the ignition but succeeded only in jabbing the steering column. He tipped his head to get a better look, and guided it toward the slot. The drawn-out creak of the sagging windscreen was abruptly smothered by a significant increase in the volume of the hyena's din, and Jay saw that the seal had given up completely on the passenger side of the windscreen and a finger-width gap had appeared. The key slid into the ignition. He turned it. The car growled at the hyenas and, as one, they retreated a couple of feet, Mohawk slithering from the bonnet. At the same moment, Al Green recommenced singing *L.O.V.E.* from halfway through the first verse. Jay punched down the handbrake, stamped on the clutch, dragged the gearstick into reverse and stepped hard on the accelerator. He took the Meriva in an arcing trajectory to the back of the car park, until he was pointing at the ramp he'd seen Ellen go up.

A hyena slammed into the front passenger-side door and the window shattered, showering Jay's backpack with fragments of glass. The hyena thrust its arm into the car. Jay stamped on the accelerator and the Meriva sped, tires screeching, toward the ramp. The hyena was dragged along for a couple of seconds before it dropped to the tarmac, to be trampled by the rest of the pack.

Jay realised too late that he was driving too fast to negotiate the tight, upward-sweeping 'u' of the ramp's trajectory. The front passenger-side wing was wrenched off and the car juddered so hard Jay almost lost his grip on the steering wheel, but he managed to keep it moving. A glance in the rear-view mirror showed nothing but hyenas.

Numerous signs recommended a maximum speed of five miles per hour, but Jay was doing closer to thirty when he came off the ramp and had to slam on the brakes to stop himself from ploughing into a concrete pillar that already bore the cracks, chips and scrapes of carelessness.

Jay looked around for any sign of Ellen. Nothing. She must have kept moving up. He tried to bring the car back round on itself to take it up the next ramp but went wide and had to reverse and adjust his approach, during which time the hyenas had reached the top of the ramp he'd just exited and were spilling across to the next, blocking his way.

He put the car into first, gritted his teeth and drove into the pack. Of the four hyenas in the Meriva's immediate path, two were knocked aside, both pirouetting, and one went under the wheels. The fourth was scooped up and hit the centre of the windscreen face first, creating a bloody cataract, before rolling off and joining its packmate beneath the wheels. To the left, the hyenas caught between the car and the wall of the narrow ramp were dragged against the concrete. One reached in, succeeded in snatching at Jay's shoulder before being rotated back along the car, shrieking. Jay had left more space on the right, and here a growing rank of hyenas kept pace with the car. The lead hyena, sporting a ragged, once lipstick-pink tracksuit, tore off the wing mirror and began using it to hammer against the driver's window. There was a series of thuds and scuffles above him as hyenas clambered onto the roof. Jay plunged down the accelerator as he came out of the turn.

A pillar that appeared to be a scrape for scrape replica of the one on the first floor reared up. Jay hit the brakes and yanked the steering wheel hard right. He succeeded in saving the wing from further ruin, but the car slid into the pillar side-on, the front passenger door taking the brunt of it. Jay felt the impact in his bones, in his teeth, and this time his hands lost their grip on the wheel and his feet were bounced from the pedals. The engine died, cutting short Al Green's backing band just as they were really beginning to enjoy themselves.

Out of the corner of his eye, he could see the top of

the ramp filling with hyenas. He turned the key back then forward. The engine grumbled to life, stuttered and died.

'Fuck!'

He gave the key another turn. The engine grumbled again. Then stuttered and died again.

The hyenas were at the door now. A hand so filthy it looked scorched punched through the glass and into Jay's cheekbone. Almost blinded by the blow, Jay turned the key backwards, then forwards. The hyena that had punched him drew back its fist to repeat the offence. The engine grumbled again. Before it could cut out, Jay stomped on the accelerator and Al's backing band surged back to life. As the Meriva lurched away from the concrete pillar, the crushed front passenger door popped open, whatever mechanism had been keeping it locked and shut, wrecked.

In his eagerness to get away from the hyenas, he'd overshot the entrance to the ramp by a good twenty feet. He put the car into reverse and ploughed into the advancing pack until the nose of the car was in the right position to turn onto the ramp.

A hyena in a denim jacket and with a face so swollen and seeping with infection that Jay couldn't place its pre-Jolt age, gender or ethnicity, threw itself onto the bonnet of the car, sliding up and onto the windscreen. The glass began to warp inward under its weight.

Jay took the car up the ramp, knowing that the steep incline would increase the hyena's weight against the windscreen but, with the flapping passenger door and his own window broken, he knew he couldn't hang around. He stayed as far right as he could as he followed the ramp's curve, trying to prevent further damage to the offside wing but only succeeding in destroying the other wing in a shower of sparks.

The hyena tried to rear back, but the momentum of the car pulled it down again. The seal on the passenger side gave up entirely and half the windscreen fell in, draping over the dashboard.

The Meriva emerged on the third floor and Jay surprised himself by taking the car up onto the final ramp with barely a scrape. He would have felt quite pleased with himself if it wasn't for the fact the windscreen was peeling inwards at an alarming rate. But there was nothing he could do about that, except hope.

Once he was out of the bend, Jay floored the accelerator and the Meriva flew out onto the roof. The hyena scuttled across the bonnet so it was directly in front of Jay, blocking his view. It tried to rear back again but Jay kept his foot down, pinning it in place. Then he stamped on the brake pedal.

But the car didn't stop. It carried on racing forward, fishtailing. He'd forgotten about the snow. Jay leaned left, to see past the hyena. He was almost at the edge of the roof, a low wall the only thing between the Meriva and a four-storey plunge. All over the roof, gulls and pigeons took flight. Jay jerked the wheel left then right but the Meriva's trajectory was set, the most he could do was exaggerate the fishtailing. He braced himself for impact, pushing himself back into the chair and scrunching his eyes shut. Al was singing something about love being as bright as the morning sun and then the noise as the car hit the wall was deafening. Despite his best efforts to remain rigid, Jay was thrown forward, his forehead hitting the steering wheel. The blow forced open his eyes and, thinking *so much for the fucking airbag*, he saw the hyena and windscreen fly beyond the crumpled bonnet of the car. Then he was thrown back into his seat so hard the air was forced from his lungs. The hyena and the windscreen dropped from view. Jay was fully expecting to follow them down to the street below, tensing his entire body in readiness, when he realised the car had stopped.

He looked in the rear-view mirror. The pack had arrived at the top of the ramp. Ears ringing and trying to ignore the various injuries that were starting fires throughout his body, Jay put the Meriva into reverse and trod down on the accelerator. Nothing happened. And then Jay realised, no Al Green, no L.O.V.E love. The engine had cut out. Jay worked the key back and forth. Nothing. Not even a cough. He tried again. Nothing. The hyenas had halved the distance, trudging through the thick snow, stalking toward the Meriva as if it was a wounded animal, exhausted and unable to escape.

Before

———

'They're a sort of artsy-fartsy community theatre group, going round schools doing plays about 'issues'. You'd hate them.'

Jay's dad smiled, shook his head.

'I'm sure I wouldn't,' he said and gulped a mouthful of Cain's bitter.

'Anyway, they're big on promoting literacy. So, I come on and just, you know, 'be myself'. I tell these kids what it's like trying to get through life without being able to read and write, and how, unlike me, they've got a choice. And I actually get paid for this. It's all government funded. We'll be going all over the North West.'

'Sounds really good,' said Jay's dad.

'The money's not much but I can pay you a bit of housekeeping now.'

'You don't have to do that, son.'

'No, I want to. I want to pay my way. I'm eighteen, now.'

Jay drained the remainder of his lager.

'Fair enough. But it's up to you. I won't be chasing you for it.'

'You won't have to. I'll leave it under the phone, every

Friday after I've been paid.'

'If you do, you do. If you don't, you don't. So, when's your first 'gig'?'

'Thursday. Holt Comprehensive, by the Fiveways.'

'Nervous?'

'A bit, yeah. Well, a lot. But I've got to do it and I've got to get it right because,' there's this girl in the group, Lucy, and she's gorgeous and she keeps smiling at me for no reason, 'I don't think I'm going to get another chance like this.'

Behind them, over by the bar, a couple of old regulars shouted abuse at the horses on a wall-mounted television.

'Fucking donkey!' one of them shouted, throwing his betting slip to the floor.

Jay's dad finished his pint then pointed at the empties.

'Another round?' he said.

Jay nodded.

'You must be excited,' said Jay's dad as he returned with the drinks, a fug of cigarette smoke parting as he approached.

'Yeah, but you know me. I can't help thinking something's going to go horribly wrong. It usually does.'

'Well, it'd be a pretty dull life if nothing ever went wrong. Great things are done when men and mountains meet. Blake.'

'But all I ever seem to meet is fucking mountains.'

Chapter Twenty-Three

Jay grabbed his pack and the rifle and fell out of the car, sprawling in the snow. Back on his feet, he looked around for a fire escape, an exit. But there was nothing. There were only two other vehicles on the roof, parked next to each other about twenty feet away, a Transit van and a Punto, both inflated with snow, neither with an open door. He put his backpack on and raised the rifle, sighting the nearest hyena. There were at least twenty on the roof now and still more spilling from the ramp. As his finger tightened on the trigger, he wondered where the hell Ellen was. Perhaps she was on the floor he'd bypassed, or maybe she had doubled back somehow, made her way down to the ground floor and got out. He hoped so and he was glad he'd told her where the boat was moored.

He pulled the trigger. The stock punched him in the shoulder, sending something like an electric shock through his arm and down into his fingertips. At the same time, the lead hyena dropped to the snow, blood as dark as oil erupting from the back of its head. The shot echoed across the city. But so what if it brought more hyenas? He was fucked anyway.

Hyenas

And then Jay's brain finally processed something he'd seen a couple of seconds ago, something he'd seen but had failed to properly notice.

There had been footsteps in the snow, leading up to the driver's door of the Transit, and the snow on the door itself had been patchy, as if disturbed.

Ellen. She was in the van. He glanced over. There was no sign of a broken window. Which meant the door had already been open. Which meant maybe there were keys. He was turning toward the van when he thought, *What if I'm wrong? I'd just be leading the hyenas to Ellen and then we'd both be fucked.*

Jay fired another shot into the pack, not targeting anything in particular. Two hyenas fell in a tangle. He wasn't sure which one he'd actually hit. He wondered how many bullets there were in the rifle's stubby magazine. Twenty? Already too few. They were nearly upon him now, less than fifteen feet away. He pulled the trigger again, surprised at how calm he was feeling, how much he was enjoying the cool breeze against his sweat-sodden forehead.

He only just heard the sound of the van's engine stutter to life over the sound of his own gunfire.

And then Ellen shouted, 'Get in! Move your arse!'

He turned to see her leaning from the open driver's door. Jay could feel the heat from the hyenas behind him as he made for the van, as if someone had opened the door to a sauna.

As he grabbed the inner door handle and planted one

foot on the bottom of the door frame, he felt a weight on his backpack. He pivoted round, rifle held at waist level and fired. A hyena with Marty Feldman eyes dropped to its knees then flopped onto its back, convulsing. Jay reversed into the van, firing off a shot at a hyena that was naked but for a pair of red Playboy boxer shorts. He slammed the door shut, then writhed out of his pack and put it, and the rifle, on the middle seat.

Strapping herself in, Ellen said, 'You can drive?' She pointed at what was left of the Meriva. 'The evidence to support that claim isn't exactly compelling.'

'Wasn't my fault,' said Jay. 'There was a hyena squatting on the bonnet.' He grinned. 'I'll try to look after this one.'

Hyenas began hammering against the side of the van. Filthy palms and faces pressed up against his window then, a moment later, Ellen's window.

'Thought you were going to leave me out there,' said Jay.

'Considered it,' said Ellen. 'Sorry, but if it's a choice between you and Lilly...'

'Lilly?'

'Just came to me.'

'What if it's a boy?'

'It's a girl. It's a Lilly. She's a Lilly.'

'Lilly it is, then,' said Jay and put the Transit into reverse. He ignored the hyenas trying to clamber up onto the van's stubby bonnet and eased the accelerator down. The last thing he needed was for the wheels to start spinning in the snow. 'It's a good name.'

The Transit trundled back in a broad arc. Once it was parallel with its starting point and facing the ramp, Jay put it into first. He stepped on the accelerator with a little more force than before. The two hyenas that had managed to hold on to the front of the van lost their grip and slid down and out of view, as if they'd been sucked under the wheels. The van hardly registered their presence.

The top of the ramp was packed tight with hyenas, a wall of filth and wild-eyed, grinning faces.

Jay pushed the accelerator down hard.

'Hold onto your seat, Ellen,' he said.

'Christ.'

A moment before they hit the pack, Jay was almost certain that the wall of hyenas was so dense he wouldn't be able to penetrate it and the Transit would just bounce off. But then most of the hyenas disappeared beneath the wheels or spun off to the left and right, slamming into the walls and each other. One was lifted up into the air and hit the windscreen head-first, leaving a bloodied frosted patch about the size of a dinner plate dead centre, before sliding off the bonnet and under the wheels.

Jay had to brake hard as he entered the bend. There was a screech of rubber and a juddering crunch as the wing scraped the wall, crumbling concrete and throwing up sparks.

'Fuck. Where did you learn to drive?'

'I didn't. Not properly. Mate taught me. Mostly in car

parks. Dad let me steer at Knowsley Safari Park. That sort of thing.'

'Great.'

As they emerged onto the third floor, Jay locked the wheel, u-turned the van and, with a minimum of damage to the paintwork, took it down the next ramp. More hyenas crowded their path. Jay drove through them. Another hyena head-butted the windscreen and a second bloody cataract appeared. The next ramp was free of hyenas and Jay noticed the long bloodstains and scraps of hair and clothing decorating the concrete walls. Without thinking, he put his foot down a little harder. The van picked up speed and Jay could feel control of the vehicle slipping away from him as he entered the final ramp and the Transit bounced from left wall to right, the acoustics of the van's interior creating a series of deafening crashes.

There was a rush of cold air from behind him. Jay glanced over his shoulder and saw that the back doors were flapping open and closed. He caught a brief glimpse of five or six hyenas in frantic pursuit, the frontrunner bounding on all fours. Jay knew he couldn't afford to take his foot from the accelerator. If even one of the hyenas got inside the van…

They came off the ramp to the ground floor so fast, the van dipped forward, dragging its nose across the tarmac for a couple of seconds, before lurching up again. At the same time, Jay had to swerve hard right to avoid a concrete pillar. The Transit lost traction for a moment, gliding left, almost colliding with a parked Golf, then Jay regained control and sped toward the entrance, which was now filled with hyenas.

'Once we're outside, we won't be able to get far, with the snow and abandoned cars,' he said. 'As soon as we stop, we'll have to get out and run.'

'Running's fine,' said Ellen. 'Compared to this, running is great.'

A few feet before the exit, Jay hit the brakes. He knew he had to slow down before the tarmac was replaced by snow. They were still doing close to twenty when they hit the hyenas, crushing and scattering them. The impact shaved a few miles per hour off, but they were still going too fast as they left the car park. The Transit slid across the snow, spinning one hundred and eighty degrees counterclockwise as it did so. The tyre walls struck the opposite curb, and the passenger-side wheels left the ground for a second before dropping back down again, almost throwing Jay and Ellen from their seats. Jay's foot jerked from the accelerator, but he kept the clutch down and the engine didn't cut out.

The back doors were wide open now, filling the interior with the sound of hyenas. Jay shifted into first gear then, as soon as the van started to move forward, quickly took it through second and up to third. The engine laboured a little but there were no wheel-spins, and he didn't get stuck in the snow. As the hyena clamour increased, the urge to drive faster was almost overwhelming but he held back. As he turned left into the narrow side street, drifting a few feet but not enough to take out the front window of the Premier Inn, hyenas began drumming against the side of the van.

Once he was on the straight, he put his foot down. Seconds later, a string of abandoned black cabs forced him to drive on the pavement.

Jay didn't even know the hyena had got in until he heard Ellen say 'Fuck!' and unfasten her seat belt and grab the rifle. Inside the Transit, the shot was so loud Jay felt needles of pain so deep in his ears he felt like he'd swallowed broken glass.

He slowed the van down as he reached the junction with Tithebarn Street then turned left in a sweeping arc much broader than he'd intended. Ellen, still facing into the rear of the van looped one arm through the rifle's strap and grabbed the back of the seat with both hands.

'Warn me next time, Lewis fucking Hamilton!'

The back end of the van whipped left and right but Jay managed to point it down Tithebarn Street toward Chapel Street, toward the Mersey.

Ellen took aim with the rifle once more. Jay, unable to take his hands from the wheel, clenched his jaw in the hope this would somehow muffle the sound of the imminent gunshot. It didn't. Wincing, he looked in the rear-view mirror and saw one of two pursuing hyenas drop to the snow, a pink mist dispersing through the air above its sprawled body. Another gunshot, and the second hyena dropped.

Jay returned his attention to his driving and put his

foot down. There were cars strewn across the wide road between the twin high arches of the Exchange Station Building and the top of Moorfields. Too many cars. He brought the van to a fishtailing stop a few feet before a too-narrow gap between abandoned cars made identical by the thick snow.

Rifle in hand, Ellen jumped out of the van. Jay grabbed his pack, hitching it back onto his shoulders before joining her.

He looked back the way they had come. Slalom tracks in the snow led back to Vernon Street sixty feet away. Already, more pursuing hyenas were beginning to appear. Jay turned to see Ellen already crossing Moorfields, passing the Lion then the Railway pubs. He sprinted to catch up.

He was only a few feet behind her, crossing Exchange Street East which ran back down to Dale Street, the Exchange Building looming ten storeys above them, when he saw a hyena emerge from Old Hall Street off to their right. And then he remembered, too late of course, that there were two entry points to Moorfields Station, one at the bottom of Moorfields itself, the other on Old Hall Street.

He opened his mouth to warn Ellen, but she was already turning down Exchange Street East, the rifle slipping down her arm on its strap and into her waiting hands. The sheer soldierly nature of Ellen's performance reawakened in Jay his feelings of woeful inadequacy in the face of the challenges of life in the post-Jolt world.

Despite these feelings, he found himself grinning and, for a moment, didn't know why. Then he realised it was because he knew that Ellen, this stroppy, pregnant woman, was going to survive. Whatever happened next, she was going to live and, inexplicably, he felt a certain amount of personal pride in that.

His grin faltered then vanished as the hyena, now at the head of a ten-strong pack, spotted them. It showed them a mouthful of oversized yellow teeth then pulled away from the dark, corrugated sandstone of Tithebarn House and cut across Tithebarn Street toward them. As Jay followed Ellen, he looked back over his shoulder. The car-park hyenas were gaining, only fifty feet or so behind them now.

'We need to go to ground, Ellen.'

'No chance,' she shouted back at him. 'Last time we went to ground we ended up in that fucking van.' About a third of the way down Exchange Street East, Ellen broke right, taking them into Exchange Flags, the plaza between the back of the Exchange Building and the back of the Town Hall. The Exchange Building seemed intent upon engulfing them, looming above them and wrapping itself about them. Jay would have been intimidated if it wasn't for the fact that the building, in all its Georgian-style excess, resembled a vast, grey wedding cake. At the centre of the plaza, the Nelson Monument was a confusion of flags, cannons and skeletons; around its base, shackled French prisoners of the Napoleonic Wars wept into their hands. Above the prisoners' heads, the words: ENGLAND EXPECTS EVERY MAN TO DO HIS DUTY. Jay had always wondered what it had said. With Ellen leading the way by a couple of feet, they crossed the plaza, keeping low, using the monument for cover, and sprinted around the back of the Martin's Bank Building.

Jay looked over his shoulder. The hyenas were closing the gap. There was no way he and Ellen were going to be able to outrun them and it was very possible they had left it too late to find a bolthole. He wanted to call out to Ellen, apprise her of the situation, but what was the point? What would that achieve? And anyway, the hyenas would reach him first. He'd keep them busy long enough for Ellen to get away. Maybe it was exhaustion making a fool of him, but he found he quite liked the idea.

The sound of the hyenas' footsteps seemed to be getting louder, deeper, as Jay and Ellen approached Rumford Street. The yellowish tinted windows of an egg-carton of a building presented their jaundiced reflections, the hyenas a smeared mass in the background. Then Jay realised the sound — a rhythmic bass rumble — was coming from somewhere up ahead, off to the left, from Water Street. Jay also realised he recognised the sound, had heard it before, recently.

As Ellen stepped out onto Rumford Street, the horse appeared from the side of the Martin's Bank Building. Even though it was the same horse that Jay had first seen with Dempsey only that morning, the same horse that had saved him from being press-ganged into the militia, it had lost its nobility. It looked, somehow, *insane*. Its eyes were rolling as if loose in their sockets, thick ropes of foaming saliva had formed a sagging web from its mouth to its chest and such improbable quantities of steam rose from its gouged and bloodied hide that it looked as if it was on the verge of combusting. But it was still huge, fierce and powerful, and it was thundering toward Ellen.

Jay tried to shout her name, but his mouth was too dry, and his lungs were incapable of drawing the necessary breath. The horse snorted dense blasts of vapour and Ellen turned, almost sprawling.

'Ellen!' Jay managed, now that it was too late.

Then the horse lurched right, away from Ellen, toward Exchange Flags. It lost its footing for a second, stumbled toward Jay, threatening to slam him into the wall of the Exchange Building, then regained its balance and galloped toward the advancing hyenas.

He heard Ellen laugh the high uneven laugh of someone who has come closer to harm than they care to think about. She said something about Emily Davison.

Maybe the horse was too tired to change its trajectory. Maybe it had seen the hyenas too late. Maybe it *wanted* to hurt them. Whatever the case, it ploughed right into the advancing pack.

Four hyenas fell beneath the blur of its hooves. Two were knocked several feet sideways — one left, one right — landing in the snow, motionless: dead or dazed.

Another hyena leapt, wrapping its arms around the horse's neck, attempting to crawl round onto its back. Coming to a standstill, the horse reared up and shook the hyena loose. Its forelegs pistoned out, driving two more hyenas down into the now-bloody snow.

The horse seemed unstoppable to Jay. The hyenas — twenty or so of the things now — circled it but kept a safe distance.

'Jay, let's go,' said Ellen. 'That horse is fucked, and we'll be next. Come *on*.'

'What?' *Fucked*? Jay couldn't see it. The horse looked strong to him. Crazy, yes, but strong, a force *not* to be trifled with. As if to prove the point, its forelegs pistoned out again. A hyena Jay was certain he recognised — pre- or post-Jolt, he couldn't be sure — lost a hoof-shaped chunk of face, its shrill laughter replaced by a dwindling whimper.

This horse was *not* fucked. The hyenas were fucked. All of them.

Then, suddenly — suddenly to Jay, anyway — the horse's rear legs gave, just *gave*, and it collapsed, almost vanishing into a cloud of snow-dust and steam.

'Fucksake Jay!' Ellen growled through clenched teeth. 'Run! Now!'

The hyenas swarmed over the horse, dodging its thrashing legs. Jay just stared. The horse made a sound very much like a scream and Jay ran.

He turned right, back toward Chapel Street, then, following Ellen, he cut left across a near-empty car park that was little more than a waste ground; the low, broken walls of which gave clues to the building that had once been there. The far-left corner of the car park was occupied by a red-brick pub, the Pig and Whistle, which still had scars from where it had once been connected to the long-since demolished building.

Halfway across the car park, Jay looked back the way they had come. He couldn't see any hyenas. They were too busy with the horse. He could hear them laughing. He could hear the horse, too. He resisted the urge to clamp his hands to his ears.

Gasping for breath, they kept moving. Out onto Chapel Street, which sloped down toward Saint Nicholas Place, between the modern, prow-like structure of the Atlantic Tower Hotel and the pale sentinel, with its lantern spire, that was the Church of Our Lady and Saint Nicholas. Beyond the elaborate spire, the verdigris-encrusted Liver Birds were visible on their domed perches.

Jay turned and looked back up Chapel Street, toward the intersection of Old Hall Street and Tithebarn Street. There were no hyenas. None visible, at least. He could hear them, though, the city centre's architecture bouncing their cackles and screeches from wall to wall, creating the impression that the things were *everywhere*.

As they reached the bottom of Chapel Street, the Church of Our Lady and Saint Nicholas above them now, Jay abruptly became convinced they were being followed, stalked. He froze and looked right, over his shoulder. But there was no silent, creeping hyena.

Instead, the dock exit of the Queensway Tunnel.

Jay had forgotten all about it. The tunnel emerged from the side of the Atlantic Tower like the opening to a huge burrow. He fully expected to see wild-eyed and filthy faces floating out of the darkness. But there were no hyenas, just a once-white, now-scorched Volvo.

He could hear them, though, the hyenas, down there in the dark, making their way toward the light.

'Christ, they could have been *waiting for us*,' said Ellen, fighting for breath. She was looking into the mouth of the tunnel, too. 'Just waiting for us, and then how fucked would we have been?'

Waiting for us, thought Jay and the words seemed to drop down into his gut, past his burning, aching lungs. He felt sick but he was also certain that his nausea wasn't instigated by a sense of what-might-have-been. It was something else.

'Waiting for us,' said Jay, and found himself looking at Ellen's rifle.

'Well, thank fuck they weren't. We better get moving. It won't take them long to find their way out.'

Ellen started to turn but Jay grabbed her arm.

'Not the hyenas. Something else. Something else is waiting for us.'

Ellen pulled her arm away.

'The others are waiting for us, Jay.'

'The others,' said Jay, straining to bring his thoughts into focus.

'Look, if you're going to have a nervous breakdown,

can you wait until we're on the boat?'

'The other two,' said Jay. 'Those militiamen, in the museum, Pete and Col, they said something like 'Let's see if we can find the other two. Pepper said there were three of them. Assuming the jokers haven't got to them already.' Something like that. I didn't really process it at the time because I was trying really hard not to shit my pants and start crying. Three of them. You, me and Brian.'

'Fuck. Sergeant Pepper's got the others. That's why the militia were around the library. They were looking for us. Which means they're probably—'

'Waiting for us.'

Before

'Four years,' said Jay. 'It took her four years to figure out that she *did* have a problem with my problem, after all.'

'I'm sorry, Jason, I really am,' said Jay's dad.

'When we first started going out, she said it was a gift. She said, 'You're not burdened by the tyranny of the written word.' It sounds so stupid and pretentious now, but at the time I felt ten feet tall.'

Jay stuffed a forkful of Lewis's egg custard into his mouth, more to stave off tears that were beginning to feel inevitable than out of any desire to eat. But he found the taste of the dessert—sweet and creamy, a perfect egg custard—wrapped him in childhood and brought him even closer to tears. He swallowed the food quickly, tried not to taste it and put down his fork.

'She said, 'You don't have to dot the i's or cross the t's. You can make up your own rules.' She even quoted Blake: 'I must create a system or be enslaved by another man's; I will not reason and compare: my business is to create.' No wonder you liked her.'

'I wish I could say I didn't like her. I wish I could tell you you've had a lucky escape. Christ, I wish I could offer you a bit more than crap about time healing all wounds and there being plenty more fish in the sea. But I can't. I'm a dad. We're terrible at this kind of thing. I wish your mum was here.' He sighed. 'Anyway.'

'Yeah. Anyway.' Jay managed a brief, bitter laugh. 'Funny thing is, just before she pulled the car over to tell me it was over, her stereo chewed up my William Blake tape. Alan Bates was reading *The Four Zoas* and next minute it started to warp and then went completely mental. And I remember thinking, 'This is a bad omen.' And, you know me, I'm not superstitious or anything. But after she told me, I thought, I might not be able to read words, but I can read fucking signs.'

Jay's dad summoned a smile and took a sip of coffee. Jay picked up his fork and poked his egg custard as if he half expected a wasp to come crawling out of it.

'So, what about the theatre group, son, your job?'

'I'm jibbing it,' said Jay.

'What? Look, I can understand why you might want to avoid Lucy for a while but—'

'It's not just that. It's been bothering me for a bit now, the way I have to stand in front of all those people and say, 'You don't want to turn out like me.' It's like, 'Behold ladies and gentlemen, the Amazing Educationally Subnormal Man! Marvel at how words a five-year-old can readily absorb from the printed page baffle and enrage him!' It's pretty un-fucking-dignified.'

Jay's dad laughed.

'It's not really like that, though, is it?' he said.

'I suppose not. Not always, anyway. But more and

more lately, it feels that way.'

'But what else are you going to do?'

Jay dropped his fork.

'Thanks a bunch,' he said.

'What?'

'What else am I going to do? You said it as if you couldn't imagine me being able to do anything else. Thanks.'

'That's not what I meant. You know that. It's just, well, it's tough for everyone at the moment. Jobs are thin on the ground and, like it or not, you've got more hoops to jump through than most. Shit but true, Jason.'

Jay nodded. 'Shit but true. Fair enough.'

'I know it's hard, but maybe you should stick it out.'

'I can't. I can't face it.'

'Give it a couple of weeks, then see how you feel.'

'I know how I'll feel. I'll feel exactly how I feel now. I'll feel precisely how I feel all the time. I'll feel like a freak. Because, when all's said and done, I am a freak, Dad. And life's just a fucking trap for people like me.'

Chapter Twenty-Four

'So, now what?' said Jay.

'What do you mean?' said Ellen, but there was a look on her face that Jay could only describe as pre-emptively guilty.

'You know what I mean. Do we just head for the boat?'

'Jesus.' Ellen tried to inject some venom into the word but with little determination. Her hand went to her belly and she sagged a little. 'I don't know.'

'I mean, what are we going to do? Take on the militia whilst dodging hyenas and come to the fucking rescue?'

Ellen shrugged and sighed. 'I don't know. I really don't.'

'We've got one gun with a few bullets and they're armed to the teeth,' said Jay. 'We have to be…'

There was someone sitting on the small flight of stone steps leading to the Deutsche Bank entrance to the Liver Building. Even at this distance, Jay recognised him.

'Dempsey,' he said.

He ran across the dual carriageway, keeping low and weaving between the cars, until he was face to face with the Dubliner.

Dempsey was dead, of course. His face was the colour of old putty but he wore an expression of mild amusement, as if he'd been sitting on the steps just watching the world trundle by in its usual silly way when death had touched him lightly on the forehead and sent his spirit off to Wherever. The deep tracks scored into the snow, spotted with blood, leading back toward Princes Parade told a different story.

'You knew him?' said Ellen, still catching her breath.

'Yes. Met him this morning. It was his boat. He came looking for a sailing book in Waterstones and stopped me getting taken to pieces by a hyena.' He turned to Ellen. 'He's the reason you're not safe and warm, painting your pictures. He's the only reason we might actually get out of this city before everything turns to shit.'

'Don't know whether to kick him or kiss him.'

Jay reached forward to close his eyes then decided against it. Let him carry on watching the world go by.

'How the fuck did he get here?' said Jay.

'Dragged himself, by the looks of it.'

'Dragged himself. Jesus. He'd lost so much blood. Then he had a heart attack or some kind of seizure and fell into the Mersey. I thought he was dead. He should have been dead. But then he pulls himself out of the icy water and starts working his way back to the city centre. Christ, he was probably looking for another sailing book.'

Jay laughed.

'What?' said Ellen.

'Dempsey asked me why I was in a bookshop when

the Jolt happened, and I was too embarrassed to tell him. Seems stupid now.'

'What does?'

'Embarrassment.'

'So, what were you doing? In a bookshop?'

As Jay spoke, he looked into Dempsey's death-glazed eyes. 'I used to go there all the time. I've got a recording of William Blake poems. I'd listen to the poems and pretend I was reading them. I'd pretend I was normal.'

Ellen laughed.

'What?'

'Well, that is pretty embarrassing.'

'That's what I thought. But now I think it was just one more thing I've done to survive.'

Ellen patted him on the arm, as if he was a rambling elderly relative. 'You keep telling yourself that.'

Jay grinned. 'Piss off.'

'We all pretend stuff,' said Ellen. 'To get by. I pretended to hate books, to make it easier. I pretended so hard, that even now I *can* read, I… well, I can't. I mean, I *will*. At some point. I suppose. Once the pretending wears off. It's powerful stuff, pretending. It stains.'

'You'd like Blake,' said Jay. 'Painting and poetry, words and images, they were all the same to him. Imagination.'

He looked up at the Liver Buildings.

'We go in, get up high and take a look. See what Pepper has in mind. Then we take it from there. If there's nothing we can do, we head for the boat.'

Ellen nodded. 'Sounds like a terrible idea.' She smiled.

'But okay. In for a penny, in for a pound. Let's find a way in.'

'Well, Deutsche Bank's closed,' said Jay pointing at the imposing oak door.

'There must be other entrances,' said Ellen. 'You go right, I'll go left. Don't go too near to the front of the building. If Pepper spots us, we're fucked.'

She didn't wait for Jay to respond, just scooted off down Water Street, staying tight to the low wrought iron railings that surrounded the building. Jay did likewise, to the right. There were double doors halfway along, closed and as impassable as the Deutsche Bank entrance. He looked around for open or broken windows. Nothing, not even on the higher storeys. He was wondering if he'd be able to break a window without alerting Pepper — just make a small hole, then pull the shards out until there was a hole big enough to squeeze through — when Ellen appeared at the corner and waved for him to follow.

'I think I've found a way in,' she whispered once he'd caught up. 'But we're going to need a bit of brute force. Man's work.' She grinned. 'But you'll have to do.'

Ellen led him to an entrance that was opposite the one he'd just come from. Three broad stone steps went up to double sliding doors, all glass but for a thin aluminium frame. The right-hand pane was all but gone, just a few jagged teeth left top and bottom. Jay followed Ellen into a small vestibule. Ahead of them, revolving doors. On the snow-dusted floor an A-board sign covered in muddy footprints read 'Staff Entrance Only. All Visitors Please Report to Main River Entrance. Thank You.' Through the revolving doors Jay could see a corridor that appeared to plough right through to the other side of the building. Past the revolving doors and immediately to the left, a narrow flight of steps led up.

'I tried moving the doors, but I can't get them to shift more than an inch or two,' said Ellen.

Jay stepped into the wedge-shaped space, put his shoulder up against the glass and put his back into it. It moved the inch or two Ellen had already achieved then stopped dead. He stepped back a couple of paces then fell against it, shoulder first. It shifted another inch, but the movement was accompanied by a small shriek of complaining mechanisms.

He looked back at Ellen and they winced in unison. Ellen shrugged and whispered, 'Try again. I'll keep dixie.' She went to the bottom of the steps and peered around the edge of the wall toward the river. Without looking back, she gave him a thumbs-up.

Jay couldn't help smiling. Dixie. He hadn't heard that one since school. He took a few steps back then threw himself at the door again, aiming for the narrow polished-steel frame. He didn't want to go through the glass, with all the noise that would make. The door moved another couple of inches, but the shrieking was louder this time. He looked back at Ellen; she was still looking toward the river, but she was no longer giving the thumbs-up.

Hyenas

'Bollocks,' said Jay and felt his own attempt to burrow up into his gut.

The thumb wavered. Then it went up again. Jay puffed out a white plume of relief. He walked back to the top of the steps then charged at the door. As he hit it this time, hard enough to hurt, there was a trio of sounds. There was the shriek, a lot louder this time, a metallic snap and a crack. Jay was already familiar with the shriek. He had no idea what the snap was until the door rushed away from him. The complaining mechanism had given up its protesting, had given up entirely. And as he staggered forward, Jay realised what had generated the crack. The pane of glass ahead of him had broken from the bottom left-hand corner to the middle of the top frame. The fissure seemed to be getting wider, then Jay realised the right-hand shard of glass was falling toward him. Without thinking and still stumbling forward, Jay grabbed at the shard, tried to stop it from crashing to the floor. He didn't feel any pain, but he did feel the glass slice into the palm of his left hand, a brief pressure followed by a sort of *spreading* of the flesh and then a numbness. He kept hold of the shard and, regaining his balance, lowered it to the floor. The door behind him slapped him on the backside, knocking him forward a couple of paces.

Jay stepped out of his wedge and found himself on the other side of the vestibule, next to the narrow flight of stairs. He looked back toward Ellen and saw she was already at the revolving doors, pushing her way toward him.

'Sorry,' he said as she emerged. 'Noisy.'

She smiled. 'Not as noisy as it sounded to you. Nobody came running, anyway.' She pointed at his hand. 'You're bleeding.'

He looked at his palm. There was a deep gash running from just below his little finger to the pad of his thumb. Blood that had been running toward, and dripping from, his fingertips changed direction as he raised his hand, dribbling down his wrist.

'Christ,' he said. Seeing the injury seemed to switch on the nerves in and around the wound. The pain was dizzying.

'Fuck me, that's nasty,' said Ellen.

'I need to sit down,' said Jay. He pointed to the narrow stairway.

Once on the stairs and out of sight, he sat down as nausea rippled up from his gut to the back of his throat. Ellen dropped down next to him, shrugged off her backpack and began rummaging around inside it.

'Think I've got a bandage in here, somewhere,' she said.

Jay risked a glimpse at his hand again. The wound looked like a mouth, thin with pale lips, blood like a reptilian tongue flickering about.

'Should consider myself lucky, really,' he said. 'I've got off relatively unscathed so far.'

Ellen, pulling the cellophane wrapping from a bandage, threw him a look of incredulity.

'What?' said Jay.

'Have you seen your face lately? It's a bit of a mess.

You look like you've been on the business end of a fucking good kicking.'

There was a door at the top of the stairs, with a small rectangular window in the centre of the top third. Jay stood, swaying a little, and walked the remaining few steps up to the door. It was dim on the other side of the window, brighter on Jay's side, so it worked well enough as a mirror. His face *was* a bit of a mess. There was a dark bruise about the width and length of his thumb across the centre of his forehead; it was raised a little, too, as if there *was* a thumb lying just below the surface and pushing outwards. He remembered how he'd got that one: when the hyena had leapt on his back and driven his head down into Waterstone's carpet-tiled floor. There were thin, bloody scratches running down from his hairline to meet the bruise, from when he'd burrowed, head-first, into the icy snowdrift at the back of Waterstones. His right cheekbone was purple and swollen, from the rifle butt driven into it by one of Pepper's militiamen. And then there were the numerous speckles and splashes of blood, from the hyenas he'd killed.

He didn't recognise himself. Who the hell was this battle-scarred veteran, this survivor, this killer? It surely wasn't the same Jason Garvey who'd hidden away for weeks, hoping the shitstorm would pass him by whilst he ate Kit Kats and blueberry muffins and drank UHT chocolate milk, the diet of a child without caring parents. It surely wasn't the same Jason Garvey who'd crammed himself under a table, watching a hyena attempt to eat the works of Byron, whilst he thought, *What the fuck? The world ended five weeks ago. There shouldn't be any more surprises.*

He was quite pleased to find his reflection reminded him of none other than Dempsey, all cuts and bruises, a boxer who'd won his fight on points but had, nevertheless, won.

He turned away from himself and looked down the stairs at Ellen as she produced a safety pin from a small first aid kit. Sarcastic, pregnant, unstoppable Ellen. Whether it had ended or not, the world was full of surprises, he realised, and he felt a little surge in his chest, a warm, velvety wave.

'What are you smiling at, dickhead?' said Ellen.

'Nothing. Just glad to be alive for a little while longer.'

'Very profound. You should get some t-shirts printed. Now, come here. Let's get this bandage on.'

Jay sat back down next to Ellen. She grabbed his hand like a mum seizing the hand of her child who's just tried to stroll across a busy road without looking.

'This is going to hurt, but I don't want to hear about it,' she said, then squeezed his hand hard, causing the lips of his wound to press together. Blood oozed out, uneven lipstick. 'Keep your hand stiff like this while I strap it up tight.'

'Ever had an exhibition?' said Jay. 'Of your paintings?'

'You're just trying to distract yourself from the pain because you don't want to cry in front of a woman.'

'No, honestly, I'm interested. And anyway, I'll cry

in front of anyone, me. I love making people feel uncomfortable.' He grinned. 'It's the only time I feel powerful.'

'Yeah, I had exhibitions. In Liverpool, Manchester, even a couple in London.'

'Wow. Cool.'

Ellen smiled. 'Yeah. It was. It was very cool.'

'What sort of things did you paint? Not hyenas, obviously.'

'Not hyenas, no. But almost everything else. People, buildings, landscapes, objects. One of the exhibitions I had in London was just paintings of keys. I'd bought this box of keys at a car boot sale and it just seemed really sad. All these keys that didn't open anything anymore. Or, if they did, would never again. There was a review in the *Evening Standard*.'

'Really? That's amazing.'

'It was. I mean, it was a really positive review. Except the writer, this art critic Paul MacLeod, said the keys represented my desire to unlock the language centres of my brain. Twat. I phoned him up, gave him merry hell. Language centres, my arse. They're just an interesting shape, keys. Nice to draw and paint. And they're the thing we lose more often than anything else. It's almost like they're meant to be lost. That's their true purpose. To not be there. Before I started painting, that was how I felt. Like I wasn't meant to be here, wasn't meant to be anywhere.'

'Yeah,' said Jay. 'Like we're a glitch.'

Ellen nodded. 'A glitch.' Then, 'Paul offered to buy me dinner, by way of an apology. One thing led to another. We were together for a couple of years. Then this happened.' She glanced at her belly. 'He didn't want to be a dad. I wanted to be a mum. I came back to Liverpool. Last I heard he was shacked up with a Pilates teacher in Chelsea.'

'Christ, he didn't hang around, did he?'

'He did not, Jay. He did not.' She sighed. 'I keep thinking about him, maybe sitting in an art gallery somewhere. The V&A, the Tate. Not looking at the paintings, but staring at the little plaques *next* to the paintings. Just staring at them and not knowing why. Poor fucker. I mean, he was a complete let-down, but my life's been full of let-downs, and he was no worse than most of them.'

Ellen finished with the bandage and, standing, said, 'Come on.'

Jay followed, trying to flex his bandaged hand a little and finding it impossible.

The door at the top of the stairs opened up onto another stairway, this one gloomy and zigzagging up to the top of the building.

Ellen had to stop, once on the second floor and again on the fourth; each time, just for a minute and then she took a deep breath, puffed it out loudly and set off once more.

They left the stairway on the fifth floor, stepping out onto a long corridor, close to a set of lifts facing each other. The floor alternated between pale, laminate flooring and blue carpet tiles. At either end of the corridor were double doors of frosted glass.

Jay got his bearings.

'This way,' he said, heading left. 'River end.'

The doors opened onto a small reception area, with two leather sofas facing a curved desk. A visitors' book was open on the desk; the pages that were on display were only half filled with signatures. A row of chest-high filing cabinets created a low wall between the reception and an expansive open-planned office. A three-cabinet gap formed an entrance in the middle of the wall. They went through the gap and made their way over to the opposite side of the office.

There was something depressing about the step-and-repeat uniformity of the rows of desks; keyboards, monitors, telephones and in-trays all identically positioned. The desks' occupants had battled against conformity with pot plants, framed photographs, toys and ornaments, but all to little effect. As they neared the windows, they could see Birkenhead on the far side of the river. Sluggish smoke trailed from a few buildings here and there, creating an illusion of snug domesticity.

The illusion was undermined by the remains of an EasyJet fuselage, one ragged wing still attached, drifting downriver. Seagulls swirled about the aeroplane's remains, swooping in and out of the carcass; Jay didn't want to think about what they might be feeding on in there. Further inland, the towers and chimneys of the oil refineries and chemical plants at Ellesmere Port were smokeless. Jay wondered if some automated safety mechanisms had kicked in after the Jolt, shutting everything down, or whether it was just a matter of time before they roared and turned the sky black.

They edged closer to the window and looked down. They saw the others immediately, standing round a bench, across the road from the Liver Buildings. There were a few stuffed bin bags on the bench and two large bottles of water, the kind that, turned upside-down, sat on top of office water dispensers.

'Where's Phil?' said Ellen.

Jay saw that she was right. There was Dave, stocky and somehow aggressive even when motionless. There was Joe, afro silvered with snow. There was Simon, his pale dreadlocks a little embarrassing next to Joe's authentic afro. And there was Kavi, his turban spattered with blood. But no Phil.

'Maybe he didn't make it,' said Jay. 'Like Brian.'

'Looks like,' said Ellen, she turned away from the window and visibly sagged. 'Jesus. He saved my life. I got cocky this one time and ended up being cornered by three of those things in the Tesco at the top of Bold Street. Phil came in with a hatchet and carving knife, cool as anything. Didn't pause. Didn't flinch. He just got to work and did what he had to do. Afterwards, he cried. He didn't full-on blub. He just cried a bit and said, 'Ellen? Can you try and be a bit more careful from now on? I haven't got it in me to do that again, love...'

'A couple of days ago, he told me he wanted to be an architect, when he was kid, back before all this happened.

Said he told the careers advisor at school. Careers advisor laughed at him. *Laughed* at him. Who does that, to a kid? And he said maybe he could be an architect now, once things settled down and people started needing buildings again. I didn't have the heart to tell him buildings are probably going to outnumber people for the next twenty years, because he looked so hopeful. It was the first time since I'd met him I'd seen him look optimistic, look anything but grim and doomed. I mean, I'm looking at a grown man with grey hair and a beard, a man old enough to be my dad, and I'm picking my way through the minefield of his feelings, and this careers advisor couldn't do that for a *child*? Because, what, 'tough love?' Because 'character building?' Fuck all that shit. If I'd been there, and little Phil said he wanted to be an architect? I'd have told him I'd see what I could do. And I'd have done everything I could to help. Everything. Because he was just a little boy.'

She turned back to the window, and Jay heard her breath hitch in her throat a couple of times. Then she said, 'What's that?'

She was pointing to a yellow DHL van, seemingly abandoned less than ten yards from the bench. Jay couldn't see anything else of note.

'Footprints,' she said. 'Around the van.'

Jay had seen them but not registered, not understood their potential significance. He widened his eyes like someone trying to stay awake whilst watching a late film. He knew he had to be on the ball. He told himself this was the endgame. Success or failure would depend on little details, like the footprints round the van, the footprints that should have set off alarm bells.

'Maybe it was Dave and the rest of them who left the footprints,' said Ellen. 'Maybe they were checking the van out, seeing if there was anything useful in there.'

'It's Pepper,' said Jay. 'Him and his militia. They're either in the van or pressed up against the other side of it, where we can't see them.'

'What makes you so sure?'

'If we'd got here first, would we be standing out in the open by a bench as if we were just killing time?'

'No. We'd stay out of sight. We'd hide until the others turned up. Fuck.'

'It's Pepper. In the van or behind it.'

'So. What now?'

'Give me the gun.'

Ellen handed him the rifle.

'What's the plan?' she said.

'You go down there. You tell the others to follow you. Not to argue. You know it's a trap. You know what's going on. They just have to trust you. Tell them you've got it covered. As soon as you start moving, Pepper will make his move. That's when I start shooting. I keep Pepper pinned down. You and the others get to the boat and wait for me there.'

'Jesus. And how are you going to get to the boat? How are you even going to get out of this fucking building? Pepper will see where the shots are coming from and he'll come after you.'

Jay shrugged.

'Just wait for me at the boat,' he said. 'Give it, I don't know, thirty minutes, then, you know, splice the main brace or whatever it is you're supposed to do.'

'And what about the hyenas? It won't be long before they start coming out of that tunnel.'

Jay shrugged again.

'I don't know, Ellen.' He grinned like a nauseous drunk. 'I just don't know. But I can't leave them down there. I can't because...'

'Because Dempsey wouldn't have left them down there.'

He nodded, opening his backpack.

'Something like that, yes. I just think it's time I stepped up to the plate, you know? For once in my fucking life.'

Ellen shook her head. 'How many times have you had to say the words 'I can't read' to complete fucking strangers, Jay? How many times?'

Jay shrugged. 'I don't know. Hundreds.'

'Well, every time you managed to get that sickening little phrase past your lips, you were stepping up to the plate. Every fucking time, Jay. Okay?'

'Okay.' Jay managed a smile but felt close to tears.

Ellen stared hard into his eyes.

'What?' said Jay. He took out the sailing book.

'Are you sure you want to do this? I mean, you don't have to. I wouldn't.'

'But you've got Lily to think about. I'd be just trying to save my own skinny little arse.' He handed the book to Ellen.

Ellen carried on staring hard but took the book.

'I don't really know you from Adam, but I can't imagine you've done much wrong in your life, Jay. Not bad-wrong at least. I'm pretty sure you've fucked up on any number of occasions. Because you do have something of the air of a fuck-up about you.' She grinned. 'But nothing to go to confession over.'

The grin dropped away.

'I had a brother, Jay. He was eight years old. We were in the cinema on Edge Lane, watching some Disney flick, talking animals and the like, when the Thing happened. When I came to, he was gone and those bastard things were everywhere. I found him in McDonalds, a couple of hours later. Except it wasn't him, it was one of those things. A hyena, a zombie, a mouth-breather. He was chewing something, blood was running from his mouth, and he had a clump of hair grasped in one hand; it still had a chunk of scalp attached to it. He snarled at me, my little brother, and there was nothing of him there. There was just this fucking animal.

'I ran, Jay. I got scared, got scared for the baby, got scared for me, mostly for me, and I ran. I just ran.'

She turned away and walked through the gap between the filing cabinets, then through the door and out of sight.

Jay took a couple of steps forward, as if to go after her then stopped because he had no idea what he would say, what he *could* say. He didn't even know what to think, what to feel.

Hyenas

He looked at the rifle and thought for a second that maybe he understood the attraction of the military life. It wasn't so much a craving for adventure, action and violence as a longing for simplicity. There was us and there was them, this side of the gun and that, safety and danger, life and death. Everything else was trivial. Of course, he knew none of that was true and that soldiers were as distracted and troubled, as dissatisfied as everyone else.

Jay opened the window five inches and there was a click as some mechanism prevented it from opening further. He wondered if it was some kind of anti-suicide lock, designed to prevent employees driven mad by the uniformity of their environment and doubtless, the uniformity of their days, from throwing themselves down to the pavement below. There would be enough of a gap to poke the barrel of the gun through and angle it toward the DHL van.

He took off his pack and dropped it onto the nearest desk. There was an unopened can of Dandelion and Burdock on the desk, between a pair of portable speakers. He picked up the can, cracked it open, took a couple of sips and smiled. The taste of childhood. He walked back over to the window. There was no sign of Ellen. The others carried on milling about. They didn't really look as if they were killing time at all. Their movements were stiff and anxious. They knew that if they tried to make a break for it the bullets would start flying and there was no real cover, and they would probably die.

He hoped Ellen could cut through their fear. He thought of how the Book Club had treated her in the office on Hanover Street and he realised that, to a man, they had respected and loved her.

They'd listen. He was certain of it. They had to.

He finished his drink, dropped the can into a wire mesh wastepaper basket and got into position. He trained the rifle on the front of the vehicle, glad that it wasn't his trigger finger that was bandaged up. That's where Pepper's militiamen would come from once they saw Ellen; that was the most direct angle of attack between the van and the others. With the gun pointing at the van, he turned his attention to the bench and Dave, Joe, Simon and Kavi. He knew they'd react as soon as they saw Ellen. They'd probably try to warn her. When they did, he'd get ready to start shooting.

And then Dave moved a couple of feet from the others, toward the Liver Building, his hands held palms out at waist height, making a pushing gesture. Jay couldn't see Ellen yet, but he knew she had arrived. He turned his attention to the van, looking down the barrel of the gun, training the sight on the far corner of the bonnet. He wouldn't be able to watch Ellen or the others now; he had to focus all his attention on keeping the militia pinned down.

Pepper stepped out first, pistol in hand. Through the open window, Jay heard him shout something but couldn't make out what exactly. Two more militia appeared behind Pepper, assault rifles at the ready.

Hyenas

Jay pulled the trigger.

A white flower bloomed from the centre of the bonnet, a good foot and a half from where Jay had actually been aiming. As the flower disintegrated, Pepper and his men froze, not entirely sure what had just happened.

Jay pulled the trigger again.

A second flower, this one closer to the edge of the bonnet, bloomed and shattered in the same instant, showering Pepper with snow. This time, the sergeant and his men seemed to understand precisely what was happening and darted back behind the van.

Jay took a quick glance over at the bench. There was no sign of Ellen and the Book Club. He wondered where they'd gone, why they weren't running toward Princes Parade, then realised that would put them in Pepper's line of fire. They must have gone back onto Bath Street; that would take them parallel to the Parade and they could just drop in when they were nearer the Alexandra Tower.

He returned his attention to the van again. One of Pepper's men was peering from the back of the vehicle, just the side of his face visible. Jay aimed at the ground close to the rear passenger side tyre and pulled the trigger. The bullet kicked up snow about two feet from its intended target, but it was enough to send the militiaman back into hiding.

Half a minute passed with no activity and Jay knew that they were conferring, putting a plan together. Then, two militiamen stepped out, one from either end of the van and fired randomly up at the Liver Building.

Without thinking, or even aiming, Jay fired back, the bullet striking the side of the van close to the rear. The militiamen scuttled back behind the van. They knew where he was now; they'd seen the muzzle-flare.

Only a couple of seconds delay this time and the militiaman at the front of the van appeared once more. Jay took aim near the militiaman's feet but before he could even think to pull the trigger he stepped back behind the van. As he was stepping from view, his counterpart at the back of the van leapt out and immediately began firing. Bullets struck the heavy blocks of the Liver Building creating a series of brittle squeals and then the next window along from where Jay was standing shattered.

Jay was about to return fire when the militiaman moved back behind the van. At the same time his front-of-van comrade stepped back into view and began firing. More brittle squeals filled the air. A third militiaman appeared from the front of the van and ran toward the Liver Building. Jay, too panicked to take aim, fired three shots in the general direction of the van, kicking up plumes of snow from the roof that did nothing to deter the returning fire. Another militiaman broke from the cover of the van and made a dash for the Liver Building, then Pepper did likewise. Jay was training his sights on the ground at Pepper's feet when a bullet shattered his window and he was showered with broken glass. He staggered back, tripped on the wastepaper bin, into which he'd dropped the dandelion and burdock can,

Hyenas

and fell onto his backside.

For a few seconds, he wasn't sure if he'd been shot. He scanned his body, arms and legs, looking for bullet wounds. Everything seemed intact. He stood up, shards of glass falling from his shoulders and head, chiming on the pale blue carpet tiles.

'Lucky,' he said. 'Fucking lucky, Jay.'

He put on his pack and ran over to the west side of the building and looked out of a window for any sign of Ellen and the others on Bath Street but they'd done the sensible thing and gone to ground rather than try to make it to the boat in a single leg. He wondered if they'd dipped into the Crown Plaza Hotel. That made sense: plenty of hiding places and they could probably exit on the far side of the building, closer to the boat and out of the militia's line of sight. They might even be able to stock up on the supplies they'd left at the bench. There was no sign of Pepper or his men, which meant they were too close to the building to be seen or had already gained access.

Jay was wondering how the hell he was going to get out unseen (shooting his way out was a non-starter), when he noticed the hyenas spilling out of the docks exit of the Queensway Tunnel. They continued across the road, twenty or more of them, heading directly for the Liver Building. There were gunshots from somewhere near the base of the building and two, three, four of the hyenas fell, but the pack was undeterred. More shots. More hyenas fell. But still they came, as even more of them emerged from the blackness of the tunnel.

Jay headed back through the reception and out into the corridor. He made his way to the stairs he and Ellen had climbed. The sound of shouts and boots below stopped him dead. He wasn't going to get out that way without a fight, a fight he couldn't conceivably win. He ran to the far end of the corridor. Another door opened up onto an identical stairway. Jay took two steps down, then stopped. Shouts and boots here, too.

'Shit. Organised little bastards.'

He went back down the corridor and into the office, making for the centre and turning on the spot until he saw a fire door on the east side of the building. There were more gunshots — from inside or out, it was impossible to tell. He hoped to God the militia and hyenas would keep each other busy long enough for him to just slip out like he was escaping a dull party.

He was almost at the fire exit when a bulky silhouette filled the translucent square of wire-glass in the door. The handle began to turn.

Jay dropped to the ground and scuttled under the nearest desk, turning into a sitting position and pulling his legs in as far as he could, knees right under his chin. He heard the door open, followed by two heavy footsteps.

'Garvey,' said Pepper.

Chapter Twenty-Five

Jay held his breath and told himself his heartbeat couldn't be heard outside of his own head.

Pepper marched across the office, his booted feet passing right by Jay. There was a crunch of glass and Jay realised Pepper was checking over by the broken window, looking for Jay's wounded or lifeless body.

'No blood, Garvey. You're in here somewhere, hiding. Aren't you tired of hiding, Garvey?'

Two gunshots filled the office, accompanied by the sound of breaking glass and splintering wood.

'Come on, Garvey. You've survived this long. We could use someone like you. Forget about the boat. We'll find it, burn it. You're going nowhere.'

Footsteps getting closer. No more than a few yards away now.

'Garvey?'

Silence.

A crackle of static.

'Any sign of him on the stairs, Lloyd?'

Laced with interference, the reply came back, 'No sir. Lot of fucking jokers, though. Fuck! Fucking... shit... past us, sir. Fuck.'

Jay could hear gunfire in muddled stereo, over Pepper's walkie-talkie and from the building's lower storeys. Then the transmission died.

'Lloyd? Lloyd? Bollocks. Come on, Garvey, everything's going to shite, so let's get this over with, eh?'

Jay ignored the request. Then he noticed a tuft of white fluff on the floor next to the tip of his left foot. It was a scrap of stuffing from his coat, the stuffing that had been dragged out by the hyena in Waterstones. He smiled. He'd been hiding under a table then, too. The smile vanished. It wasn't fucking funny. After everything that had happened today, here he was skulking under a desk, just as scared and useless as he'd been at the start of the day. And this wasn't even a hyena; it was just a bloke, some chancer who'd probably been one of Liverpool's unwanted and unusable before the Jolt had turned everything inside out.

The heavy footsteps came closer.

'Garvey? I'll be honest with you. I don't want to put a bullet in your head — I could have shot you before, on Lord Street, but I didn't — but if you don't come out on the count of five, I swear to God, I'll shoot you in the gut and watch you die.'

The footsteps came closer.

Then Pepper's booted feet stepped into view.

'Come on out, Garvey.'

For a second, Jay thought that Pepper was addressing him directly, that he knew where he was hiding, but then he started turning on the spot and said, 'Garvey?

For Christ's sake, lad.'

Jay heard the sound of a door being flung open on the far side of the office.

Pepper's feet turned toward the reception.

A hyena cackled.

'Fuck!'

A gunshot.

The hyena shrieked laughter.

Pepper started moving away from Jay, toward the reception and the hyena.

Another gunshot.

Jay crawled out from under the desk and stood.

Pepper, his back to Jay, was standing a few yards away, pistol held in two hands. The hyena — a shaggy ape of a thing who would have been intimidating prior to the Jolt — was running across the banks of desks, scattering pens and paper and personal effects, stooped, intuitively presenting as small a target as possible. It was about ten yards away and closing fast.

Pepper pulled the trigger. A chunk of something flew from the hyena's right arm and deep red spilled over filthy flesh. But the hyena kept coming.

Jay pointed his rifle at the back of Pepper's head.

Pepper fired again.

The hyena placed the palm of its hand flat against its chest and kept coming. Only five yards away now.

Pepper fired again. The hyena's head flipped back, as if it was trying to flick the greasy ropes of its hair from its face. It dropped from view between two desks.

'Jesus,' said Pepper.

The hyena lurched to its feet. Its face was gleaming with blood. No wound was visible. Jay assumed the bullet had struck its scalp. The hand pressed to its chest was similarly red and glistening now. It grinned with bloody teeth and stumbled forward.

Pepper pulled the trigger again, but the revolver just clicked.

'Bugger.'

Still grinning, the hyena let out a wet, wheezing sound and crashed to the floor.

Pepper's shoulders dropped and he sighed loudly.

Jay pushed the barrel of the rifle into the base of Pepper's skull.

'Move and I'll fucking kill you, Pepper.'

Pepper tensed and Jay thought he was going to spin round, try and knock the gun from his hands. Instead, he let the pistol fall to the ground and put his hands on top of his head.

'Why don't you, Garvey? Kill me? Just do it. There's no Geneva Convention anymore, lad. Point of fact, there are no conventions, at all.'

'I don't want to kill you. But I will. Not out of anger or malice but because I'm so fucking tired that anything more than pulling this little trigger here is just too much like hard work. Does that make any sense?'

Pepper laughed. 'Perfect sense. I admire your honesty. Why not help me out? We could win back this city. This is your city, too, Garvey. You're born and bred, I can tell.

Your accent, it's rich, it's got the life in it.'

'Don't get me wrong, Pepper, I like The Beatles, I really do, but I'm not going to die because the man who wrote She's Leaving Home happened to be born here. Besides, he fucked off as soon as he could afford the fucking air fare.'

'It's not about—'

The hyena let out a final rattling breath, a terrible slaughterhouse sound.

It was all the distraction Pepper required.

He turned, a blur.

Jay pulled the trigger.

But Pepper was already knocking the barrel up with the back of his hand. The bullet shattered a polystyrene ceiling tile above Pepper's head.

Pepper snatched at the gun, but Jay leapt back and levelled the barrel at Pepper's gut.

'Don't,' said Jay.

'Fuck you,' said Pepper.

He lurched left, then right. Jay tried to keep the gun on him.

Pepper lunged, dipping low, trying to stoop under the firing line.

Jay pulled the trigger.

The rifle produced a click.

'All out,' said Pepper. He reared up to his full height, a good few inches over Jay, and punched him in the right temple.

Blinded by the blow, Jay staggered back, but as he did

so, more by instinct than design, surprising himself, he lashed out with the rifle.

He felt it connect, a juddering crunch.

The anticipated retaliatory strike didn't come and, a second or so later, Jay's vision returned, foggy but functional.

Pepper was on his knees, left hand clamped to right cheek. Blood seeped from between his fingers.

'Had worse,' said Pepper. He let his hand fall, revealing a deep gash beneath his eye, then launched himself at Jay.

Jay swung the rifle like a baseball bat but missed.

Pepper threw his shoulder into Jay's gut. All but a few useless dregs of air left Jay's lungs and Jay left the ground. He smashed down on the desk behind him, the back of his head cracking the dead screen of a computer monitor before sending the whole thing, monitor, CPU, keyboard and mouse to the floor.

He'd still managed to keep hold of the gun and, as Pepper came at him again, he shoved it hard into Pepper's hip. The resulting crack brought a grimace to Pepper's face and stopped him in his tracks.

'Motherfucker!'

He lunged again, but Jay was already rolling off the desk and down onto the floor. He got to his feet as Pepper slammed both fists down on the desk where Jay had been sprawled only a moment before. Jay, dragging thin streams of air into his lungs, brought the butt of the rifle down toward Pepper's shoulder. But Pepper twisted away from the blow then backhanded Jay across the face. Jay staggered back. He could taste blood. He could feel blood, too, running from his scalp and down the back of his neck from where he'd hit the monitor.

Jay swept out with the rifle. Pepper dodged the blow. With one hand bandaged and the other greased with sweat, Jay lost his grip on the gun. It sailed across the office, landing on top of a bank of filing cabinets, sending several neatly stacked towers of CDs flying in a glittering cascade.

Pepper moved in close and delivered two blows to Jay's ribcage, left then right. What little air Jay had managed to pull into his lungs abruptly departed.

Jay tried to shuffle back, out of range, but he immediately reversed into a desk. He tried to sidestep but Pepper inflicted two more body blows and Jay felt and heard bone crack.

Ignoring the pain, he threw a wild haymaker in the general direction of Pepper's head. Pepper dipped enough to avoid taking it in the face, but Jay struck a glancing blow to the top of his head. It was enough to delay Pepper's next assault. Jay threw another punch, but Pepper ducked it and threw one of his own. It caught Jay on the cheek, rocking him back on his heels. A second punch landed on his other cheek and Jay was hard pressed to remain standing. His head was starting to spin.

He reached behind him, grabbed whatever he could find and swung it at Pepper.

Pepper leapt back, a pencil protruding from the side of his forearm. His teeth were clamped together, his eyes hyena-wild with pain and disbelief.

'Jesus!' he hissed.

Jay backed away. Gasping for breath, he spat blood onto the tiles.

With an animal grunt, Pepper yanked the pencil from his arm and threw it on the floor.

Jay couldn't help but grin.

'You must really love The fucking Beatles, Pepper.' He pointed to the crimson pencil. 'What's that worth to you? A couple of bars of Yellow Submarine?'

'Fuck you. You don't actually think this is all about The Beatles, do you?' He rushed toward Jay. 'You fucking brain donor.'

Jay sidestepped but Pepper adjusted his trajectory and caught Jay with a dipped shoulder.

Jay spun on the spot one hundred and eighty degrees then hit the floor face first.

Pepper kicked him in the back, once, twice, three times.

'What about the world's first school for the blind? The world's first school for the deaf? The first public washhouses in the UK? The first social housing? The first free school meals? The first nurses paid to look after the poor?'

Jay tried to crawl away, but Pepper stomped on the backs of his thighs, pinning him.

'What about the first anti-tuberculosis campaign? The first city to employ a municipal bacteriologist? What about the fact that the RSPCA, NSPCC, the Citizens' Advice Bureau and legal aid all started in some shape or form in Liverpool? We were the first city to really start looking after its vulnerable. Christ, compassion was practically *invented* in Liverpool.'

Jay dragged his legs free, rolled onto his back and scuttled away from Pepper.

Pepper followed.

'And then there's the first lifeboat station in the world. The first purpose-built public library. The first public art gallery. The first x-ray medical diagnosis. The first school of tropical medicine. The first mosque. The first municipal Jewish cemetery. Britain's first Chinese newspaper.'

Pepper shoved a heel into Jay's gut.

'Christ, The Beatles are fucking great, don't get me wrong. I mean, *A Day in the Life*? Beautiful. But it's just five and a half minutes. Five and a half fucking *minutes*.'

He stomped again, but Jay rolled aside, and Pepper only succeeded in grinding his heel into the floor.

He came at Jay again.

'This is a city, Garvey. A whole fucking city. Eight-hundred years old, on paper, older in reality. The Beatles? Jimmy Tarbuck? Do you think that's all this city is?' He stomped again, but Jay rolled aside and the boot heel ground into carpet tile once more. But he could feel what little energy he had left leeching away from him and he knew it was only a matter of time. 'Do you think that's all Liverpool's made of? Pop music and celebrities who piss off once they've got a bit of dosh?' Another heel stomp, this one catching the sleeve of his coat.

Pepper sensed the hyena a second after Jay saw it lurching up behind him. It was probably male, ginger hair like rusty bed springs, one ear reduced to an angry stump. Pepper turned as a fist caked in dried blood and clustered with tarnished jewellery slammed into the side of his head.

Pepper tried to counterattack but the blow had done its work and the man's legs buckled. He dropped to his knees. The hyena leapt on him, fists falling.

Jay got to his feet, spat out another mouthful of blood.

Pepper looked at him with eyes that were beginning to glaze.

Jay started for the reception area and the door to the stairs.

He stopped — 'Fuck!' — turned around and marched back toward Pepper, who had curled into a tight ball. The hyena was clawing at him, trying to find a way in, an animal endeavouring to get at the soft flesh beneath the tough outer rind of a new and intriguing fruit.

'Oi! Laughing boy!'

The hyena glanced back at him.

His stomach flipped as he realised he had no idea what he was doing, no idea what he'd do if the hyena came charging at him.

'Yeah, you,' he said, voice warped by the onset of panic. 'Mick Hucknall meets Stig of the Dump. I'm really sorry to be the one who has to point this out to you, but you smell worse than hot dog shit on a cold day.'

As Jay spoke, the hyena tipped its head at a quizzical angle and its eyes darted about, seeming to track the words as they left Jay's mouth. Its behaviour reminded Jay of Hello Kitty and he almost felt sorry for the thing.

It traced the bluebottle flight path of the last couple of words, and then turned its attention back to Pepper, raising a fist in readiness to strike.

Jay took a breath.

'And did those feet in ancient time walk upon England's mountains green?'

The hyena's fist remained aloft. It turned and looked at Jay.

'And was the holy lamb of God on England's pleasant pastures seen?'

The arm dropped, limp. Its eyes were darting about now, as if it was watching a firework display.

'And did the Countenance Divine shine forth upon our clouded hills?'

Jay was no grandstanding slam poet. He just let the words out, slow and steady. Even so, it was clear he was creating nothing less than a pyrotechnic display; the hyena's head was darting about as it endeavoured to capture every flash, every detonation. Jay thought, if you like this, you'd fucking *love* Alan Bates.

'And was Jerusalem builded here among these dark Satanic Mills?'

The hyena took a couple of loping steps toward Jay. Something about its face was all wrong and it took Jay a couple of seconds to realise what it was. The hyena was smiling. Not grinning. Smiling. It was a proper smile, not a putrid split in a grimy face. It took a couple more steps forward and stopped.

'Bring me my bow of burning gold! Bring me my arrows of desire!'

The hyena's head jerked about as it tried to keep up with what was to the hyena, Jay imagined, an *eruption* of Blake.

Pepper unfurled and got to his feet, swaying like a drunk. Blood streaked his face.

'Bring me my spear! O clouds, unfold! Bring me my chariot of fire!'

The hyena looked like it was in ecstasy. Saliva drooled from its smiling mouth.

Pepper grabbed something from a nearby desk tidy, Jay couldn't make out what.

'I will not cease from mental fight, nor shall my sword sleep in my hand, till we have built Jerusalem in England's green and pleasant land.'

Pepper buried whatever it was he'd snatched into the side of the hyena's neck.

A pair of scissors.

The look of delight left the hyena's face. For a second, it wore no expression at all, and Jay felt a surge of grief so deep, he let out a sob.

Then the look of hyena savagery and insanity returned, and it spun round to face Pepper. But Pepper was ready. He stomped down on its shin. The bone broke with a grinding crunch. The hyena let out a gurgling howl and dropped onto its side.

Pepper kicked the scissors further into its neck, until they were buried up to the handle. Blood sprayed from the wound, alternating between a thick jet, like a writhing wire, and a fine mist. The hyena convulsed for a full minute then lay still.

Not looking at Pepper, seeming instead to address his remarks to the dead hyena, Jay said, 'I can't do this anymore. I just can't fucking do it. I know it's not about The Beatles. I know Liverpool's worth saving. But I can't help you. I'm not like you. You're an ex-con for fuck's sake. All I've ever really wanted was to find a quiet spot and read a book. How shitty an ambition is that?' He finally looked at Pepper.

Pepper helped himself to a handful of tissues from a box on someone's desk and wiped the blood from his face as best he could.

'Fair enough,' he said. 'Fair enough. I understand. I know you probably think I'm some kind of nutter, but I'm not. I'm just someone who had to... someone who had to...' He sat down on the edge of the desk. 'Christ.' He stared down at his feet. 'I'm not a convict. I was *working* in the prison. Well, in the prison grounds. I was a gardener.' He grinned. 'A gardener. That's why I was there. The prisoners, the ones that hadn't become those things, hadn't become jokers, were terrified, disorganised. I got them out, led the way. We went to the Territorial Army base in Aintree and tooled-up. Then,

Hyenas

I went home. The suburbs were a fucking nightmare, Sunday morning, jokers everywhere. Except I didn't call them jokers back then, didn't know what to call them. My wife was gone, but my boy, Edward, my six-year-old boy, was still there. He was sat in the kitchen, sat in his own shit, eating chocolate buttons and Kinder eggs. He attacked me, fucking flew at me. I'd fend him off, but he'd come at me again, seconds later. He kept coming at me and coming at me. It went on for hours. Hours. He didn't seem to get tired and I was fucking exhausted. I tried talking to him, calming him, soothing him, but it just made him worse, the words. The words made him worse. Every time he got close, I'd look into his eyes, trying to see if there was something there, something that could be brought back, something that could be... I don't fucking know... fixed? But there was nothing. There was nothing of Edward left. Just *nothing*. The last time he came at me, I... I had to... I held him tight and put my... I put my hand over his mouth and kept it there until... kept it there until... until he stopped breathing.' He showed Jay the palm of his hand, it was purple and knotted with scar tissue that looked infected, looked like it would never heal. 'He fought to the end,' he said and smiled, as if his son's determination and relentlessness was a weird source of pride. 'So, I'm going to fight to the end, too, just like Edward. To the end.'

'I'm sorry,' said Jay. 'About your son. I'm sorry.'

There were tears in Pepper's eyes as he said, 'I know it sounds stupid, and I know I can't bring Edward back, but sometimes I think if I could just put everything else back the way it was... And even if it doesn't bring him back — and I know it won't; of *course* it won't — at least I can lie down and die and just be finished. Does that make any sense?'

Jay nodded. 'Yes.'

Pepper said nothing for a while. Then, almost a whisper, 'I buried him in the garden. The hole... the hole in the ground was... so *small.*'

He let out a couple of harsh sobs, then ground his teeth together and stood up straight.

'Right, how the fuck are we going to get out of here, lad?'

It was only then that Jay became fully aware of the sound of hyenas swarming up through the building. There was no gunfire. Pepper's men had either been defeated or they'd fled.

Pepper pressed a button on his walkie-talkie. 'Anyone receiving me? Anyone?'

A hiss of static.

He turned a small knob, pressed the button again. 'Could do with a little help boys. Anyone in the vicinity of the Liver Building?'

Not even static this time, just dead air. Pepper shrugged then clipped the walkie-talkie back to his belt.

'We're on our own,' he said.

Chapter Twenty-Six

―――

Jay looked around frantically, hoping a solution might present itself.

'Calm down,' said Pepper, fully composed now. 'We've got a minute or two before they get up here. We'll figure something out.' He retrieved his pistol and reloaded it from a carton of shells pulled from his jacket pocket.

'That's not going to be enough,' said Jay.

'No, it isn't. Better than nothing, though.'

Pepper jogged over to where Jay had played sniper. He craned his head out of the broken window and looked down.

'We could climb,' he said. 'It's icy as fuck but we could do it. Possibly.'

'Well, I supposed we'd get down there one way or another,' said Jay. He walked over to Pepper. 'And if we fucked up, at least it'd be quick.'

Jay's backpack was where he'd left it. He picked it up.

'Any better ideas?' said Pepper. 'You've survived for weeks on your own, without firearms and a small army, so you must know a thing or two about resourceful.'

'I hid,' said Jay. 'A little rat in a hole. Nothing to be proud of.'

Hyenas

'You survived. Not to be sniffed at.'

The hyenas were getting closer. Only a couple of floors away now.

'Christ,' said Jay. 'Sounds like a fucking bus-load of the bastards.' He started to shoulder his pack, as if he was getting ready to get going.

'Maybe it's a coach party, come to attend one of your poetry recitals. Apparently, they're very popular amongst the more cultured elements of Liverpool's joker population.'

Jay stopped. He shrugged off his backpack.

'What?' said Pepper.

'Speakers,' said Jay. 'I saw some before. Those little ones you plug into a computer. I saw some. Where?' He pointed to the desk from which he'd filched the can of dandelion and burdock. 'There. And I need some tape as well. Find some.'

'Yes, sir,' said Pepper and began scouring desks and dragging open drawers.

Jay grabbed the speakers, yanking them free of the computer. He gathered up the cables until the jack was in the palm of his hand. He examined it. 'Perfect.'

He opened his pack and took out the personal CD player. He unplugged the headphones, plugged in the speakers and pressed play.

The same voice, the same warm, measured Scouse accent, spoke.

'I wander thru' each charter'd street, near where the charter'd Thames does flow, and mark in every face I

meet marks of weakness, marks of woe.'

He pressed the skip button a couple of times. Then turned the volume up as loud as it would go, on the CD player and the speakers.

'*Of the primeval priest's assum'd power, when eternals spurn'd back his religion, and gave him a place in the North, obscure, shadowy, void, solitary.*'

Jay pressed stop. He retrieved the rifle from the top of the filing cabinet, where he'd inadvertently flung it.

The hyenas were on the final flight now. Jay imagined he could smell their foulness, like the rush of exhausted air that precedes a train in an underground station.

Pepper returned to the desk at the same time as Jay. He handed two rolls of tape over, both half-used-up.

'It was murder finding them. White-collar reprobates always stealing the fucking stationery. Never saw any of those bastards in prison.'

Jay laughed and took the rolls of tape. 'Should be enough,' he said.

Jay taped the speakers to either side of the end of the barrel of the rifle. As he worked, he said, 'What about football? You never mentioned it in your little why-Liverpool-is-so-fucking great speech. You know, while you were kicking the steaming crap out of me? How come?'

Pepper smiled, but it was a serious smile. 'Because football's too pure to mix up with all this shit. The Spasm, jokers, the end of the fucking world. Football's too pure. It deserves to be left out of it. Maybe, when things have settled down a bit, me and whoever's left standing can have a little kick-about. Might even get a bit of a league going. I can think of worse foundations for a new civilisation.'

'Fair enough,' said Jay, taping the CD player close to the trigger. 'But you could have used football to bring people together, instead of The Beatles.'

'Too divisive, red or blue, all that,' said Pepper. He laughed. 'Besides, everyone I met was a fucking Bluenose, like you.'

'How'd you know I'm a Blue?' said Jay.

'You've got that look of ground-in disappointment. Can't mistake it.'

'Fuck you,' said Jay, grinning. When both rolls of tape were finished, Jay lifted the rifle and gave it a shake, to make sure everything was secure.

'You have *got* to be fucking kidding me, lad,' said Pepper, but he was smiling as he spoke, his voice shaded with both disbelief and admiration. 'Well, it's a plan. And it's a fuck sight more than I've got to offer.'

'It'll work,' said Jay. He smiled weakly. 'It'd better work.'

A chorus of barked laughter, only slightly muffled, told him the hyenas were here. He looked toward the reception. Through the frosted glass of the double doors he could see the twitching, ragged silhouette of several hyenas. The silhouette grew larger, and then filled the glass.

The door shook.

There was a click as Pepper pulled back the hammer on his pistol.

'Don't use it unless you have to,' said Jay.

'That's going to be a tough one to judge.'

The doors flew open and the hyenas spilled in. The first couple fell to the floor and were trampled by the seven or eight that poured in after.

They spotted Jay and Pepper immediately and charged toward them, a couple of them, the frontrunners, leaping up onto tables.

Before the doors could fully close, they flew open again, and more hyenas fought their way through.

'Jesus,' said Pepper. He lowered his gun. There was a quaver of fear in his voice. 'If this doesn't work, we're fucked.'

'It'll work,' said Jay. 'Trust... Shit.'

One of the two frontrunners had taken the lead. Jay recognised her. A surge of nausea strained to empty his already empty stomach.

It was Alice Band. Her bare arms were evening-gloved in red. She'd lost a clump of hair since Jay had last seen her, muscle gleaming wetly where a chunk of her scalp had been torn away. Her hair band was still in place, somehow obscene next to that glistening sore.

Jay remembered her punching her way into her victim's skull, effortlessly it seemed, and he thought: It won't work on her, the Blake. It won't work.

Her face was contorted with rage, a bruised and scratched and bloodied mask of savage hatred. It couldn't possibly work on her.

Her? Jay reminded himself. It wasn't a 'her' it was an 'it', a vicious, brutal 'it'.

He wanted to turn to Pepper and scream, Shoot it! That one! The nearest one! Shoot it!

Instead, he pressed the play button.

'Eternals! I hear your call gladly. Dictate swift wingèd words, and fear not to unfold your dark visions of torment.'

As one, the hyenas paused. Then, almost tripping over themselves, they stopped.

Except for Alice Band. Alice Band kept coming.

Pepper raised the gun to shoot her.

'No,' said Jay. He wasn't sure what the noise of the gunshot would do to the hyenas whose faces had already lost their fury, replaced by a kind of thuggish reverie.

Alice Band's fury had remained in place. She was only a few yards away now and Jay could see every rage-induced groove in her face, like cracks in sun-baked mud.

'Christ, Jay.' Pepper's hand was shaking so much, it looked like he was trying to conduct an orchestra with the barrel of his gun.

'... self-clos'd, all-repelling. What demon hath form'd this abominable Void, this soul-shudd'ring vacuum? Some said it is Urizen. But unknown, abstracted, brooding, secret, the dark power hid.'

Some of the hyenas were sitting down, attentive as school children. A few seemed to have discovered the rhythm and melody of Blake's words and had begun to dance, a jerky to and fro. The rest stood motionless, staring, half smiling.

Alice Band continued to bound across the desks.

Any second now, she'd slam into them. The CD player might get damaged. Jay couldn't risk that.

He turned to Pepper.

'Shoot,' he said.

Pepper lowered the gun.

'Shoot! Jesus!'

Pepper grinned at Jay, then looked at Alice Band.

Jay followed his gaze.

She, it, she — Christ, it was hard to know what to call them anymore — was standing on the desk nearest them, swaying and smiling, like a drunk at an office party that had got shockingly out of hand.

'*...ninefold darkness, unseen, unknown; changes appear'd like desolate mountains, rifted furious by the black winds of perturbation.*'

'Now what?' said Pepper.

'We just walk out of here, I suppose,' said Jay and, keeping his steps slow and steady, he made his way toward the reception.

Pepper fell in behind Jay, Alice Band behind Pepper, the remaining hyenas behind Alice Band, until a procession had formed.

There were more hyenas on the stairs, emerging from the gloom, heading up, snarling, but as soon as they heard Blake's words read aloud in that soft Liverpudlian accent, their savagery evaporated. Swaying, staring, some giggling like children, they stepped aside, waited for the procession to pass, then attached themselves to its tail.

'*...rolling of wheels, as of swelling seas, sound in his clouds, in his hills of stor'd snows, in his mountains of hail and ice; voices of terror are heard, like thunders of autumn, when the cloud blazes over the harvests.*'

The heat on the stairwell was almost overwhelming, a foetid sweat lodge. Jay kept his breathing brief and shallow, convinced that the hyenas would take offence if he started retching uncontrollably, and then all bets would be off.

'*Earth was not, nor globes of attraction; the will of the immortal expanded or contracted his all-flexible senses; death was not, but eternal life sprung.*'

One of the hyenas, a stocky teenager who appeared to have modelled himself on James Dean, sidled up to Jay, smiling dreamily. He placed a hand, hot and crusty, flat against Jay's face. Jay managed to flinch only slightly.

'Jesus,' Pepper muttered, his grip on the pistol tightening.

Contact made, James Dean seemed satisfied and rejoined the parade.

They had just passed the landing to the first floor and begun the descent to the ground floor, when Jay noticed the small red light flashing on the edge of the CD player.

He turned to Pepper, mouthed 'Fuck!' and flicked his eyes at the red light. Then he mouthed the word 'Battery.'

Pepper rolled his eyes and almost seemed amused.

'Here alone I, in books form'd of metals, have written the secrets of wisdom, the secrets of dark contemplation, by fightings and conflicts dire with terrible monsters sin-bred, which the bosoms of all inhabit: seven deadly Sins of the soul.'

At the bottom of the stairs, they pushed open the door and stepped out into the foyer. The place was packed with hyenas.

'How much longer before that thing gives up the ghost?' said Pepper.

'A couple of minutes, maybe. Probably less. Any thoughts?'

'Okay. Thoughts. Right. As soon as we get outside, find the deepest bit of snow you can. Plant the rifle in the snow. The jokers carry on listening to Poetry Please with Roger McGough and we fuck the fuck off. You to your boat, me back into the city.'

'You could come with us,' said Jay.

'Thanks. But no. No, I couldn't. This is it now for me, until it's finished, until, one way or another, I'm done.'

'Fair enough.'

'Rage, fury, intense indignation, in cataracts of fire, blood, and gall, in whirlwinds of sulphurous smoke, and enormous forms of energy, in living creations appear'd, in the flames of eternal fury.'

They paraded down the steps of the side entrance and out onto Water Street, Jay, Pepper and the hyenas. Jay wasn't certain why, but he continued around the building to where Dempsey sat, somehow as determined and carefree in death as he was in life. Feeling as if he were planting a flag in some unexplored territory, Jay gently eased the butt of the rifle into the deep snow drift at the bottom of the stone steps close to Dempsey's feet.

The snow was falling heavily now, a swarm of white. Jay could only just make out hyenas emerging from the Queensway tunnel across the road. As with the hyenas inside the Liver Building, they charged forward, intent upon harm, but their viciousness faded as soon as they fell under the spell of Blake.

'Okay,' said Pepper. 'We need to back away now. Slowly.'

'But not too fucking slowly.'

'Yeah, not too fucking slowly.'

As if they were retreating from a watchful tiger, they reversed away from the rifle-mounted CD player, which looked oddly totemic to Jay now that he was no longer holding it, now that it was a thing on its own, the hyenas staring on with something not unlike reverence.

The low-battery light flickered red.

'In fierce anguish and quenchless flames to the deserts and rocks he ran raging, to hide; but he could not.'

Jay and Pepper backed through swaying, transfixed hyenas, down the side of the Liver Building, toward the Mersey.

The red light flickered.

'...in howlings and pangs and fierce madness, long periods in burning fires labouring; till hoary, and age-

broke, and agèd, in despair and the shadows of.'

The red light winked out.

The silence following the CD player's death was somehow intrusive, worming its way into Jay's ears.

Pepper saluted then sprinted off upriver, toward the Cunard Building and the lifeless black wedges of the Mann Island Apartments. A second later, Jay headed pell-mell in the opposite direction, toward Princes' Parade.

Behind him, there was silence from the hyenas and for a moment, even though he knew it was ridiculous, he thought the hyenas had died, that the sudden cessation of poetry, of Blake, had proved too much of a shock and their hearts had stopped.

Silence.

Silence.

Then, an explosion of rage. Jay wasn't entirely certain he only imagined the outer rim of its shockwave pushing against his back, pressing him forward with such urgency that it was an effort to stop himself from lurching ahead of his own feet and falling over.

Before

———

'Make us a cuppa, eh, son?' his dad asked as Jay closed the front door behind him. 'I'm gasping, but you know how it is.'

Jay took off his jacket and draped it over the bottom of the banister.

'Okay, Dad. You want anything else? Toast? Biscuits?'

'No thanks. How'd it go at the job centre?'

'Shit. I've got a new Employment Guidance Officer, or whatever the fuck they're calling them now, and she can't quite grasp the fact that every job requires at least some degree of literacy. Even when I told her about that cleaning job I lost because I couldn't fill in the audit sheet, she was like, 'Well, there must be something,' all exasperated as if I was just being awkward.'

'Well, you probably *were* being a little bit awkward, knowing you,' his dad replied as Jay stepped into the living room, grinning.

'Maybe a little bit. Can't help it. They wind me up. I've had nearly five years of this shite.'

His dad looked terrible. Thin, grey and practically hairless. There was a faint stink in the air that Jay could only think of as sickness.

Hyenas

'Did you do the other thing?'

Jay sighed. 'Yes. I've done the other thing.'

The Other Thing was arranging for someone at Social Services to come around and assess Jay's 'special needs' because his dad—who never tired of reminding him—was not only not going to be around forever, he wasn't going to be around for long.

'They're coming next Tuesday,' said Jay. 'Half eleven. Have you taken your pills?'

'Will do once you get a wiggle on and brew up.'

As he made the tea, Jay noticed, as if for the first time, the alien squiggles on the side of his dad's mug that said *World's Greatest Dad*. At least that was what his mum had told him it said when they'd bought it in Woolworths all those years ago. It could have said, European Body Popping Champion 1986, for all Jay knew.

When he brought the tea in, his dad was up from his armchair, checked green pyjamas hanging limp on his sticklike frame, shuffling over to the computer desk by the bay window.

'Where do you want the tea: computer or armchair?'

'Armchair. Just getting this.' He pressed a button on the PC, a tray slid out and his dad removed a CD before pressing the button again and sending the tray back once more. He took a marker and wrote something on the disk then returned to his armchair. 'Here,' he said, holding the CD out for Jay. 'I made it for you.'

Jay took the disk and sat down on the settee, moving

blankets aside that were still a little warm from his dad's afternoon nap.

'What is it?' he asked.

'It's Blake. Well, it's me reading Blake. I recorded it on the computer then burnt it to disk. Took me a few weeks. I get tired.' He smiled. 'I'm no Alan Bates but, you know, it's better than a kick in the teeth.'

'Thanks.'

'It's nothing, really. Dads, eh? We're a pretty useless bunch. Mums do all the real work. Dads are only there to save your life if you do something *really* stupid.'

Jay looked at the disk, at his dad's writing. He recognised it even though he had no idea what it said and, for a moment, he felt a hot fist deep in his chest, tears threatening, and it meant everything to him that his malfunctioning, fucked-up brain had allowed him that one small mercy, the ability to recognise his own father's handwriting.

And then he thought how like his dad's voice the handwriting was. It undulated gently. There were no angles, no sharp peaks or jagged troughs. There was a warmth to it. It looked like a series of interconnected smiles, all expressing varying degrees of amusement.

The hot fist in his chest opened up and he started crying.

'It's alright, son. It's alright, lad.'

An arm around his shoulders, thin, almost muscleless, but strong all the same.

Chapter Twenty-Seven

Princes' Parade seemed endless, the Alexandra Tower concealed, despite its boastful height, by the whipping, twitching fabric of the snow.

Behind him, the snarling and snickering of the hyenas seemed to coordinate with the frenetic, jerky movement of the falling snow, a conspiracy of sound and motion.

He filled his lungs with icy cold air and tried to transmute it into energy by force of will. Then he mentally pushed that real or imagined energy down into his legs.

It actually seemed to work. He could feel himself picking up speed. The hyenas' din was falling away. But with the roar of blood in his ears, he couldn't be sure. Flakes of snow, fat and wet, stuck to his eyelashes, further blurring and confusing his vision. If it wasn't for the river to his left, its rolling surface greasy with snow, he could easily have strayed off course. Even without looking, he could sense the Mersey, a different quality of air, livelier somehow, against the left-hand side of his face. He felt energised for the first time since... The truth was he couldn't remember the last time he felt this strong, this focused, this able. He threw each foot down and pushed it back as if he wasn't so much driving himself forward as turning the Earth, a mammoth treadmill, bringing his destination toward him, one step at a time. There was a pain in his side and the insides of his lungs felt scoured by the icy air, but he could take it. It was no big deal.

The Alexandra Tower appeared, the snow seeming to part, the big reveal at the end of a magic trick. He veered toward the river, toward the railing, beyond which the boat and Ellen and everybody else would be waiting.

And then he saw Simon, lying in the snow, face-up, bloodied mouth catching snowflakes, eyes rolled back to reveal whites like ice. His pale dreadlocks were splayed out across the snow in a neat, symmetrical pattern that looked almost deliberate, arranged.

What happened next seemed to take place in entirely the wrong order.

Jay fell, sprawling in the snow, and for a fraction of a second he thought he'd tripped on something, the outstretched arm of one of Liverpool's dead, perhaps. Then he felt a pain he could only describe as an icy burning halfway up the side of his right thigh, followed by a bone-deep numbness from his hip to the tips of his toes. And then he heard the gunshot.

He rolled onto his back and looked down at his leg. Tendrils of blood, like the roots of some crimson plant, stretched out from a single, small point on his thigh into the snow.

The hyenas — at least fifteen of them — stopped and

turned toward the source of the gunfire. A figure, little more than a silhouette in the swirling snow. A man with an assault rifle.

'Told you'd I'd take you down, you little cunt, didn't I?' the silhouette snarled. 'Fucking told you!'

Jay couldn't even process what was being said. The pain in his leg, the after-whistle of gunfire in his ears, the proximity of the hyenas: a blizzard of distractions.

The figure took a step forward. Jay could see his face now. He looked familiar.

'Been following you since the museum, you little shit,' he said. 'Lost you a couple of times. But the thing with snow is, you leave footprints. Smart, me.'

He tapped the barrel of the assault rifle to his temple to demonstrate just how smart he was, and Jay couldn't help laughing.

'It's Pete!' said Jay, through gritted teeth. 'Of 'Colin and Pete'. How you doing, Pete?'

'What you fucking laughing at?' said Pete.

And then the hyenas bore down on him and Pete began firing enthusiastically into the pack.

Jay tried to get to his feet, but his lifeless leg was impossibly heavy and the most he could manage was to sit up. He looked to his right. The guard rail wasn't as close as he'd hoped but he had no other options; he flopped onto his belly and, clawing through the soft top layer of snow and driving his fingertips into the frozen crust beneath, dragged himself toward the river, pushing with his uninjured leg, dragging its useless associate behind.

There was a gunshot accompanied by a high-pitched ping; an unspectacular spark appeared briefly on the top rung of the guard rail. Jay kept moving. The numbness in his leg was beginning to lift. He wished it hadn't.

There were more gunshots, followed immediately by the sound — somehow hard and wet — of bullets thud-ripping into hyena flesh.

'Fucking jokers!' Pete all-but shrieked. 'Get out of the fucking way!'

Three, four, five more gunshots. Then one, two, three clicks.

'Bollocks!'

The hyenas erupted into snarling laughter.

Pete whimpered. Then he started to scream. Started but didn't finish, the emerging sound muffled as the hyenas fell upon him. Jay might have felt sorry for him, if it wasn't for the sight of Simon, like a trophy on display.

Jay grabbed the lowest rung of the guard rail, the first of four, with his right hand and dragged himself closer. He threw his left hand up onto the second rail and pulled himself closer still.

There was a series of thuds as the hyenas slammed their fists into Pete, the sound becoming progressively more liquid, a kind of slow-motion version of the thud-tearing of the bullets.

Jay grabbed the third rail and pulled himself up onto one knee. He didn't dare bend his wounded leg; he just let it jut out. Even so, as he seized the top rail and pulled himself up onto his feet, the pain was extraordinary, as if some gruesome Jack Horner had rammed a thumb deep into the muscle of his thigh and was wriggling it around in search of a plum.

The liquid thudding behind him, like children stomping in muddy puddles, was now accompanied by the snapping of bones. Jay was certain that, any second now, the hyenas would break open Pete's skull, if they hadn't already, find disappointment and turn their attention to him.

Crying out in pain, he threw his injured leg over the top rail, straddling it like a child attempting to mount a bicycle that was too big for him. He let the leg drop to the ground but didn't put his weight on it, instead letting his wrists and torso take the strain as he pulled his good leg over and planted his foot on the ground.

He looked over at the pack. Pete was in ruins now, motionless. Rearing over him, face awash with blood to which fat snowflakes adhered briefly before melting, was Alice Band. She met Jay's eye and grinned.

Jay looked down into the Mersey and saw the great worn steps onto which Dempsey had fallen before plunging into the waters, temporarily as it had turned out.

Jay saw the steps, but no boat.

'And there it was, gone,' he muttered.

Alice Band roared with laughter.

Chapter Twenty-Eight

He couldn't blame them, Ellen, Dave, Kavi and Joe. They didn't need Jay anymore, didn't know him, owed him nothing. The city was crawling with hyenas now. They'd done the right thing, the sensible thing, casting off from dry land, away from all the horror, doubtless with Pete raining gunfire upon them. He couldn't blame them. He really couldn't.

'Miserable fucking bastards,' he said.

Alice Band coughed phlegmy laughter. Closer.

Jay turned. She was only a few yards away, almost strolling toward him, the ragged remains of her flower-print dress flapping about legs blue with cold where they weren't brown, grey or black with dirt.

'I can't believe they've fucking ditched me,' he said. 'I mean, I don't blame them, not really, but... Miserable fucking bastards. You can't rely on anyone these days, can you?'

Alice Band watched the words as they emerged from Jay's mouth. The movement of her eyes and head suggested she was tracking something with an easy, undulating motion. Jay thought: Is that the Liverpudlian accent? Is that what it looks like to the hyenas? Fluid, informal, almost dreamy? Is that how we spoke, this entire city? Were our voices that beautiful?

'So, what now?' said Jay. 'Maybe we could just talk for a while. I could bore you to death, then maybe you'll get fed up and, you know, fuck off. How does that sound? Fair enough?'

Alice Band, almost within arm's reach now, continued to follow the lazy trajectories of his words, smiling a little. For a second, Jay thought perhaps she would be content just to hear him talk, but then her legs bent, tensed and she leapt up onto the top rail, balancing with simian ease.

'Fuck,' said Jay. He stepped back and immediately began to lose his footing, his heels hanging over the edge of the promenade wall.

Alice Band dropped onto him, wrapping her arms around his neck and her legs around his waist. Her forehead cracked against his.

Maybe it was down to the wooziness caused by loss of blood, the blow to the head or just plain exhaustion, but as they arced down toward the water it felt less like an assault and more like an embrace.

For a moment after they hit the water, it seemed as if the oily surface would hold them, that they'd just lie there on that thick undulating skin, like the heavy flakes of snow that refused to melt or sink.

Then an aperture opened in the river's skin and the Mersey sucked them under.

The cold was so immediate, so intense, Jay felt his

skull would implode, as if it was being crushed between tectonic plates. His eyes were clamped shut, his jaw locked, every muscle rigid. Alice Band's fingers dug into his back, her forehead pressed hard against the side of his neck. For a moment he could feel himself sinking, could feel the water rushing upward away from him, then all sense of direction abandoned him, and he had no idea which way was up.

The pain inflicted by the freezing Mersey was unbearable. He was certain it would kill him long before his lungs filled with icy water and he drowned. Then Alice Band's grip suddenly relaxed and she dropped or rose away from him, and he knew he was doomed. If she couldn't survive, how could he?

It was over. Finished.

He felt himself relax then, as if injected with some powerful sedative. The cold was there, the pain was there, but that was all on the surface; deep down he was calmer than he'd ever been. He felt almost happy, the weight of striving lifted from him. He felt warm and buoyant with failure.

Despite a mouth clenched tight against the Mersey, he smiled.

A line from Blake leapt into his forebrain.

Can I not flow down into the sea and slumber in oblivion?

It was something his dad had always said when woken from a deep sleep to get up for work or, in his last days, to take his medication.

Hyenas

Can I not flow down into the sea and slumber in oblivion?

He could see his dad now, mumbling those words before ducking back under the duvet. And then, an explosion of memories, roaring through his mind just as the icy waters roared around his head, tearing at his face and scalp.

His dad dripping iodine onto a graze on Jay's knee and wincing more than his son, as if he was willing the pain away from Jay and onto himself.

His dad marking schoolbooks, scowling, then looking at Jay and saying, 'You're ten times brighter than most of these indolent little bastards, Jason. Ten times brighter. And better looking.'

His dad teaching him chess and insisting upon calling the pawns 'prawns' no matter how often Jay rolled his eyes.

His dad laughing uncontrollably, actual tears rolling down his cheeks, as he watched Laurel and Hardy attempt to push a piano up a huge flight of stairs.

His dad sewing buttons onto one of Jay's school shirts then getting angry just for a second before belly-laughing when he realised he'd sewn through the back of the shirt.

His dad pitching a tent in torrential rain near Delamere Forest while Jay watched, sheltered under a picnic table. Every now and then, he'd turn to Jay and give him a thumbs-up, as if to say, I've got it, I've got it, before witnessing the whole thing collapse again.

His dad walking out of a smoky kitchen, wafting his arms around to disperse the haze, saying, 'Christ, I could set fire to soup, me,' then clapping his hands together and asking, 'What do you fancy from the chippy, then, son?'

His dad picking him up and nuzzling his stubbly chin into Jay's neck and saying, 'Happy birthday, little man,' and not letting go for a long time.

His dad, only a few weeks ago, saying, 'It's nothing, really. Dads, eh? We're a pretty useless bunch. Mums do all the real work. Dads are only there to save your life if you do something *really* stupid.'

Jay started kicking his legs and thrashing his arms, trying to propel himself in whatever direction he happened to be pointed. He still had no idea which way was up, which way was down, but he just couldn't allow himself to slip silently away, couldn't allow his dad to fail.

The pain, which had retreated when Jay had accepted defeat, returned ten-fold. The freezing water crushed his bones. His lungs were on fire. He'd never known pain like it, never known terror like it, a biological horror, not existential dread, but an almost feral reaction to the prospect of being swiftly snuffed out. He couldn't help thinking of the horse, snorting great plumes of steam as it ran and ran and ran, preferring to burst its own heart than accept its fate.

He opened his eyes, desperate to get his bearings, to identify some kind of light, no matter how weak, and begin swimming toward it. But there was no light, just a grainy, textured darkness swirling all around him.

So, he just kept kicking and thrashing and hoping he was moving in the right direction.

The burning in his lungs was too much. He exhaled, feeling bubbles hard as stones erupt around his face. If he'd expected relief to follow, he was disappointed. The vacuum that replaced the burning was even worse. The urge to open his mouth and draw in something, anything, was rapidly becoming impossible to resist. A lungful of Mersey River water was better than the agonising void that threatened to shred him from the inside out. He was about to inhale when he realised he'd felt those stone-hard exhaled bubbles run from his mouth, past his nose and into his hairline. He knew which way was up. He was swimming in the right direction.

He clamped his jaw even tighter, as if he was holding onto a rope by his teeth, dangling over a vast chasm, and kicked and scrabbled at the vicious water with what he knew to be the last of his strength. The pain in his skull was like an icicle rammed into the centre of his brain, an icicle that was expanding by the second. His body was almost entirely numb now and he realised he couldn't be at all certain that he was kicking and scrabbling anymore, that all this frenetic activity might very well be taking place in his delirious, near-frozen brain.

But he kept kicking, kept thrashing.

His lips parted. He couldn't stop them. They had a will of their own. Metallic-tasting water, so cold it shouldn't have been liquid at all, seeped between his teeth and onto his tongue. He tried to tense his throat, to seal it against the incursion, but it was no good, the water oozed in. Suddenly he was coughing and with each spasm he drew in another mouthful of Mersey. He thought maybe he was crying now, but he really couldn't be sure.

And then his head split through the thick skin of the river's surface and he could hear and see. The light was feeble but blinding all the same. He retched up foul-tasting water and drew in chill air that was swarming with snow. A second or two of retching and gasping and then the river tried to drag him under again. What felt like coils of current wound round his legs and tugged him downward. Jay kicked against them, tried to pull his legs free. He had some measure of success, disentangling himself a little, but he could feel his energy dissipating and knew it was only a matter of seconds before he went under again; and once down, he knew he'd never get up and out, and he would slumber in oblivion.

As he struggled, he turned on the spot and looked around for any sign of the promenade. There was nothing, not even buildings, just water as far as he could see; rubbery, oversized waves, flexing. He had no idea where he was. He felt as if he was racing along, out toward the Irish Sea, but it was impossible to be sure with the writhing fabric of snow all around him.

'Ellen!' He coughed the name as much as shouted it. 'Ellen!'

Hyenas

The current's tentacles snatched at his legs again, latched on and tugged him down. His head dropped below the waterline. He kicked as if he was kicking at some creature, something he could persuade to let him go if he hurt it badly enough. It worked and he was able to push his face up into the wintery air and draw breath, but only for a second as the trough he found himself in warped upward and submerged him once more.

He kicked again at the current creature and again succeeded in pushing his face up through the water's skin. He sucked in a little air and used it to cry, 'Ellen!'

The shark, pale and vast, struck his shoulder with its snout and spun him like a buoy. Jay couldn't help laughing. A shark? A fucking shark! Christ, he thought, the universe really wants me dead and it's not taking any fucking chances, is it?

But then he saw that the shark had *Jerusalem* tattooed on its side.

'Ellen!' he tried to shout but the name emerged as little more than a croak.

But from high above him he heard Ellen say, 'All right, stop harping on. Heard you the first time.'

Hands gripped his shoulders and arms, and he was dragged out of the water.

Chapter Twenty-Nine

Kavi said, 'Lucky, lucky boy. Bullet went right through. He should survive. God is great.'

'Yeah, but not that fucking great,' he heard Dave reply, 'or none of this fucking shite would have happened in the first fucking place, would it?'

'God is great,' said Kavi, but he sounded a little doubtful this time.

Time passed and somebody, Jay thought it might have been Joe, said something about 'more antibiotics.'

A little later or a lot later, Ellen placed a cool palm flat against his forehead and said, 'Seems to be coming down.' She smiled at him.

Jay ducked in and out of sleep or consciousness. Every now and then, he heard his dad reciting Blake, but he knew that couldn't be happening.

'Father! Father! Where are you going? O do not walk so fast. Speak, father, speak to your little boy, or else I shall be lost. The night was dark, no father was there, the child was wet with dew, the mire was deep and the child did weep, and away the vapour flew.'

At some point, the boat was hit by a storm. Or maybe it wasn't, and Jay just dreamed the whole thing. In the dream, if that's what it was, Dave reared above him, face screwed up with fury and said, 'This is all your fault, you little cunt! Oh, I've got a brilliant idea! Let's escape in a fucking sailing boat even though none of us has ever sailed before. Don't worry, we'll be fine, we've got a fucking book out of the fucking library! Twat!'

When Jay woke up, he was back in Waterstones, hiding, the pale wooden underside of the tabletop above him; out of sight, just inches away, the hyena gorged on Byron. Then he realised it was the ceiling of the *Jerusalem*'s cabin he was seeing, and the sound of the hyena's gorging was entirely imagined, the remnants of a nightmare that had piggybacked into the waking world.

It was quiet and bright. Gusts of impossibly fresh, chilly air came in through the glaring rectangle of the cabin doorway. Then the doorway filled with shadow, and the shadow morphed into Ellen.

Smiling, she said, 'Get off your lazy arse, Jay. It's a gorgeous day.'

He thought of his dad ducking back below the duvet, mumbling, *Can I not flow down into the sea and slumber in oblivion?*

He sat up. Every muscle ached and where the bullet had passed through him felt like he had a splinter the size of a broom handle lodged just below the surface of his skin, but he felt good.

Ellen helped him stand, then, taking his hand, led him out onto the deck of the *Jerusalem*.

The sky was cobalt blue and glassy, the sun a blinding white hole. The sea, motionless, did its best impression of the sky.

Joe was pulling on some rope or other, smiling; he looked as if he was having the time of his life. Dave and Kavi were both holding paperbacks and steaming mugs of tea. They were talking with a kind of easy earnestness and Jay knew they were discussing their books. Dave had a battered copy of *The Call of the Wild*; Kavi was clutching an equally decrepit *Eric Morecambe Unseen*.

Jay experienced a sudden urge to read, to grab a book, any book, and devour its every word. It was all he could do to stop himself from snatching Dave's book or Kavi's.

'Where are we?' he said, as much to distract himself from his sudden bibliophilia as to ascertain their location.

'I've no idea,' said Ellen and she seemed perfectly happy about that.

'We've pretty much mastered the sailing bit,' said Dave.

'But we can't navigate for shit,' said Joe.

Ellen pointed at the horizon.

'We're heading for that,' she said.

'But we don't know what 'that' is,' said Kavi. He grinned.

Jay squinted at the horizon.

Between sky and sea was a short sliver of green.

'Maybe we should name it after you,' said Dave. 'You brought us here.'

Jay scrutinised Dave's face, searching for evidence of

sarcasm or spite, but Dave was smiling too, just like Ellen and Joe and Kavi.

After a while, Jay started smiling, too.

If you enjoyed *Hyenas*, you might also enjoy
The Girl Beneath the Ice, **available**
now at Northodox.co.uk

Acknowledgements

I would like to thank:

Clare Coombes and all at The Liverpool Literary Agency.

Sarah Moorhead for publishing advice and making connections.

Jeff Fullerton and Alex Bentley for helpful suggestions when Hyenas was a scraggy first draft.

J.A. Sullivan, W. Sheridan Bradford and Christopher Henderson for their enthusiasm for an earlier incarnation of this book.

Catherine McCarthy for being a cheerleader for my writing, and boosting my confidence when I really needed it.

Everyone at Northodox Press for making me a part of their proudly Northern publishing project.

NORTHODOX PRESS

HOME OF NORTHERN VOICES

FACEBOOK.COM/NORTHODOXPRESS

TWITER.COM/NORTHODOXPRESS

INSTAGRAM.COM/NORTHODOXPRESS

NORTHODOX.CO.UK

Printed in Great Britain
by Amazon